Lords & Ladies of Mayfair

Laura Beers

Chapter One

England, 1813

Lady Esther Harington found herself to be in a terrible predicament. Her stepmother was insistent that she should marry a man who was older than her father; a man that had already outlived his three other wives. It wasn't that she objected to the thought of marriage, she just wanted a say in *who* she married.

She stared out the window of her bedchamber and watched as the birds danced merrily in the trees. How she envied them. No one told them what to do or how to dress. They were free to come and go as they pleased.

It hadn't always been like this. She hadn't always felt so trapped. She'd had a happy childhood with doting parents. But it all changed when her mother died. Her father quickly got remarried to a young woman that was only a few years older than her; a childhood friend of hers. Now she felt like an interloper in her own home.

The life that she had always envisioned for herself was

slipping away and she was scared that she would be miserable for the remainder of her days.

A knock came at the door.

"Enter," Esther said.

The door opened and her young, freckle-faced lady's maid stepped into the room. "Lady Mather is requesting your presence in the drawing room," Anne announced.

With dread in her voice, she asked, "Is he here?" She couldn't bring herself to say anything more. She didn't want to say anything more.

Anne winced slightly. "I'm afraid so," she replied. "His lordship arrived a short time ago and has been conversing with your stepmother."

Esther turned her attention back to the window. As far as she was concerned, she had two options. She could do what was expected of her, just as she always did, and meet with the Marquess of Warley or she could climb out the window. She sighed. Even if she managed to climb down the wall without seriously injuring herself, where would she go?

Anne spoke up, drawing back her attention. "If I may, my lady, running away won't solve your problems," she counseled.

Had she been so transparent in her thoughts that her lady's maid had seen right through her? "No, you are most assuredly correct," Esther responded.

Anne probably thought that she was being ridiculous. She was about to be presented to a marquess and receive an offer of marriage. But she wanted more out of her life than an arranged marriage. She wanted what her parents had- love.

Esther knew that she had tarried long enough. She wasn't brave enough to run away, leaving her with only one choice. She would go down and speak to Lord Warley. With any luck, he would find her dull and withdraw his suit.

"It will be all right," Anne encouraged.

"I don't see how," Esther said as she approached the door. "I am leaving one gilded cage for another."

Anne went to open the door. "Don't despair. Things have a way of working themselves out for the best."

Esther gave Anne a weak smile, knowing she was trying her best to be encouraging. "Thank you for what you are attempting to do, but life isn't always fair. I must change what I am able and accept what I can't."

As she walked down the corridor towards the stairs, Esther's legs felt like they were made of lead and every step seemed to take a considerable amount of effort. Most people would consider her fortunate for snagging a marquess, but she would have rather secured a love match.

Her blonde-haired stepmother stepped out of the drawing room and watched her descend the stairs with a look of annoyance on her sharp features. She had once been close to Susanna but that had all changed when she had married Esther's father. Now the distance between them seemed to grow with every passing interaction, making her wonder if she had perhaps imagined their childhood bond.

Susanna placed a hand on her increasing stomach and waited for Esther to come to a stop in front of her. "Lord Warley does not like to be kept waiting, for anyone," she chided. "You would be wise to remember that."

Susanna didn't give her stepdaughter an opportunity to speak before she continued. "Speak loudly and concisely when addressing the marquess. It is imperative that you make a good first impression."

"And if I don't?"

Susanna pressed her lips together, clearly displeased by Esther's response. "Cheer up," she said. "If all goes well, you will become a marchioness soon enough and will be the envy of the *ton*."

"This isn't what I want," Esther admitted.

"Trust me, this is what you *need*," Susanna declared. "You will thank me later when you are living at your grand townhouse and have a myriad of servants tending to your every whim."

Why did her stepmother always dismiss her thoughts or concerns as unimportant? Susanna only seemed to hear what she wanted to hear, nothing else. It was like talking to a wall.

A short, dark-haired man stepped out from the drawing room and met Esther's gaze. "Lord Warley would like to speak to you now." He paused. "Alone."

Susanna nodded her permission. "Very well," she said. "I shall remain here."

Esther hesitantly walked towards the drawing room, wishing that she had the strength to run away. But she didn't. To do so would embarrass her and her family. She had no choice but to go through with this.

She stepped into the drawing room and saw the marquess standing by the mantel. Taking a moment to quietly observe him, she didn't quite understand what was so intimidating about the man. He was short, had a round belly and his white hair was thinning on the crown of his head. His clothes were made of the finest quality but that did little to distract from his pasty skin.

Lord Warley turned to face her with a frown on his lips. "I am glad that you finally decided to grace me with your presence."

Unsure of what to say, Esther dropped into a low curtsy. "I apologize for being late, my lord."

The marquess shuffled over to her, stopping in front of her. His critical eyes swept over her and it made her feel small, inconsequential. "You are taller than I imagined."

"I'm sorry," she attempted. There was nothing she could do about her height.

"May I see your teeth?"

Fearing she'd misheard him, she asked, "I beg your pardon?"

"Your teeth," he responded harshly. "Let me see your teeth."

Esther opened her mouth as he studied them. "Your teeth will do," he said, taking a step back.

Good heavens, what was this man about, she wondered. She felt like a stallion being put on the auction block.

"You are young and have nice, wide childbearing hips," Lord Warley went on to say. "That will do well for you when you bear me a son."

Esther was at a loss for words. Did she thank him for making such outrageous remarks about her person, especially since they seemed more like observations than compliments?

"I am a busy man, but I find myself in need of a wife. You will do, I suppose," Lord Warley said. "I see no reason to wait. Do you?"

Esther blinked. How did she respond to such a ridiculous question?

Lord Warley turned his head and shouted, "Clawson!"

The man stepped back into the drawing room and bowed. "Yes, my lord."

"Lady Esther will suit just nicely," the marquess said. "Bring me the wedding contract."

She felt panic well up inside of her as Clawson removed papers from his jacket pocket and walked them over to the desk that sat in the corner. He picked up the quill and dipped the tip into the ink pot. "I will just need both of your signatures," he informed them.

Lord Warley accepted the quill from his solicitor before he signed the document. He turned back towards her and held the quill up. "Lady Esther, if you will."

Esther found that she couldn't quite seem to move. She no more wanted this marriage with Lord Warley than she wanted to chew glass. If she married him, she would be entirely at his mercy and she would be miserable. He was not the type of man that she could grow to love, she was sure of that. By the way he'd already treated her, it proved to her just that.

"Lady Esther," the marquess repeated. This time, his voice held a sternness to it. "I do not have all day for you to dilly-dally."

Her stepmother had entered the room and said through gritted teeth, "Just sign the contract, Esther."

The time had come for her to speak her mind. If she didn't, she would be trapped in a loveless marriage, and it didn't matter to her that he was a marquess. She couldn't do this... no, she *wouldn't* do this. She did not want to throw her life away for a title.

"No," Esther said, her voice no more than a whisper.

Lord Warley gave her a puzzled look as his solicitor's mouth dropped open. "No?" he asked. "What is 'no'?"

In a soft voice, Esther said, "I don't want to marry you."

"What?" Lord Warley asked. "Speak up, Child."

Esther squared her shoulders and mustered all the courage she could gather. "I don't want to marry you," she confessed, hoping her words sounded more confident than she felt.

Lord Warley stared at her for a moment before a smile broke out onto his face. "You are teasing me, aren't you?"

She shook her head.

The marquess' smile dimmed. "You are rejecting my offer of marriage?"

"I am," she said. She didn't mention that he had failed to ask her to marry him. He more or less commanded her to do so.

Placing the quill down onto the desk, Lord Warley considered her for a moment. "No one has had the audacity to turn me down before, and that includes my three wives that came before you," he growled.

Her stepmother stepped forward and said, "Please, my lord, she is just overwhelmed with your generous offer and needs some time to process this momentous decision."

Some of the anger dissipated from the marquess' expression. "You make a good point, Lady Mather." He turned his attention towards Esther. "I shall wait for your answer this evening at Lady Morley's ball. If you are in agreement, we will dance two sets to announce our engagement."

"I do not think——" Esther started.

Her stepmother cut her off. "Esther will think on this most thoughtfully, knowing her entire future is at stake." She shot Esther a warning look to be quiet.

Lord Warley approached Esther and reached for her gloved hand. "I know women's minds can get easily befuddled but do not try my patience again, my dear."

Esther resisted the urge to cringe at his touch as he kissed the air above her knuckles and released her hand. Lord Warley spun on his heel and departed from the room without another word.

Clawson's mouth still hung open, as if he couldn't quite fathom what had just happened. "I shall leave the contract here for you to sign."

"Thank you," her stepmother said.

Once the main door was closed, Susanna walked over to the window and watched as the marquess' crested coach traveled down the road.

Esther had expected her stepmother to be disappointed in her but she hadn't expected the deafening silence that filled the room. The only noise was the ticking of the long clock in the corner, timing her misery.

Susanna turned purposefully towards her. "Wait until your father hears what you have done," she said.

"I had no choice," Esther attempted. "I couldn't marry him."

"You did have a choice, and you almost made the biggest mistake of your life."

"I don't think I did."

Her stepmother frowned and raised her hand to her brow,

disapproval etched into her features. "You singlehandedly managed to embarrass this family in front of Lord Warley. Do you not think there will be repercussions to your actions?"

"Susanna…"

"Go to your bedchamber," her stepmother ordered.

"If you will just listen to my reasonings—"

"No!" Susanna exclaimed. "I will not. Do you know what great lengths your father had to go to so Lord Warley would even consider you for his bride? Do you even care?"

Esther just stared at her stepmother, knowing nothing she said would quell the woman's anger.

"I have never met a more ungrateful person in all my life," Susanna declared. "You have been handed everything your entire life and you have no idea how cruel life can truly be."

"I just feel—"

"You don't get to feel anything," Susanna stated. "You have a duty to the family and it is time that you pay up."

Susanna walked over to the door and stopped. "Lord Warley is an old man. All you have to do is marry him and bear him a son. If you can accomplish that, your life will be one of ease and comfort. You won't want for anything. Does that mean nothing to you?"

"I don't want to marry him."

"Marriage brings forth security, and that is the most important thing for a woman," Susanna said before she departed from the drawing room.

Once she was alone, Esther lowered herself onto the camelback settee. She was pleased that she had stood up for herself, but she knew this battle was far from over. She would need to continue to be strong to turn down one of the most powerful men in England… again.

Mr. Samuel Moore sat at his desk in his office as he reviewed the documents for his upcoming case. He had never lacked for work, but he had been inundated with people wanting to hire him as their barrister. And it was all thanks to Lady Eugenie Lancaster. Once she had been exonerated, the newssheets had reported that he had worked tirelessly to get her released from prison. Which was true, but he also had help from Lord Rushcliffe.

He glanced at the pile of files that sat on the edge of his desk and sighed. He needed to review them and decide which cases he would accept. There was no way he could handle all of them since there were just too many. He should be grateful for the work, but he was tired. The monotony was starting to take a toll on him, taking with him every ounce of joy that he had once felt for his work.

When he had started working as a barrister, he was determined to fight for the poor, the wrongly accused, and the misunderstood. But now, he didn't know who he was fighting for. It wasn't for himself anymore, that much he knew.

It was an odd thing for him to work as a barrister. He was his father's heir, but he didn't care much for what Society expected him to do. He preferred to do what his conscience dictated.

Placing the file down, he realized that he wouldn't get much more done this afternoon. Which wasn't necessarily a bad thing. He had been working since the early morning hours and needed a break. Perhaps a drink at White's would be just the thing to lift his spirits.

Samuel shoved back his chair and rose. He walked out of his office, being mindful to lock it behind him, and departed from his building. He wasn't far from White's so he decided a walk would do him some good. It would allow him to collect his thoughts.

He kept his gaze straight ahead as he walked past the street vendors that were hawking their goods along the crowded pavement. The smell of fresh baked bread wafted through the air and he realized that he had skipped breakfast that morning.

A woman blocked his path as she held up a bouquet of flowers in her hands. "Do ye want some flowers, Mister?"

"No, thank you," Samuel replied as he attempted to side-step her.

The woman moved with him. "Don't ye want to get some for yer wife?"

"I don't have a wife."

"That is a shame," she replied. "A man as handsome as ye should have a wife to keep ye company."

"I thank you kindly, but I am not interested."

The woman's posture drooped, emphasizing her slender shoulders. "Please, sir, will ye not reconsider? I need to feed my kids this evening."

Samuel knew that the cost of flowers was inconsequential to him, but it could be the difference between putting food on the table or not for this woman. Or the woman knew precisely what to say to tug on his heartstrings. It was most likely the latter, but he didn't want to take that gamble.

He reached into his waistcoat pocket and pulled out a gold coin.

The woman's eyes lit up when he extended her the coin. "Thank ye," she said as she accepted it.

As he moved to walk around her, the woman shoved the flowers towards him. "Here are yer flowers."

He put his hand up. "You may keep them."

The woman huffed, clearly offended by his request. "I will do no such thing," she responded. "Ye paid for them. They are yers."

Samuel reluctantly accepted the flowers, wrapped in a brown wrapping, wondering what in the blazes he was going to do with them. But he didn't want to insult this woman by refusing them again. "Thank you," he said before he walked away.

With a bouquet of flowers in his hand, Samuel approached White's and a liveried servant opened the door wide for him. He stepped inside and his eyes roamed over the main hall until they landed on his friend, Mr. Whitmore, who was sitting near the back wall.

He approached the table and Mr. Whitmore gave him a curious look. "Are those for me?" his friend asked, pointing at the flowers in his hand.

"Of course not," Samuel said as he laid them down onto the table. "I bought them from a street vendor."

"For what purpose? You have no wife."

"Thank you for the reminder," Samuel muttered.

Mr. Whitmore raised his glass up. "That is a fortunate thing, my friend. A wife is like a shackle around one's foot. Given time, a sane man will try to gnaw off his foot to be set free."

Samuel pulled out a chair and sat down. "That is a little drastic, but I see your point."

His friend lowered his glass and grew somber. "My father has informed me that I must do my duty and marry, for the sake of our family."

"I never thought I would see you settle down and get married."

"It is not by choice, mind you, but I need an heir." Mr. Whitmore reached into his jacket pocket and pulled out a piece of paper. "That is why I created a list."

"A list for what?"

"I am on the hunt for the perfect woman, so I made a list of qualities that I want her to be in possession of," Mr. Whitmore informed him.

Finding himself curious, he asked, "Pray tell, what qualities have made the list?"

Mr. Whitmore cleared his throat, loudly, before reading,

"Her ears must be the appropriate size for her head, she must chew quietly, as not to disturb me while I eat, and her feet must be dainty." He looked over at him. "I do not like women with overly large feet."

Samuel wasn't sure which item should be addressed first, but he decided to focus on the feet. "You don't like women with large feet?"

"Heavens, no," Mr. Whitmore replied. "What if they step on me? They could break my toes."

"In this scenario, are you wearing boots? Because if you are, I doubt your wife stepping on your boots would hurt."

"Can I take that chance?"

"Very well, but what of the ears?"

Mr. Whitmore shrugged one shoulder. "I do not want to marry a woman that has ears that remind me of an elephant."

"Whyever not?" Samuel asked. "I would imagine they would be ideal for listening to you babble on and on."

"I do not babble."

"You are babbling right now," he joked. "Although, just so we are clear, do you know the difference between qualities and physical attributes? I only ask since you did not list one quality."

"I haven't gotten to those yet."

With a flick of his wrist, Samuel said, "My apologies, please proceed then."

Mr. Whitmore brought his list back up. "I do not want a woman that interrupts me or has an opinion."

Samuel just stared at his friend. He knew he should be surprised by Mr. Whitmore's outrageous remarks, but he wasn't. "What woman do you know that doesn't have an opinion?" he questioned.

"I know. That is why I find myself in an impossible position," Mr. Whitmore said with a dramatic sigh. "Women are drawn to me, but I have yet to find one that keeps my interest. It is a terrible burden that I must bear. You wouldn't understand since you scare women away with the perpetual scowl on your face."

"I do not scowl."

"You scowl, all the time," Mr. Whitmore said matter-of-factly. "But that works for you since you have no interest in marriage or having any friends."

"I have friends, but you are right about the marriage part," Samuel contended.

Mr. Whitmore placed the list down onto the table. "You cannot understand the pressure that I am under to find a wife."

"Are you sure no one has sparked your interest this Season?"

"A few have, but then they start talking and they ruin everything."

Samuel chuckled. "You do realize that once you are married you will have to converse with your wife about her thoughts and feelings."

Mr. Whitmore shuddered. "What a terrible thought."

Pointing at the list, Samuel said, "My advice is to get rid of that list and have an open mind when you are being intro-duced to the ladies."

"An open mind? Are you mad?" Mr. Whitmore repeated. "No, this list will help me eliminate the ladies that are not up to my high standards."

A server approached the table and placed two drinks down into the center of the table. "Will there be anything else?" he asked.

"Not at this time," Mr. Whitmore replied.

As the server walked off, Samuel reached for a glass and took a sip. His friend's list was ludicrous, but it was on par for the man.

"How was work today?" Mr. Whitmore asked.

"It was busier than usual."

Mr. Whitmore took a sip of his drink before saying, "You

don't have to work. You are the son of a highly respected- and wealthy- viscount. You can close up shop and spend more time with me."

"As fun as that sounds, I enjoy being a barrister. It gives me a purpose."

"You work entirely too hard." Mr. Whitmore tightened the hold on his glass as he said, "Join me tonight at Lady Morley's ball."

With a shake of his head, he replied, "I could think of nothing worse to do with my time."

"I need your help with the ladies."

"I have no doubt that you will do just fine on your own."

Mr. Whitmore grew uncharacteristically solemn as he leaned forward in his seat. In a low voice, he asked, "Did you hear that Phoebe has returned to Town?"

Samuel took a moment to collect himself. Even now, after all this time, just hearing her name caused his heart to do inconvenient things. He had worked so hard to banish Phoebe from his thoughts, but he was never quite able to do so.

Trying to appear indifferent, he asked, "Why should I care?"

"I think you do care."

He couldn't let on to Mr. Whitmore about how much he *did* care or else his friend would pity him. "You would be wrong. Phoebe made her choice when she married Lord Bedlington."

"But Lord Bedlington died nearly two years ago and Phoebe is a widow."

Samuel was well aware of Phoebe's widowed status but that didn't mean he would pursue her. He had already gone down that path and his heart had yet to recover. Phoebe had left him as a broken man and it had taken a long time for him to pick up the pieces and move on. No. He refused to make that mistake again.

He pushed away his drink and said, "I do not want to speak about Phoebe."

Mr. Whitmore gave him a look that could only be construed as pity. "I know she hurt you, but you have a chance with her again."

"I think not." Samuel shoved back his chair and rose. "With that said, I do believe it is time for me to depart."

With a glance at his nearly full glass, Mr. Whitmore said, "But you haven't even finished your drink."

"I am not thirsty."

A sigh escaped Mr. Whitmore's lips and his expression seemed to grow more sympathetic. "You can't keep on running whenever Phoebe's name is mentioned. Eventually, your past will catch up to you."

"It is a past that is better forgotten."

As he turned to leave, Mr. Whitmore said, "Prove it, then. Join me tonight at the ball and show me that Phoebe has no power over you."

"What would that accomplish?"

Mr. Whitmore gave him a knowing look. "It would help you to move on."

"I have moved on."

"Have you?" Mr. Whitmore asked. "Because you have shown no interest in any other lady since Phoebe turned down your offer of marriage."

Samuel was done with this conversation. He didn't want to think on that fateful day when Phoebe had informed him that she was marrying another. He thought they had an understanding, but he had been wrong. She had chosen to marry for security, rather than love.

However, he didn't dare admit to his friend the depth of feelings that he still held for Phoebe. There was a reason why every other woman paled in comparison to her.

"Fine, I will go this evening, but do not expect me to dance," Samuel said. Quite frankly, he knew his parents would be pleased that he was going to a ball, as well. He could kill two birds with one stone, so to speak.

Mr. Whitmore smirked. "I wouldn't dream of it."

"Are we done here?"

Leaning back in his seat, Mr. Whitmore reached for his glass. "I think so," he replied. "I will see you tonight."

"Yes, you will," Samuel said before he turned to leave. He would go to the ball and prove to himself that he was doing just fine on his own. Phoebe be damned. He didn't need her in his life. She had made her choice and he refused to let her back into his life. So why was his heart still pounding at the mere thought of seeing Phoebe again?

Chapter Two

Esther sat in the library as she read a book. She was biding her time until her father returned home so she could appeal to his sense of decency. She couldn't marry Lord Warley. He may be old, but he had already outlived three wives. What if he outlived her? The thought caused her to shudder.

She was already on her fourth Season but she refused to entertain the thought of not marrying for love. Her mother and father had a love match and they had been so happy. That is what she wanted. So why was her stepmother pressuring her into marrying an old man? It didn't matter to her that he was a marquess.

How had it gotten this far? She had told her stepmother and father, repeatedly, that she did not want to marry Lord Warley. When would they stop this madness and listen to what she wanted? It seemed the more she tried to make her opinion known, the more they dismissed what she said as unimportant. She felt unheard, and that made her feel alone.

A young maid stepped into the room and announced, "Lord Mather would like to speak to you in his study, my lady."

"I shall be right down."

The maid tipped her head before departing.

Rising, Esther placed the book onto the table and knew this was a fight worth fighting. Ever since her father had married Susanna, he had changed. He wasn't as approachable as he had been when her mother was alive. At times, she wondered if she'd lost both of her parents the day her mother died. But she refused to believe her father would force her into a marriage that she didn't want, knowing how unhappy she would be.

She was already at a disadvantage. Susanna had no doubt shared her opinion on the matter with her father and, knowing her, added a few tears to ensure she got her way.

Esther exited the library and headed towards the study on the main level. She had a fairly good idea of how her father would react to her turning down Lord Warley, but she hoped she was wrong. Her father's temper was not one that she wanted to stoke.

As she stepped into the study, she saw her stepmother was sitting next to her father on the settee. It was just as she'd predicted- Susanna had red-lined eyes. She had been putting on a show for her father and she had no doubt that he had fallen for it.

Her father looked up when she came into the room. "Come have a seat, young lady."

This was not starting out well. Her father only used "young lady" when he was upset with her, which was starting to become more frequent.

Esther sat across from her father and stepmother, clasping her hands in her lap. She was waiting for the tongue-lashing that would undoubtedly come.

Her father shifted in his seat to face her, his expression unreadable. "I understand that you had a visitor today."

"I did."

"Will you kindly tell me why you would turn down Lord Warley's offer of marriage?" Her father's words sounded pleasant enough but there was a sharpness to his tone that put her on edge.

With a glance at Susanna, Esther replied, "I do not want to marry him, Father." She spoke gently, yet with an air of conviction.

"Pray tell, why would you turn down this advantageous marriage?" her father pressed.

"He is old."

Her father looked unimpressed by her admission. "That is your only concern?"

"No." She paused. "I know I could never grow to love him."

Susanna let out a slight huff but remained quiet.

Reaching for his wife's hand, her father said, "Susanna and I feel that you should reconsider for the sake of your future."

Esther stared at her father in disbelief. Surely he didn't mean that. Her father was many things, but he tended to be reasonable. So why was he pressing this marriage? "You wish for me to enter a loveless marriage?"

"It is not as if you have received any other offers," her father replied. "You are on your fourth Season and you have yet to attract a husband."

"I didn't realize you were so anxious for me to wed," Esther remarked as she attempted to keep the bitterness out of her tone.

"What happened?" her father asked. "Your first Season seemed so promising, but you failed to secure a suitor. Now I fear that you are welcoming spinsterhood."

Esther shook her head. "I do not wish to become a spinster. I just have failed to find the right person to marry."

"What, exactly, are you looking for?" Susanna asked.

In an unwavering voice, she answered, "A relationship built on love." She shifted her gaze back to her father. "I want what you and Mother had."

Her father's eyes softened at the mention of her mother, but only for a moment. "Sometimes, we have to make our own happily ever after," he counseled.

"Do you truly think that Lord Warley will make me happy?" Esther asked.

"Lord Warley is a good man and he has treated all his other wives with respect," her father replied.

"Is that what you want for me- respect?" Esther pressed.

She watched as her father pressed his lips together, hoping her words had resonated with him. "You have given us little choice in the matter," he replied. "If you had only shown more interest in your suitors, we wouldn't be having this conversation."

Esther bit her lower lip as she said, "You seem to forget that Mother died during my third Season and we went into mourning."

"Yes, but that was long ago," her father stated. "It is time for you to move on. I have." Her father exchanged a glance with Susanna. "Time doesn't stop when someone you love dies. You just have to learn to live without them."

"I am not like you," Esther said. "I am still mourning my mother."

"I will always mourn the loss of your mother..." her father started.

Unable to bite her sharp tongue, she interjected before he could finish. "I doubt that. You married Susanna only six months after Mother died. How much did you truly mourn her if you got over her so easily?"

Susanna gasped. "That was uncalled for," she chided.

The emotion her father had written across his face was difficult to interpret, but the sorrow in his eyes was unmistakable. "It is all right," he responded. "I was lonely, and I needed an heir to secure our family's legacy. Susanna was the logical choice."

Esther couldn't help but notice that Susanna flinched at

his words. It was so subtle that she feared she had imagined it. Apparently, Susanna didn't like being called "a logical choice."

Her father continued, unaware of how his words had affected his wife. "I won't always be around, and I need to ensure that you are taken care of. If you marry Lord Warley, you will have a brilliant future. Just think of the doors that will be opened to you."

"But I will be trapped in a loveless marriage," Esther argued.

"You don't know that for certain," her father responded. "Besides, you might develop mutual respect for Lord Warley. That is the best you can hope for."

Esther didn't know what to say. Why was her father pushing her into a marriage that she did not want? Did he care so little for her?

Susanna spoke up. "I know you think we are being terribly unfair but you will come to see that marrying Lord Warley is the logical choice." There were those words again- *logical choice.*

"I don't want logical. I want love," Esther stated.

Her stepmother placed a hand on her increasing stomach and said, "Then perhaps you should have made more of an effort to obtain it."

Esther grew quiet. She would never agree to a marriage with Lord Warley but what if she came up with another solution? Would that appease them? "What if I entertained suitors this Season?" she suggested.

"No," her father replied. "I can't keep paying for you to have a Season only for it to end in disappointment."

"This Season will be different," Esther asserted.

"I doubt that," Susanna said under her breath.

"It is true," Esther remarked. "If I don't find a husband by the end of the Season, then I will agree to an arranged marriage."

Susanna did not look pleased by her proposal. But, then again, when had her stepmother ever been pleased with her?

"I doubt that Lord Warley will wait that long for you," Susanna said before she addressed her husband. "Will he?"

"I don't rightly know," her father replied. "I agreed to throw my support for his bill in Parliament for a union between our families."

"Why would you agree to such a thing?" Esther asked.

Her father met her gaze, and for the briefest of moments, it reminded her of how he used to look at her with admiration. But that was long ago.

"It is the least I could do for you," he replied. "Furthermore, we want you to establish your own household and not be underfoot when the baby comes."

"You have already banished me to the other wing of the townhouse," Esther said. "Is that not far enough?"

Susanna merely shrugged one shoulder. "Your bedchamber was the perfect location for the nursery. I didn't realize you had such an objection."

"Of course I had an objection!" Esther shouted, tossing her hands up in the air. "That has been my bedchamber since I have been out of the nursery."

Her father gave her a pointed look. "There is no reason to raise your voice. Everyone has to make some sacrifices for the baby."

Esther doubted that. What did her father and stepmother have to give up? They seemed to only be asking her to make sacrifices.

"Regardless, I do not think we should delay announcing the engagement between you and Lord Warley," Susanna said. "We don't want to risk his interest waning."

"If his attention would wane so easily, is he even truly interested in me?" Esther argued.

"You would be the Marchioness of Warley," Susanna said. "Do you know how much power that wields in high Society?"

"I don't care about my place in Society," Esther countered.

Susanna awkwardly rose from her seat and said, "This conversation is going in circles and I need to rest."

Rising, her father asked, "Would you care for me to escort you to your bedchamber?"

"That won't be necessary," Susanna replied with a wave of her hand. "Just try to talk some sense into your daughter."

"Very well," her father responded.

Neither of them spoke as Susanna departed from the room and Esther was grateful for the silence. She wasn't ready to back down but, then again, neither would her father. He was entirely too stubborn for that.

Her father walked over to the drink cart and poured himself a drink. As he picked up the glass, he asked, "What am I going to do with you, Child?"

Knowing her father wasn't expecting a response to his rhetorical question, she remained quiet. She didn't want to aggravate him any further.

He walked back over to the settee and sat down. "I understand your reservations, but sometimes we need to look at the whole picture before we come to a decision. Lord Warley might be your only chance to wed and establish your own household."

"I won't marry him, Father."

"You would willingly choose spinsterhood over Lord Warley?"

Esther knew her father wouldn't like her response, but she had to speak true. "If those are the only two options, then I would choose spinsterhood."

Her father frowned, his displeasure evident in the lines creasing his forehead in response to her words. "I'm afraid I can't allow you to throw away your future. You must trust me on this."

"Trust you?" Esther asked. "How can I trust you when you

know nothing about loyalty? You betrayed Mother by marrying Susanna."

"I do not see it that way," her father responded. "Besides, I thought you would have welcomed Susanna with open arms since you were friends."

"We were friends, Father, but that all changed when she became my stepmother," Esther stated.

"Regardless, I need an heir. I cannot stand the thought of Daniel inheriting everything that I have worked so hard to obtain," her father said. "He would squander it all on the horse races."

Esther was all too aware of her cousin's less than stellar reputation and she understood her father's reluctance to allow him to inherit. But that didn't mean he had to marry Susanna. There were plenty of women that would have been thrilled to be a countess.

After taking a sip, her father placed his glass down onto the table. "I have decided that we will announce your engagement with Lord Warley tonight at the ball."

She was speechless, her jaw dropping open in astonishment. It took her a few seconds to regain her composure. "You can't be in earnest, Father."

"I am," her father said. "You are angry now, but I assure you that, one day, you will thank me for pushing you into this marriage."

"What would Mother say about this?"

Her father's face grew solemn. "Do not bring your mother into this!" he shouted. "You are my daughter and I will do with you what I think is best."

Esther knew precisely who had arranged this marriage. She was no simpleton. "No, you are doing what Susanna thinks is best."

"Susanna wants what is best for you, too—"

She huffed. "I doubt that."

"You may as well come to terms with your engagement because I have no intention of changing my mind."

"We shall see." Esther rose from her seat. "If you make me go forth with this engagement, I will never forgive you."

A grayish flush spread over his face, dissolving all his expressions into a man she hardly recognized. "I am sorry you feel that way, but my mind is made up."

Esther couldn't believe her father would be so callous as to force her into an arranged marriage. He had changed since he had married Susanna, and not for the better.

With tears pricking at the back of her eyes, Esther ran from the room. She didn't want to cry in front of her father and show him how much he had hurt her. She needed to find a way out of her current predicament, and quickly.

It wasn't as if she could run away since she had no place to go. No, she needed a miracle.

Samuel stood in the back of the ballroom as he listened to the patrons being announced. He tried to pretend that he was uninterested in what was going on around him, but he was anxiously waiting for Phoebe's name to be announced. He hadn't seen her since she had turned down his offer of marriage. He just wanted one glimpse of her. That was all. Then he could move on.

Mr. Whitmore approached him with a flute of champagne in his hand. "Why are you hiding all the way in the back?"

"I am not hiding."

"What are you doing then?"

"I am merely observing."

Mr. Whitmore didn't look convinced. "Observing what, exactly?" he asked. "Because it almost appears as if you are trying to keep yourself hidden from Phoebe."

Samuel stiffened. "I am doing no such thing," he lied. How had his friend been able to see right through him?

"It is all right if you want to admit that you still desire her," Mr. Whitmore said with a knowing smile.

Turning towards his friend, he asked, "What is it that you want?"

"I just heard the most tasty piece of gossip," Mr. Whitmore replied. "Apparently, Lord Warley is going to announce his engagement this evening."

"Who is the unlucky lady?"

Mr. Whitmore shrugged. "I don't rightly know, but it would appear that she has gone missing."

"Missing?"

"Yes, but she will turn up," Mr. Whitmore said. "Whoever this lady is would be a fool to turn down an offer of marriage from Lord Warley."

"Perhaps she is wise to turn him down."

Mr. Whitmore took a sip of his drink before saying, "Lord Warley has wealth, power and is old. No doubt, he will die soon and this lady will be free to do as she pleases."

As he opened his mouth to reply, his friend, Lord Brentwood, broke through the crowd and stopped in front of him. "There you are," he said, his voice breathless. "I have been looking for you everywhere."

"Why?" Samuel asked.

Lord Brentwood grew somber. "Phoebe is here," he hesitated, "and she is on the arm of Lord Leyburn."

Samuel tried to appear indifferent. "Why would I care a whit about that?"

"I think we both know that you do," Lord Brentwood replied. "There is a rumor that they are about to announce their engagement."

"Already?" Mr. Whitmore asked. "Phoebe has only just reentered Society's ranks."

"I cannot speak on that, but I wanted to give Samuel fair warning," Lord Brentwood said, his eyes holding compassion.

Samuel was fine. Just fine. He was a grown man and he didn't need his friends to coddle him. It wasn't as if he planned on pursuing Phoebe… again. No, she had made her choice and he must accept it. So why did his heart ache at the thought of her getting engaged to another man?

Botheration. His love had never waned for Phoebe and he knew it. Had he no shame? She had led him on, pretending that she cared for him, but she had chosen a man with a higher rank than his. All she cared about was her place in Society and love was just a trite detail to her.

His mind barely registered Phoebe's name being announced but he heard it, nonetheless. His eyes shot up and he saw Phoebe gliding into the ballroom. She was dressed in a gold-colored gown and an ornate diamond necklace hung around her neck. Her blonde hair was piled high atop her head and small curls framed her face.

Good gads, she had grown even more beautiful since he had last seen her. How was that possible?

He had been so distracted by Phoebe that he failed to notice her silver-haired companion, Lord Leyburn, had escorted her into the ballroom. He leaned closer to her and whispered something, causing a bright smile to come to Phoebe's face. That was the smile that still haunted his dreams.

Lord Brentwood had a look of concern etched on his features. "Are you all right, Samuel?"

No. How could he be all right when Phoebe had once again moved on from him? He wasn't surprised by her lack of suitors, but he had been secretly hoping that she would recognize that she had made a mistake when she had turned him down. But it appeared that was just a fantasy on his part.

"Excuse me," Samuel said. "I need to step outside for a moment."

"Would you like us to join you?" Mr. Whitmore asked.

Samuel needed air and he needed it now. It was entirely too stuffy in the ballroom. "I would prefer to be alone," he replied before he headed towards the French doors that led out to the veranda.

He didn't stop on the veranda but continued down the path towards the rear of the gardens, passing by patrons that were taking advantage of the cool night air. He decided to step off the path and approach a cluster of trees that lined the back gate.

While he headed towards the trees, he saw a shadowed figure attempting to climb one of the tall birch trees in a ball-gown. He should just walk away and leave this lady alone, but he found himself curious as to what she was attempting to do.

The young lady was so engrossed in her efforts to climb the tree that she failed to notice him approach.

"Pray tell, what are you attempting to do?" he asked.

Without sparing him a glance, she replied, "Isn't it obvious, sir? I am attempting to climb this tree."

"Attempting is a good word for it."

"It is harder than I thought to climb a tree in a gown and slippers, and I would ask you to keep your voice down."

Samuel leaned his shoulder against a tree and asked, "May I ask what you hope to accomplish by climbing that tree?"

She let out a puff of air. "I am trying to escape."

"Escape from what, exactly?"

"The ball," she said as she reached for a branch above her head and tried to pull herself up. But she failed, time and time again.

"Why would you wish to escape the ball?"

"My reasons are my own," she responded.

"Do you know how to climb a tree?"

"I used to climb trees when I was younger," she said. "Would you kindly assist me up?"

Samuel shook his head. "I will not."

"Are you not a gentleman? Will you not help a woman in distress?" she asked.

"I am a gentleman, but I cannot in good conscience help you climb a tree," he replied. "Where is your companion?"

She huffed as she placed both of her feet back down onto the ground. From where he stood, he could see the straight bridge of her nose and thin lips pursed into a tight arc, showing her determination. "You need not worry about that. If you are unable to assist me, then be on your way," she said with a wave of her hand.

"I never said I was unable. I am just unwilling to do so."

The young lady turned to face him as the moonlight hit her face. She was stunning, with her delicate complexion, defined nose and slender jaw. Her golden tresses were formed into ringlets atop her head, and a single strand of pearls encircled her neck.

His heart beat a little faster as their eyes met. She was enchanting. Who was this young woman, he wondered. And why did he have such a reaction to meeting her?

The young woman placed her hand on her hip. "You are drawing unwanted attention to my predicament and I think it would be best if you left." She looked up at the tree. "I will find a way to escape on my own."

"Perhaps you could try the gate?"

She rolled her eyes. "That was the first thing I tried, but it was locked," she informed him. "My only recourse is to climb this tree and drop down onto the other side of the gate."

"That is your only recourse?" he joked.

With annoyance in her voice, she asked, "What is it that you want?"

Samuel smiled. He didn't know why but he found her to be quite amusing. "Nothing," he replied. "I just find myself curious as to how you are going to accomplish your escape."

The young lady dropped her hand from her hip and said,

"I am not here to entertain you, and I do not owe you an explanation."

"I am well aware, but perhaps we could find another solution to your problem." Good heavens, had he just offered to help the young woman? Why would he do such a thing? If anyone saw them together- alone- the consequences could be dire.

With a glance towards the direction of the townhouse, the young lady said, "I'm afraid no one can help me now." Her voice was sad, resigned.

The way she spoke tugged at his heartstrings and he found himself moving closer to her. "Surely nothing could be as bad as you are making it out to be."

"I'm afraid it is," she replied. "My father wants me to announce my engagement this evening to a man that I utterly do not care for."

Realization dawned and he realized that this was the missing young woman from the ball. Why was she running away? Was the thought of marrying Lord Warley so repulsive to her?

The young lady's shoulders slumped slightly. "You must think me silly to run away, but I do not want to marry this man. He is old and only wants to marry me so I can produce an heir."

"I must assume you speak of Lord Warley."

She met his gaze with astonishment. "How did you know that?"

"I will admit it wasn't that difficult to deduce," he said. "I hope this is not too presumptuous, but you would become a marchioness. Isn't that what all ladies want?" He worked hard to keep the bitterness out of his tone.

Her eyes were full of reflective sincerity. "I do not care for a title if it means I am not able to marry for love."

"Love?" he repeated. "You do not know what you speak of. Love is an elusive thing amongst high Society."

"Should I not at least try?"

Samuel couldn't quite believe what he was hearing. This young woman was willing to throw everything away- security, position in Society- for a chance at love. Was she brave or an absolute fool? He couldn't answer that. But he found her intriguing. He had never met someone quite like her.

An idea suddenly came to him. It was a stroke of genius on his part. What if they could help one another?

"I think I have a solution that might benefit both of us," Samuel said.

The young woman gave him a curious look. "What might that be?"

"What if we pretend to form an attachment with one another for the Season?" he asked. "It would buy you some time to find a suitor that you could fall in love with."

"But my father is adamant that I marry Lord Warley."

"Let me deal with that," Samuel said with a smile. "I have been told that I can be rather persuasive."

"What would you get out of it?"

Samuel paused to collect his thoughts before speaking, searching for the most effective words to sway her opinion. "I find that I am in need of a distraction."

"A distraction?" she asked. "Is that what you think I am?"

"Does it matter what I think? I found a solution to your problem. You just have to pretend to be enamored with me when we go speak to your father."

The young woman bit her lower lip. "What about after the Season?"

"You go your way, and I go mine," Samuel said. "Do we have a deal?"

She considered him for a long moment before saying, "I don't even know who you are."

"You make an excellent point. Allow me to rectify that right now." He bowed. "My name is Mr. Samuel Moore and I am the eldest son of Lord Harrogate."

Her eyes grew wide. "You are the barrister that helped to exonerate Lady Eugenie."

"That I am."

"I read all about you in the newssheets," she admitted. "You were brilliant."

He puffed his chest out with pride. "Thank you. I had some help, but I was happy that Lady Eugenie was freed."

The young woman stepped closer to him, but still maintained a proper distance. Not that there was anything proper about this situation. Emotions flickered across her face as she considered him, and he realized that she was terrible at hiding what she was feeling. He rather liked that about her. He was so accustomed to being around people that felt the need to hide behind a mask of their own making that he appreciated her vulnerability even more.

He could tell that she was nervous. And she should be. He was a practical stranger to her, and what he was proposing was pure lunacy. But he couldn't face Phoebe as he was. She would know that he hadn't moved on and she would only pity him. The mortification of it all would be too much for him. Quite frankly, he would rather pretend to pursue a young woman that he didn't know than admit he still harbored feelings for Phoebe.

In a voice that betrayed her hesitancy, she said, "You have a deal."

Chapter Three

Esther was going mad. That had to be it. Why else would she put her trust in a stranger? But her father had left her with little choice in the matter. If it was between Lord Warley or Mr. Moore, she was going to put her faith in Mr. Moore.

It had nothing to do with Mr. Moore's extremely handsome face. He had dark hair, brown eyes and his skin was rather tanned for a gentleman. Furthermore, he was much more pleasant to look upon than the old, pasty-skinned Lord Warley.

When Mr. Moore smiled, she felt a wave of hope wash over her. She believed that, though it may take time, things would eventually be all right. Maybe not now, maybe not tomorrow, but soon. She was risking everything when she agreed to this madcap plan.

"I am glad that we have come to an understanding, but I'm afraid I am at a disadvantage by not knowing your name," he said.

Esther went to drop into a curtsy but stopped when Mr. Moore reached for her gloved hand. She looked at him in surprise.

"I would prefer it if there were no formalities between us," Mr. Moore said as he still held her hand in his.

"Very well," she replied, secretly pleased by his request. "My name is Lady Esther Harington, and I am the daughter of Lord Mather."

Mr. Moore tipped his head. "It is nice to meet you, my lady." He paused. "May I call you Esther?"

"You may, sir." She found she rather liked hearing her name on his lips, but she couldn't quite bring herself to say his given name.

"I would prefer if you would call me Samuel," he corrected.

Esther had never called a gentleman by his given name, at least one that wasn't a family friend, but she knew she had little choice in the matter. They had to convince everyone that they had formed an attachment with one another.

Knowing he was still waiting for her response, she said, "Samuel."

"That wasn't so hard, was it?" he asked.

"No, it was not," she agreed.

Samuel released her hand but made no effort to create more distance between them. "May I escort you back inside?"

"Must we?" she asked. "I am not ready to face my father or stepmother."

He looked at her with compassion, as if he saw the difficulty of the situation she was in. "I have learned it is best to do the hard things first, so they are out of the way."

"I prefer to avoid doing hard things and pretend that all is well."

"Says the lady that tried to climb a tree to escape a ball," he teased.

Esther gave him an amused look. "I can assure you that climbing a tree is much more preferable than speaking to my father."

"I doubt that," Samuel said. "You seem to forget that I argue for a living."

"But for a good cause."

"Not always."

Esther could hear the pain behind his words and she decided it was best if she didn't press him. After all, she hardly knew the man. It wouldn't be fair of her to dig into his past.

Samuel continued. "The hardest part is starting. Once you get that out of the way, the rest of your tasks seem much more bearable." He held his hand up. "Let's do this together."

"Together," she replied, placing her hand into his. She quite liked the sound of that. She had been on her own for so long that it felt nice to have someone on her side for once.

"All right, Lady Esther Harington of..." His voice trailed off. "Where do you hail from, exactly?"

"Rothbury," she replied.

"Lady Esther Harington of Rothbury," Samuel started, "I propose we enter the ballroom and dance a set before we go speak to your father."

"What if he refuses to go along with our plan?"

"That is why we will dance a set first and have the *ton* see us together. It will force his hand," he replied as he placed her hand into the crook of his arm. "Furthermore, I can be very persuasive when I want to be."

It was important to her that Samuel understood her father's true character: a kind and caring individual, yet somewhat overbearing since his marriage to her stepmother. "My father believes this match with Lord Warley is the best for me," she said, "and I must warn you he can be quite stubborn."

"We share that trait in common, then," Samuel said.

Esther felt her heart pounding in her chest as they left the safety of the trees and approached the townhouse. She didn't know how her father and stepmother would react to Samuel and that made her even more nervous.

If their plan didn't work, she would find herself engaged to Lord Warley by the end of the evening. No, she wouldn't let that happen. This plan had to work.

She knew that this plan came with great risks to her. Once the *ton* discovered that Samuel was pursuing her, her reputation would become tarnished when he withdrew his suit. But it was a risk worth taking. She would rather be a spinster than marry Lord Warley.

Samuel paused on the veranda and turned to face her. His face was etched with concern. "I want to make sure that you are comfortable with this plan," he said. "I wouldn't want to do anything that would make you feel uncomfortable."

She found herself touched by his words. It had been a long time since someone seemed truly concerned for her well-being. "You are kind to say so, but I assure you that I am eager for this plan to unfold."

His astute eyes watched her for a long moment, and she was fearful of what he saw. Had he changed his mind? Was she not enough for him? She hoped not because she truly didn't want to go back to climbing a tree to escape the ball.

Finally, after what felt like hours, but was probably only mere moments, Samuel said, "Very well. Just follow my lead and all will be well."

As he led her into the ballroom, she kept her head held high as they headed towards the chalked dance floor. She noticed a few people acknowledge them, but she didn't get the gawking stares like she had been anticipating.

Her stepmother's voice came from behind her. "Where have you been?" she asked in a hushed but accusatory tone. "Lord Warley has been waiting for you."

Esther stopped and turned around to face Susanna. "There has been a change of plans," she revealed.

With pursed lips, Susanna said, "You can speak to your father in the library about this." Her stepmother's eyes flicked towards Samuel. "You will wait here."

"Mr. Moore will be accompanying me." Esther wasn't going to let her stepmother dictate her actions, especially now. Having Mr. Moore by her side provided her with much-needed strength.

Esther knew her stepmother was angry, but she wouldn't make a scene- not in the middle of a ballroom. Susanna just nodded her head in acknowledgement and headed towards the front of the hall.

Once they stepped into the entry hall, her stepmother glanced over her shoulder. "Follow me, and do not dally."

Samuel leaned closer to her and whispered, "I must assume that is your stepmother."

"It is," Esther replied.

"She is a delight."

Esther giggled, but schooled her features when Susanna shot her an irritated glance.

Susanna came to a stop outside of a door and said, "There is nothing funny about this situation. I would remember that when you are speaking to your father."

In a swift motion, Susanna opened the door and stepped inside, leaving the door wide open.

Esther went to follow her stepmother into the room but was stopped by Samuel. "Do not let your emotions get the best of you," he advised. "Keep a clear head and avoid arguing with your father."

"That is easier said than done."

"I am aware, but we must take control of the narrative," Samuel said. "You must trust me."

"Trust is to be earned."

"Then I shall strive to earn your trust," Samuel stated before he escorted her inside, stopping only to close the door behind him.

With his arms crossed over his chest, her father stood near the mantel with a stern expression on his face, eyes locked in a piercing gaze that she had never seen him use before.

She resisted the urge to move closer to Samuel. Her father had never given her a reason to be afraid of him, until now.

"Father," she said.

Her father's eyes shifted towards Samuel. "Mr. Moore," he growled. "Whatever are you doing here and with my daughter on your arm?"

Mr. Moore bowed. "Good evening, my lord. I would like to speak to you about my intentions towards your daughter."

"Absolutely not!" her father declared. "You may have won the *ton* over by exonerating Lady Eugenie, but you have not fooled me. I know the type of man you are."

Esther withdrew her hand from Samuel. "What do you mean, Father?" She hoped she hadn't misjudged Mr. Moore.

With a clenched jaw, her father replied, "He is a Whig, a reformer. I will never have my daughter associate with such a man."

She almost felt like laughing in relief. She knew her father was a staunch Tory, but Samuel's political views did not define him as a person.

Samuel did not appear concerned with her father's outburst. "Be that as it may, I intend to pursue your daughter."

"Did you not hear what I said?" her father snapped.

"I heard you, but I chose to respectfully ignore you, my lord," Samuel replied.

Her father dropped his arms to his sides. "Regardless, you are too late," he declared. "Esther is to be married to Lord Warley."

"I do believe that Lady Esther objects to that union," Samuel remarked.

Her stepmother spoke up as she walked to stand by her husband. "Esther doesn't even know what she wants."

"You insult the lady," Samuel said. "Lady Esther is a capable young woman who knows her mind. In fact, I found her trying to climb a tree to escape the betrothal to Lord Warley."

"Good heavens, what if someone had seen you?" her step-mother cried. "You would have been ruined and no one would have wanted to marry you."

"That is preferable to marrying Lord Warley," Esther said.

Her father stood there, stewing. "You would willingly give up being a marchioness to marry the son of a lowly viscount?" he asked, gruffly.

"No one said anything about marriage," Esther said as she snuck a peek at Samuel.

"That is even worse," her father stated. "You are risking everything, including your reputation, to be pursued by Mr. Moore. Think on that, young lady."

Esther bit her lower lip as she tried to find the strength to say her next words. "I have, and I do not intend to change my mind."

Susanna let out a cry as she tossed up her arms. "All of our work has been wasted."

"It has not been wasted because Esther will marry Lord Warley," her father said with a swipe of his hand.

Samuel stood his ground and his next words were full of conviction. "If you attempt to force Lady Esther into an arranged marriage then we will have no choice but to elope to Gretna Green."

Esther turned towards him with wide eyes. Surely he wasn't serious? Samuel gave her a pointed look and she real-ized that he was trying to force her father's hand on this.

"Do be serious," her father said. "This is Esther's future we are discussing."

"I know, and I am fighting to give her the future that she deserves," Samuel stated in a firm tone.

"You hardly know Lady Esther. You must trust us that we know what is best for her," Susanna stated.

Esther knew it was time that she took a stand and hoped

her father and stepmother would finally listen to her. "I know what is best for me." She took a step closer to Samuel and addressed her father. "And I would like your permission for Samuel to pursue me."

Her father stared at her, his face unyielding in its disapproval. She returned the look, daring him to stop her from deciding her own future. This was a side of Esther he hadn't seen before, but she had no intention of backing down. She refused to let him plan her future.

After a long moment, her father put his hands up in surrender. "I will not fight you on this, not anymore, since you have finally put forth an effort in finding a suitor," he said. "But I hope you know what you are doing."

"But David..." Susanna started.

Her father put his hand up, stilling his wife's words. "This is what Esther wants. At least now I don't have to back Lord Warley's bill."

"Thank you, my lord," Samuel said.

"Do not take this for my approval," her father responded. "I wanted more for my daughter but you will do, for now."

Samuel appeared to be unperturbed by her father's prickly words as he turned towards her. "Shall we return to the ball?" he asked.

Esther accepted his proffered arm and he started to lead her out of the library. She stopped by the door and turned back around. "Thank you, Father."

Her father's expression showed no signs of softening. "I will inform Lord Warley of your decision at once."

She offered him a grateful smile as Samuel led her out of the library. Once they stepped into the corridor, she leaned closer and said, "Thank you for what you did back there."

"I didn't do much."

"You did enough."

Samuel patted her hand. "That was the easy part."

"It was?"

"Now we need to convince the *ton* that we are enamored with one another," Samuel said. "They will be much harsher in their assessment than your father, especially when word gets out that you turned down an offer from Lord Warley."

"How would the *ton* know?"

"I'm afraid a tasty piece of gossip is too much for members of high Society to ignore."

Esther took a deep breath and lifted her chin as she prepared to face the patrons in the ballroom. She knew they were about to fight an uphill battle, but she wasn't as afraid as she was before. There was something about Samuel that made her hope for a better future.

With Esther on his arm, Samuel stepped into the ballroom with a renewed sense of confidence. He was well aware that they had to convince the *ton*- and, more importantly, Phoebe-that they were enamored with one another, but he wasn't overly worried. Esther appeared to be a clever young woman who knew what was at stake.

He truly hoped that Esther's reputation didn't suffer too much when they ended this farce of a relationship, but he didn't want to think about that now. He was solely focused on making sure that Phoebe knew he had moved on from her. He didn't want her to think he was still pining after her. The mere thought of that was mortifying.

Samuel watched as the dancers started to line up on the chalked dance floor and he decided it would be in their best interest to join them.

As they approached the dance floor, Esther looked over at him with questions in her eyes. "This dance is to be the waltz," she said.

"I am well aware."

Esther looked hesitant as she admitted, "I have never danced the waltz before, at least not with a gentleman."

"Just follow my lead and you will be fine."

Samuel came to a stop on the dance floor and turned to face her. He gave her an encouraging smile before he slipped his hand onto her waist. He reached for her hand and brought it up as the music started to play.

He started leading her around the dance floor and he could feel how tense Esther was. He watched as her eyes darted around the room, landing on everything but him.

"Esther," he said. "If we want this to work, we have to appear as if we genuinely enjoy one another's company."

Esther brought her gaze back to meet his, but he could see the doubt in her eyes. "But everyone is staring at us."

"Do not worry about that," he encouraged as he brought their hands above their heads, bringing them closer to one another. "Just focus on the dance."

"I just fear that everyone will know what a terrible dancer I am."

"You dance superbly," he attempted.

She let out a slight huff. "I daresay you are prone to exaggeration, sir."

"Try to relax and let me lead you."

"I will try but I don't want to relax too much or else I might do something intolerably clumsy like trip over your feet."

"Surely you are not that bad of a dancer."

"I assure you that I am."

Samuel tightened his hold on her waist. "Fortunately for you, I am an excellent dancer and I promise that I won't let you fall."

He could feel Esther relax in his arms and he considered that a small victory.

Esther seemed to study him for a moment before asking, "Will you tell me the real reason why you agreed to this plan?

I know you said it was because you were looking for a distraction, but I do believe there is more to it."

Samuel knew it was best if he just told her the truth and hoped she would understand his plight. "Are you acquainted with Lady Bedlington?"

"I am not."

"Before she married Lord Bedlington, I offered for her and she turned me down," he explained. "Now she is a widow, and there are rumors that she is about to become engaged again."

Understanding dawned on Esther's features. "And you don't want her to think you are still pining after her."

"That is correct."

"Are you still pining after her?"

With a shake of his head, he replied, "I am not. The past is best if it is left behind."

"Did you love her?"

Samuel grew silent. "I did once," he revealed softly. "I loved her more than anything else in the world, but I wasn't enough for her in the end."

"I'm sorry," Esther murmured.

"I do not want your pity."

"Good, because you aren't going to get it," she said. "I am going to help you, just as you have already helped me."

Esther started blinking profusely, prompting him to ask, "Is something in your eye?"

"No, I am batting my eyelashes at you," she replied. "Is it not working?"

He chuckled. "I think it would be best if you stopped."

"I'm trying to appear enamored with you."

"You are trying too hard," he said. "Just stare deep into my eyes."

Esther's steady gaze held his. Her blue eyes were bright, and perfectly brilliant. He had known many people with blue eyes, but all of them paled in comparison. Her eyes reminded him of the sky without any clouds.

"Am I doing this right?" Esther asked.

"I do not think there is a wrong way to stare at someone," he joked.

Esther smiled, just as he had intended. "I hope Lady Bedlington is watching and is terribly jealous of us."

"I hope so, as well."

The music came to an end and Samuel went to escort Esther off the dance floor. His eyes roamed over the room but he saw no sign of Lord Mather or his wife.

"I do not see your father or stepmother," Samuel remarked.

Esther didn't appear concerned. "I would much rather go speak to Lord and Lady Rushcliffe," she said.

Samuel followed her gaze and saw Lord and Lady Rushcliffe a short distance away. He shifted his course and headed towards his friends.

As they approached, Lady Rushcliffe smiled broadly, as if she were privy to a secret. "I hadn't realized that you two were acquainted with one another."

Esther exchanged a glance with Samuel before saying, "Yes, we are becoming better acquainted."

"That was rather clear when you two were dancing the waltz," Lady Rushcliffe said, her smile still intact. "You two dance superbly."

"That is kind of you to say," Esther responded.

Samuel knew it was time for him to depart and leave Esther with Lord and Lady Rushcliffe. He had done what he had set out to do and now it was time for him to depart from the ball. He saw no reason to tarry any longer. If he did, he took the chance of speaking to Phoebe and he didn't dare take that risk. His heart couldn't take that, not this evening, not ever again.

"If you will excuse me, I will leave Lady Esther in your capable hands," Samuel said with a slight bow.

Lord Rushcliffe gave him a knowing look. "Are you to depart so early?"

"I am," Samuel replied. "I have work that I need to see to tomorrow and I will need a clear head." He turned towards Lady Esther. "If you have no objections, I shall call upon you tomorrow."

She nodded. "I would like that."

"Very good," Samuel said.

They stared at one another for a moment, knowing there was still much to discuss between them. But some things were better left unsaid, at least for the time being. So why was he so captivated by her eyes? They were the kind that you could get lost in.

"Mr. Moore," Lord Rushcliffe said. "I thought you were leaving."

Samuel blinked, realizing that he had been caught staring at Esther. "Yes, I intend to leave… right now, in fact."

He spun on his heel and walked away from Esther. His plan was simple. He would call upon her a few times and take her on a ride through Hyde Park during the fashionable hour. If he did those two things, he could easily convince everyone that he held Esther in high regard. It was almost too simple. The *ton* could be easily manipulated to his advantage.

Mr. Whitmore's voice came from behind him. "What are you about?"

Samuel stopped and turned towards his friend. "What do you mean?"

His friend smirked. "You went outside to get away from Phoebe, and you returned to dance the waltz with the beautiful Lady Esther."

"That I did."

"Would you care to explain why that is?"

"I would not."

Mr. Whitmore's smirk vanished and he lowered his voice. "I watched Phoebe as you danced with Lady Esther and she looked crestfallen."

Samuel resisted the urge to smile. His plan was working. "Why should I care how Phoebe was feeling?"

"I think you do care," Mr. Whitmore pressed.

"I have decided to pursue Lady Esther for the time being."

"Obviously," Mr. Whitmore responded. "When, pray tell, did you decide this? Was it by chance when you were smelling the roses?"

"It happened rather suddenly," he replied vaguely.

Mr. Whitmore looked as if he wanted to say more on the matter, but thankfully, he reached into his jacket pocket. "Now it is my turn," he announced, removing a piece of paper. "Fortunately, I brought my list with me."

"Yes, fortunately," Samuel muttered.

Holding open the paper, Mr. Whitmore said, "I need to find a young woman that looks pleasing in blue."

"Why is that?"

"My favorite color is blue, and I want to ensure she will not ruin it for me."

Samuel shook his head. "That is idiotic."

"So say you. I think it is quite brilliant on my part," Mr. Whitmore said. "Make yourself useful and help me sort through all the young women in the room."

"I am not going to do that."

Mr. Whitmore heaved a sigh. "All right. I will amend my list to include the color jonquil. Is that sufficient?"

"You should rid yourself of the list and look for a young woman who makes you want to be a better man."

"That seems tiresome."

"Finding a wife is not meant to be easy."

Mr. Whitmore tucked the list back into his jacket pocket. "I suppose I could put my list away for now and revisit it later." His eyes roamed over the room. "I see many beautiful young women that would look pleasing on my arm."

"How fortunate for you."

"It is hard being this attractive," Mr. Whitmore declared. "I never know if the women are interested in me or my handsome face. It is a terrible burden and it is not something you are forced to deal with."

Samuel looked heavenward. "And with that deprecating remark, I'm afraid I must depart for the evening. I have work that commands my attention."

"No, you can't leave yet," Mr. Whitmore asserted. "I need your help with the ladies. Perhaps you can create a line for when the ladies wish to speak to me."

"You will do just fine on your own."

With a frown on his face, Mr. Whitmore said, "You used to be a lot more fun."

"I grew up."

"I do not like this side of you. It is very unbecoming."

Samuel gave his friend a knowing look. "You don't need me because I assure you that there will be no line of ladies coming to speak to you. There has never been one before."

Mr. Whitmore puffed out his chest as he feigned outrage. "How dare you! Be off with you before you scare the ladies off."

He grinned. "I wish you luck."

"I do not need luck," Mr. Whitmore stated.

Samuel chuckled as he walked away. His friend was rather dramatic, and he truly wondered if he believed half of what he said.

But one thing was for sure: life was a lot more interesting with Mr. Whitmore in it.

Chapter Four

Esther came to a stop in the doorway of the dining room when she saw her stepmother sitting at the table, reading the newssheets. Susanna was the last person that she wanted to speak to at the moment. She had no doubt her stepmother would have some harsh words for her, especially since they had hardly said a word to one another as they rode home from the ball last night.

With any luck, Susanna wouldn't notice her, and she could request a tray be brought to her bedchamber. It would be much preferable than to converse with her stepmother.

Susanna lowered the newssheets and met her gaze. "How long do you intend to loiter in the doorway?" she asked. "You may as well come join me and eat some breakfast."

That was the last thing that she wanted to do but it would be rude to refuse her stepmother's request. It would make her look petty.

Esther sat down across from Susanna and thanked the footman as he placed a cup of chocolate in front of her. She reached for her cup and took a sip. At least she had chocolate. That always made her feel better.

Susanna folded the newssheets and placed them onto the

table. "I have it on good authority that Lord Warley intends to wed Lady Selina."

"When was this decided?"

"Last night," Susanna replied. "It was right after your father was forced to tell him that you had no intention of marrying him."

"Clearly, he wasn't too devastated by the news."

Susanna frowned, her eyes holding disappointment. "You were given the opportunity to have a bright future, but you squandered it."

"It was not the future that I envisioned."

"Your father may not know what you are about, but I do," Susanna said. "You have no intention of marrying Mr. Moore, do you?"

How was Susanna able to deduce that? She was right, but Esther didn't dare admit that. "I haven't decided yet."

Susanna looked at her like she was a simpleton. "I had fantastical notions like you once, but I realized that life has a way of ruining your dreams."

Esther leaned to the side as a footman placed a plate of food down in front of her. "Thank you," she murmured as she reached for her fork and knife.

"Don't you realize that I was trying to help you?" her step-mother asked.

"How? By arranging a marriage for me to a man that is older than my father; a man that I could never love?"

Her stepmother nodded. "Yes, and you would have had the safety of your husband's name."

"I would rather fall in love and marry the man of my choosing."

With a disbelieving huff, Susanna said, "You have been reading too many fairy tales. Women must marry for security."

"I want more out of life."

"But what if you don't find a love match?" Susanna asked.

"You are left as a lone, dreary woman that becomes a burden to her family."

Esther took a bite of her eggs before saying, "I am only twenty-one."

"You are in your fourth Season and are no closer to finding a match than you were before," Susanna said. "I don't know how you convinced Mr. Moore to go along with your little charade but it comes at a great risk to you."

Esther was well aware of the risks but it was far preferable to marrying the ageing marquess. She had made the right decision; she was sure of it. She would help Mr. Moore with his situation and he would help her. It was a simple transaction. So why was the doubt starting to creep in?

Susanna glanced at the doorway before she lowered her voice. "I know you want a love match but it is time that you come to terms with the truth."

"The truth being?"

"Not everyone is lucky enough to secure a love match," her stepmother said. "We have had the disadvantage of being born women. We must rely on others for support."

Esther could hear the sadness in her stepmother's voice, which prompted her to ask, "Do you not love my father?"

Her stepmother placed a hand on her increasing stomach and replied, "I love that he treats me so well."

She couldn't help but notice that Susanna didn't answer her question. "But do you love him?" she pressed.

"I was in my fourth Season when my father arranged the marriage between David and me," Susanna shared. "He felt that I would become a drain on our family's finances and he wanted to secure an advantageous marriage before my looks started to fade."

Unsure of what to say, Esther remained quiet.

"I was grateful to leave my childhood home behind and enter a union with your father," Susanna said. "He has been nothing but kind to me, and I will always be appreciative of that. You should be so lucky to find a man such as your father."

Esther wasn't quite sure what to make of Susanna's admission. She had never considered that her stepmother had been forced into a marriage with her father. She had always just assumed that Susanna was more than eager to become a countess.

Her stepmother started rubbing her protruding stomach. "If I hadn't married your father, then I wouldn't have been able to have a family of my own."

"But you don't love him," she said. It wasn't accusatory, but rather a fact.

"Real love isn't a spontaneous feeling; it is a deliberate choice," Susanna said. "I may not have fallen in love with him, but I walked into love with him."

Esther considered her stepmother for a moment. It was evident that Susanna cared greatly for her father, but was it truly love? She suspected that Susanna wanted it to be love.

Her father stepped into the room and went to sit at the head of the table. "Good morning, ladies."

"Good morning," they both said in unison.

After her father placed a white linen napkin onto his lap, he reached for the newssheets and asked, "Dare I ask what you two were discussing?"

Susanna exchanged a glance with her before saying, "We were just discussing how lovely everyone looked at the ball last night."

"Very good," her father said. "I am glad that you two are finally putting your differences behind you. As my Hyacinth always said, 'No good comes out of family fighting'."

"Yes, she sounds very wise," Susanna said, her words coming out tight.

Her father didn't seem to notice that Susanna appeared upset by the mention of her mother. That was interesting. Could Susanna be jealous of her mother?

Bringing the newssheets up, her father grew quiet as he read the articles.

Susanna spoke up, directing her attention towards Esther. "Does Mr. Moore intend to call upon you today?"

"He said that he would."

"Wonderful, but you must not be disappointed if he doesn't," Susanna counseled. "He has a very important job as a barrister."

"I am aware," Esther said.

Susanna reached for her teacup and brought it to her lips. "He handled Lady Eugenie's case rather nicely. If it wasn't for him, she would have been hung and no one would have been the wiser that she hadn't been the murderer."

Her father folded the corners of the newssheets to glance at his wife. "I am baffled as to why Mr. Moore works as a barrister since he is Lord Harrogate's heir."

"Does it matter?" Susanna asked.

"No, but I find it rather curious. Most gentlemen in his position find the idea of work to be off-putting."

Esther interjected, "I find it admirable. He is making something of his life and not just waiting for his father to die so he can inherit."

"I suppose so," her father said, not appearing convinced. "He is still a Whig, though. Their views are far too radical for my tastes."

Susanna let out a slight gasp as her hand flew to her stomach. "The baby is kicking my ribs again," she revealed.

Her father puffed out his chest. "Our son is strong."

"We don't know if I am carrying a boy," Susanna said. "I just don't want you to be disappointed if we have a girl."

"You need not concern yourself with that," Esther's father responded. "When Hyacinth was increasing with Esther, she wasn't nearly as large as you, leading me to believe you are carrying my heir."

Susanna stiffened. "I am not large."

Her husband smiled, no doubt in an attempt to flatter her. "I meant that as a compliment," he said. "It is a good thing to be as large as possible when increasing."

His words didn't seem to appease Susanna by the frown lines that were starting to deepen around her mouth.

As her father returned his attention towards the newssheets, he announced, "Our Esther has made the Society page." His eyes roamed over the article. "Apparently, Mr. Moore has never shown interest in a young lady before and it is causing quite the stir amongst the *ton*."

Susanna pressed her lips together. "What wonderful news." Her words weren't the least bit convincing.

Lowering the newssheets, her father gave Esther a pointed look. "I do hope you know what you are doing taking Mr. Moore on as a suitor."

"I do," Esther lied.

Her father looked as if he wanted to say more on the matter, but instead he placed the newssheets down onto the table. "I would have preferred if you had secured a Tory as a suitor, but I should not look a gift horse in the mouth."

"There is nothing wrong with being a Whig," Esther attempted.

He swiped his hand. "Their heads are filled with nonsensical ideas about parliamentary and philanthropic reforms."

"Is it not good to challenge what has always been done?" Esther asked.

Her father did not look pleased by her question. "You know not what you speak of. The Whigs' fundamental belief is that political power belongs to the people and the monarchy is only in power because of the will of the people."

"Perhaps that isn't such a terrible thing, especially with the current state of affairs."

He sucked in a breath. "What do you know about the state of affairs?"

"I know a little…" she started.

"You know nothing," her father said, speaking over her. "It is unsavory for women to talk about politics with a man."

"But you are my father," Esther argued.

Her father shoved back his chair. "I will not stand by and have you insult the monarchy. Not after everything they have done for us."

"I don't mean to insult the monarchy but the poor—"

"How is it that you know so much about the poor?" he demanded.

Esther knew it might not be the best time to mention that she had read articles in the newssheets about the plight of the poor. It would only stoke her father's anger and that wouldn't help the situation.

To her surprise, Susanna interrupted, "Look at the time, dear. If you don't hurry, you will be late for the House of Lords."

Her father glanced at the long clock in the corner and said, "You are right. I best leave now or else I might not make the vote." He rose and addressed Esther. "We will continue this conversation later."

Lucky her, she thought. With any hope, her father would forget what they had been discussing when he returned home.

After her father left the dining room, Esther turned her attention towards Susanna. "Thank you for your help with my father."

Susanna rose from her seat. "My brother was a Whig, defying my father's wish, and I have a great deal of compassion for what they are attempting to accomplish."

"I hadn't realized that Phillip was a Whig."

"It wasn't until he went to Oxford that he changed his alliance," Susanna revealed. "My father was furious but there was little that he could do."

"I suppose not."

Esther watched her stepmother as she departed from the room and wondered what had just happened. For the briefest of moments, they hadn't been at odds with one another. It felt nice, familiar, but she didn't dare believe that anything had changed between them.

Samuel sat at the desk in the study as he reviewed his case files. He had a lot of work that he had to see to before he called on Esther. She was an interesting young woman. Her eyes spoke of a keen intellect, which was something that he didn't see often enough with young women in high Society. They said what they thought others wanted to hear and lacked sincerity in their speech and actions. But Esther was different. She wore her emotions on her sleeve, but it wasn't because of her innocence; rather, she was confident enough to do so.

He let out a sigh. He had been thinking about Esther and he hadn't retained any of the information that he had just read.

Placing the paper down onto the desk, Samuel leaned back in his seat. He wondered how Phoebe felt about him showing favor to Esther. He hoped that it disrupted her thoughts, constantly, and she would come to regret turning down his offer.

Why did his heart still ache at the thought of Phoebe? He was better off without her. Hadn't he proved that? He was a competent barrister, one of the best in London, and he hardly lost any cases. He had thrown himself into work after Phoebe had rejected him and it had paid off, tenfold. He was not the same man that he was when she was in his life. Yet he couldn't seem to move on, and even hatched a plan to make Phoebe jealous.

Botheration. Wasn't he better than this? No, apparently not. A part of him wanted Phoebe to suffer, even if it paled in comparison to what he had felt. He knew that wasn't very gentlemanly of him, but he didn't care. Her betrayal had cut him deep, and the scar had yet to heal.

His tall, thin mother stepped into the room with a look of annoyance on her face. "You missed breakfast."

"I wasn't hungry."

"You need to eat." She came to sit down on the chair in front of the desk. "Not that you care, but I was forced to dine alone."

"That must have been awful for you," he said with a teasing lilt in his tone.

"It was," his mother replied. "Although it is far preferable than eating with your father."

Samuel closed the file in front of him. "I do wish that you two would at least try to be civil with one another."

"We are long past civility."

"That is a shame," Samuel said.

His mother shrugged one shoulder. "It would hardly make a difference anyways since he is always with his mistress."

"You don't know that for certain."

"Why else wouldn't he come home, night after night?" his mother asked.

Samuel knew that his mother had a point, especially since his father hadn't tried very hard to hide the fact that he had taken on a mistress many years earlier. It was common in their circles for the men to take on mistresses, but he wished that his father had stayed true to his mother. Perhaps he had expected too much of him?

"You don't need to protect him," his mother said. "Your father made his choice, and now he must live with the consequences. I just wish he was more discreet with that whore."

"That is rather harsh of you to say."

His mother let out an indignant huff. "Are you truly defending the woman who is sleeping with my husband? A woman who is stealing from our coffers."

"She is not stealing from us."

"But she is," his mother claimed. "Where do you think the money is coming from to ensure your father's favorite whore is well-kept? That is your inheritance."

"You are in a particularly ornery mood this morning," Samuel remarked.

With a wave of her hand, she responded, "I am because my son, my own flesh and blood, didn't stop working long enough to join me for breakfast."

"I was busy."

"You are always busy."

Samuel nodded. "I won't dispute that, but my caseload has only increased in these past few weeks."

His mother looked unimpressed by his admission. "You were always too smart for your own good, but you need to take time for yourself."

"I attended the ball last night."

"That you did, and I was proud of you, but you need to start attending more social events. How else do you intend to find a wife?"

Samuel should have known that his mother would bring up finding a wife. She brought it up in nearly every conversation they had. It was exhausting, but he knew she meant well. She wanted what was best for him, but would a wife truly make him happy?

He wasn't opposed to the thought of marriage, but he wasn't ready to tie himself to one woman for the remainder of his days. He thought he had been when he had offered for Phoebe, but she had crushed his dreams.

His father stepped into the room with the newssheets in his hand. "Is it true?" he asked, not sparing his wife a glance.

"Is what true?" Samuel asked.

"Are you pursuing Lady Esther Harington?" his father half-asked, half-demanded.

Samuel saw the hopeful look on his mother's expression and knew that he couldn't let her down. "Yes, it is true."

His father smiled broadly. "This is wonderful news, Son. You will finally produce an heir."

"Let's not get ahead of ourselves," Samuel said. "I am showing Lady Esther favor, but I have said nothing about marriage."

"But you will since that is the natural progression of such things," his father pressed.

Samuel closed a file that was in front of him. "I do not want either of you to be disappointed if things don't work out between Lady Esther and me."

His father walked over to the desk and placed the newssheets down. "This is promising. I was wondering if you would ever get married."

"Again, I have said nothing about marriage," Samuel said as he worked hard to keep the irritation out of his voice. Were his parents even listening to him?

His mother leaned forward in her seat. "I am not acquainted with Lady Esther or her family. What is she like?"

"She is…" His words trailed off. What could he say that would appease his mother but not give her too much hope for a union between him and Esther? He decided to settle on the truth. "She is unlike any woman of my acquaintance."

Clasping her hands together, his mother said, "I cannot wait to hear the pitter-patter of feet in the nursery from your children."

Samuel shook his head. His parents were getting way ahead of themselves, and it would only end in disappointment for them.

His father interjected, "Lord Mather is a staunch Tory, though. I do hope that Lady Esther does not share her father's political views."

"Even if she did, I am sure she was brought up correctly, knowing a woman never discusses politics with a man," his mother remarked.

"Good. A woman should never voice her opinion unless called upon to do so," his father said.

His mother visibly tensed. "Why is that, Paul?" she demanded. "Is it because you can't handle a woman who knows her own mind?"

"I can handle women who speak their minds, but I can't handle women that nag relentlessly," his father responded.

"Perhaps I wouldn't have to nag you if you didn't constantly disappoint me."

With narrowed eyes, his father asked, "Why do I even bother conversing with you? Every time I do, you give me a reason to stay far away from you."

"I have no complaints," his mother said with a tilt of her chin.

Samuel resisted the urge to groan. His parents couldn't seem to be in the same room without fighting. It had been this way for as long as he could remember. They had always seemed to loathe one another, making his life rather difficult.

"Regardless, I did not come here to fight with you," his father said.

"What a shame," his mother muttered.

His father shot his wife a look of disdain. "I have come to inform you that I am cutting your allowance."

"I beg your pardon?" his mother asked, jumping up from her seat.

"I believe I spoke plainly enough that even you could understand me," his father responded dryly.

"You can't cut my allowance!" his mother shouted. "That is my money."

"No, it is *my* money and you are spending entirely too much of it."

His mother turned towards him with a desperate look on her face. "Samuel, you must do something!" she urged. "You can't let your father treat me like this."

"Stay out of it, Son," his father ordered. "This should have been done a long time ago."

Samuel knew it was only a matter of time before his parents included him in their argument. It was so predictable, but he was a smart enough man to stay out of it.

As he collected his files on the desk, he said, "I believe I will depart so I can get work done at my office."

"You are leaving?" his mother asked. "Now?"

"There is no point in me remaining here," Samuel replied. "This fight will continue, whether I am here or not."

His mother let out a dramatic sigh. "You would let your father treat me like one of his whores?"

"Mother, please, I would prefer to stay out of this," Samuel replied.

"Fine, go!" she exclaimed. "I can fight my own battles."

His father scoffed. "There is no battle. I have already informed my solicitor to reduce your allowance, effective immediately."

His mother spun on her heel and faced her husband. "You seem to forget that you were broke before you married me. I saved you from debtor's prison."

"That was nearly thirty years ago," his father remarked.

"It makes it no less true."

Samuel placed the files into his satchel and hung it around his shoulder. "Good day," he said before he started walking towards the door.

"Before you go…" his father started.

So close.

Samuel turned back around and addressed his father. "Yes?"

"It is time that you do your duty and help manage the estate," his father said. "I have indulged your pastime for far too long."

"My pastime?" Samuel asked. "You mean my profession?"

His father bristled. "You are my heir and never had to work."

"Let him continue to work as a barrister," his mother encouraged. "He isn't hurting anyone by doing so."

Ignoring his wife's words, his father said, "I need to properly train you on how to manage an estate and it is going to take all of your attention."

"I have no intention of quitting my position as a barrister," Samuel admitted. "It gives me a sense of purpose."

"A purpose?" his father repeated back. "Our estate employs over a hundred people. You will be responsible for their livelihoods. Is that not enough of a purpose for you?"

"Father…" Samuel started.

His father raised his hand, a resolute expression on his face. "I do not wish to debate this. As my heir, you have certain responsibilities that you inherited from birth. It is time for you to live up to those."

"I shall think on it," Samuel responded. He understood where his father was coming from, but he wasn't ready to give up being a barrister. He couldn't. It was so much more than a job to him. He felt like he was finally doing something important with his life. Why would he want to give that up to run his family's estate?

"There is no thinking," his father asserted. "We start your training in two weeks' time. That should give you enough time to get your affairs in order."

Samuel felt no need to respond to his father's command. He was far too old to be manipulated by anyone, much less his father. He would decide what was best for him and inform his father of his decision.

Chapter Five

Esther sat in the drawing room as she waited for Samuel to call upon her. He hadn't specified a time so she was just playing the pianoforte in an effort to pass the time.

Her hands moved quickly over the keys of the pianoforte as the notes filled the rectangular-shaped drawing room. The melody had a way of conveying her emotions, and at that moment, she was feeling quite anxious. She hoped that she had placed her trust in the right man. But she didn't know if she had, especially since she hardly knew him.

The tall, broad-shouldered butler stepped into the room and she removed her hands from the keys in anticipation. "Miss Bolingbroke and Lady Lizette Westcott have come to call. Are you accepting callers, my lady?" Gibson asked.

"I am," Esther said. "Please send them in."

Gibson turned on his heel and departed from the room to do her bidding. It was only a moment before Miss Bolingbroke and Lady Lizette stepped into the room.

Esther rose from her seat and greeted them. "What a pleasant surprise." She waved her hand over the tea service as she asked, "Would you care for a cup of tea?"

Miss Bolingbroke frowned. "How could Lizette possibly

drink a cup of tea at a time like this?" She placed a hand up to the corner of her mouth and lowered her voice. "She is furious with you."

Esther shifted her gaze towards Lizette and she didn't appear to be holding any animosity for her. If anything, the twitching of her lips indicated she found the whole situation amusing.

"I am not upset at you," Lizette revealed. "But I daresay that Anette is."

Anette bobbed her head. "Of course I am upset with Esther," she said. "She is one of my dearest friends and she failed to mention that she held Mr. Moore in high regard. I had to discover that fact alongside everyone else when you danced with him at the ball last night."

"I know that it may have seemed that way but I assure you that I do not hold Mr. Moore in high regard. We are merely acquaintances," Esther rushed to confess.

Anette didn't look convinced by the pursing of her lips. "Acquaintances don't usually dance the waltz. It is the dance of love."

"No, it is not," Esther contested. "It is merely a dance, which allowed me the chance to learn more about Mr. Moore."

"I saw you batting your eyes at him," Anette said with a knowing look.

Esther knew that she owed her friends the truth, no matter how embarrassing it may be. They would keep her confidence; she was sure of that. "Come sit and I will tell you what is truly going on."

Anette and Lizette sat down on a camelback settee as Esther closed the drawing room door. She wanted this conversation to remain private.

As she sat across from her friends, Esther said, "My father and stepmother were insistent that I announce my engagement to Lord Warley at the ball last night—"

Anette spoke over her. "But he is so old."

"Precisely," Esther agreed. "That is why I tried to climb a tree to escape the ball last night."

"That is logical. I would have done the same thing," Anette said.

"I know you would have," Esther responded. "But as I was attempting to climb the tree, Mr. Moore came across me and he was sympathetic towards my plight. We decided to hatch a plan that would benefit both of us this Season."

"A plan?" Lizette asked with hesitancy in her voice. "Why does this already sound like a terrible idea?"

"I assure you that it is not," Esther said. She hoped she seemed more confident than she felt because she had her own doubts. But she didn't dare admit that to them.

Anette gave her a curious look. "What is this so-called 'plan'?"

Esther held her breath for a moment before revealing, "Mr. Moore will act the part of a devoted suitor until he withdraws his suit. Then, we shall part ways."

Her friends stared back at her and the only sound was the ticking of the long clock in the corner.

The silence between them stretched out and it was on the verge of becoming awkward, prompting Esther to say, "I know what you are going to say…"

"I doubt that," Anette muttered.

"… but Mr. Moore and I understand the risks and we are prepared for the repercussions of our actions."

Lizette moved to sit on the edge of her seat. "Esther…" She paused. "Do you not understand that your reputation will be tainted when Mr. Moore withdraws his suit?"

"I do, but it is far preferable than marrying Lord Warley," Esther replied.

"I won't disagree with you there, but you must realize you could end up as a spinster because of this," Lizette stated.

Anette perked up. "We can be spinsters together," she

declared. "We can live in a cottage in the countryside and read books all day long. Wouldn't that be fantastic?"

"That does sound rather ideal," Esther replied.

Lizette gave them both an amused look. "In this scenario, how will you provide for yourselves?"

"I shall write my book and we will live off the income," Anette announced.

"I imagine that very few people get rich off their first book," Lizette mused.

Anette acknowledged Lizette's words with a bob of her head. "We would just have to be frugal with our money, then. Perhaps we might even take in work as seamstresses."

"You, a seamstress?" Lizette asked.

"I can be a seamstress," Anette said. "I am quite talented with a needle, and it would give me a unique perspective for my next book."

Lizette shook her head. "You are a daughter of a viscount. I doubt your mother would let you work as a seamstress."

At the mention of her mother, Anette grew despondent. "My mother might welcome the chance to wash her hands of me."

"How can you say that?" Esther asked. "Your mother loves you."

"She does, but I am just a grand disappointment to her," Anette said. "I dream of writing a book, not finding a husband. My mother was a diamond of the first water in her first Season. And I am anything but."

Lizette's eyes held compassion. "Everyone has their own journey and you mustn't compare yourself to others."

"It is impossible not to," Anette said. "I am a bit odd."

"Who decides what is odd?" Esther asked.

Anette offered them a weak smile. "I know what you both are trying to do and I appreciate it, I truly do. But I know I can never live up to my mother's impossible standards. I must be true to myself."

"That is precisely why we are friends," Lizette remarked. "I do not have time for people who aren't genuine."

The door to the drawing room opened and Susanna stepped into the room. No, it was more of a waddle. "Hello," she greeted. "I apologize I wasn't here to greet you when you arrived, but I am moving much slower as of late."

Susanna walked to the settee and claimed the seat next to Esther. She then addressed their guests. "How are you both faring?"

Any sign of anguish that Anette had been feeling earlier had been replaced with a smile. "I am more interested in how you are faring."

"I am doing as well as can be expected," Susanna replied. "I feel like a hippopotamus every time I walk around."

Anette laughed. "Did you know that hippopotamuses are fast on land, much faster than humans, in fact, and they use that advantage to chase prey?"

"I did not know that," Susanna replied.

With animated hands, Anette shared, "They may be large animals but they are very nimble. They are second in size to only the elephant."

Susanna leaned back against the edge of her seat. "How do you know all of this?"

"I have read many books about animals," Anette responded. "It is research for my book."

"You are going to write about a hippopotamus?" Susanna asked with disbelief on her features.

Anette shrugged. "I haven't quite decided what I want to write about. I thought I knew, but it changes every time I sit down at my writing desk. Although I have decided I won't write about the mating habits of any animals."

"Thank heavens for that." Susanna turned her attention towards Esther. "Have you offered your guests some tea?"

"I did, but we got to talking instead," Esther said.

Susanna did not look pleased by her admission. "That is

not an excuse. A good hostess will ensure their guests have a cup of tea in their hands."

Esther resisted the urge to roll her eyes at her stepmother. She wasn't entirely wrong, but she knew how to be a good hostess. Her mother had ingrained it in her.

Waving her hand over the tea service, Esther asked, "Would anyone care for a cup of tea?"

"I would," Lizette said.

"As would I," Anette chimed in.

Esther reached for the teapot and poured two cups of tea. After she handed them to her friends, she shifted to face her stepmother and inquired, "Tea?"

"No, thank you," Susanna replied.

Gibson stepped into the room and announced, "Mr. Moore has come to call. Would you care for me to show him in?"

As Esther went to respond, Susanna spoke first. "Yes, send him in."

After the butler departed, Mr. Moore stepped into the room and he was dressed in a rich green jacket with buff trousers. His dark hair was parted on the side, and his lengthy sideburns had been carefully clipped. With his handsome features and brown eyes, he was quite captivating.

He bowed. "Ladies," he greeted politely.

Susanna nudged Esther's arm. "Rise," she whispered under her breath.

Rising, Esther gave Mr. Moore a nervous smile. She wasn't entirely sure how she should act around him. They were hardly acquaintances, but they were pretending to be interested in one another.

Mr. Moore returned her smile, but it appeared genuine. It even reached his eyes, making her relax around him.

"It is so good of you to come," Esther said as she dropped into a curtsy. At least she remembered her manners. That was one less thing her stepmother would chide her on later.

"Lady Esther, you look enchanting," Mr. Moore said.

Esther could feel the warmth of a blush as it crawled up her neck. His words almost seemed real. "Thank you, sir," she replied.

Susanna cleared her throat and tipped her head towards her friends, reminding her of the duty as hostess.

How had she so quickly forgotten that her friends were in the room? "Are you acquainted with Lady Lizette Westcott and Miss Bolingbroke?" Esther asked, placing her hand out towards them.

"Enchanted," Mr. Moore replied as he acknowledged her friends.

Knowing what was expected of her, Esther asked, "Would you care for some tea, sir?"

Mr. Moore shook his head. "No, thank you," he replied. "I was hoping you would give me a tour of your lovely gardens."

"Yes, I most assuredly can do that," her words tumbled out. "We have the most beautiful gardens. Lots of people have told us so." Drats. Why was she rambling on?

"I am looking forward to it." Shifting his gaze towards Susanna, Mr. Moore said, "This is assuming that we have your approval, my lady."

Her stepmother looked pleased by his request. "Yes, of course, but I will be watching from the window."

"I would expect no less from you," Mr. Moore said.

Esther made the mistake of glancing at her friends and they both were hiding smiles behind their gloved hands. For some reason, they thought this was very amusing.

Mr. Moore stepped forward and extended his hand towards her. "Shall we, Lady Esther?"

With only the slightest moment of hesitation, she placed her hand into his proffered one and allowed him to lead her from the room.

Samuel led Esther down a path in the gardens as he attempted to think of something clever to say. Normally, he was never at a loss for words, but he found he was in a most uncomfortable situation. He wasn't opposed to getting to know Esther better, but that was not part of the deal. They would spend some time together then they would part ways, hopefully as friends.

Esther removed her hand from his arm and moved to create more distance between them. She glanced over at him and said, "I'm sorry about earlier. I don't usually get so nervous."

"I hardly noticed."

"That is very kind of you to say, but I don't normally blather on."

He smiled at her choice of words. "Blather?"

She returned his smile. "Yes, my mother used to say that I blathered on as a child, relentlessly. She said there wasn't a time when I wasn't going on about something."

"You do not seem like a young woman that just speaks to hear her own voice."

"I'm not; at least, not anymore," Esther admitted. "At a certain age, you are forced to grow up."

He looked at her curiously. "Why is that?"

"We can't always go on as we have. Society dictates how we should act, and we must fall in line or else face being ostracized."

"I'm not entirely sure I agree with you," he said. "Society may tell us how they think we should act, but it is ultimately our decision."

"You were fortunate enough to be born a man. A woman has so very little rights as it is. If we don't conform, we risk our reputations, as well."

"Yet are you not the woman that I caught climbing a tree?" he teased.

Clasping her hands in front of her, Esther said, "That is because I was left with little choice to do so. I refused to marry Lord Warley."

"I do not blame you." Samuel led Esther over to a bench and asked, "Would you care to sit for a spell?"

Esther nodded before she sat down. "My stepmother isn't fooled by us, though. She is worried about me."

"Your stepmother is rather astute for her age."

"You mean because she is only a few years older than me?" Esther asked with a hardness in her voice that hadn't been there a moment ago.

Samuel claimed the seat next to Esther. "I take it that you and your stepmother aren't close."

Esther gave him a weak smile. "We used to be, but it all changed when she accepted my father's proposal," she revealed. "My father is determined to have an heir, but I never thought he would marry someone so much younger than him."

"No doubt Lady Mather considered her marriage to be advantageous."

"I want more in a marriage than a title. I want a love match."

Samuel shifted in his seat to face her. "You are an anomaly amongst the *ton*, then. It has been my experience that women do just about anything to obtain their places in Society."

"I daresay that you are associating with the wrong women," Esther said. "A few of my friends were fortunate enough to marry for love."

"Most people never find love and your friends should count themselves blessed that it came their way," Samuel said.

Esther cocked her head. "You found love once. Do you consider yourself blessed?"

Samuel grew quiet. How could he adequately explain how

he felt about Phoebe? "Falling in love was not a mistake, but thinking that she loved me back was," he said. "I used to think that love would conquer all, but I was wrong. I do not believe everyone finds their match."

"Just because you made a mistake in love once doesn't mean you are doomed to repeat it."

"I'm not quite sure what to believe."

Esther's eyes held compassion as she said, "The things we have encountered in our lives, good and bad, shape us into the people we are now. You couldn't be the man you are today without Phoebe in your life."

"It would have been much easier."

"But would you have learned anything if it had been?"

Samuel wondered what he had learned. He had placed barriers around his heart, closing himself off from the possibility that he might one day find love again. He couldn't risk the chance of making the same mistake. If he did, he knew he would never recover.

"I apologize if my bold speech offended you," Esther said.

"It did no such thing," Samuel assured her. "I just can't seem to convince myself that my life was better because Phoebe was in it."

"People come into our lives and we don't realize the impact they have on us until they are gone," Esther said.

Samuel shifted his gaze towards the townhouse and saw Lady Mather was watching them from the drawing room window. He tipped his head and she responded in kind.

"Your stepmother doesn't seem too evil," he joked.

Esther pressed her lips together. "She isn't evil, but she most assuredly is not my mother," she said.

"Is she trying to replace your mother?"

"At times, I feel that she is," Esther replied. "I do believe she is doing the best that she knows how, but I miss my friend."

"Have you told her this?"

Esther shook her head, causing the ringlets that framed her face to sway back and forth. "Heavens, no. It would just encourage her to try to lord it over me. She has my father wrapped around her little finger."

"It didn't appear that way when your father released you from having to marry Lord Warley," Samuel remarked.

"That was surprising," Esther admitted.

Samuel glanced up at the position of the sun and realized that they had tarried long enough, especially since Esther had not brought a hat with her. He knew that women cared about such things.

He rose from his seat and extended his hand towards her. "Shall I escort you back to the drawing room?"

"That would be for the best," she said as she slipped her hand into his.

Once Esther rose, Samuel withdrew his hand and said, "I must admit that I find you impressive, my lady. You are not one to shy away from a frank conversation."

"I prefer speaking plainly."

"Very few women do."

Esther gave him an amused look. "Again, you must not be associating with the right women, sir."

"I think you are right."

As they started down the path, Esther asked, "Will you tell me about yourself?"

"That is a terribly vague question," he teased. "Where should I even begin?"

Esther grinned. "Perhaps we should start with an easy question. Did you attend Eton or Harrow?"

"Eton."

"You were most fortunate," she said. "My parents were insistent that I be educated at home, even though most of my friends were sent to boarding school. Although, now I cherish the time I was able to spend with my mother."

"My parents were all too willing to send me away,"

Samuel admitted. "Besides, I preferred to be far away from my home."

Esther turned towards him. "Why was that?"

"My home wasn't exactly filled with love," Samuel said. "My parents fought constantly, and they expected me to pick sides."

"That is a terrible position to put a child in."

Samuel shrugged. "It was why I preferred to be anywhere but home. Luckily, I was able to forge friendships that are still strong today. They became my family."

"I am glad to hear that," Esther said. "Everyone should be surrounded by people who are cheering them on."

With a smirk, Samuel shared, "You might not say that when you meet my friends. One of them is a very interesting character."

"I look forward to meeting this person."

Samuel placed his arm out to assist Esther as they walked up two steps to the veranda. "My friend, Mr. Whitmore, created a list to find the perfect bride."

"A perfect bride? Is there such a thing?"

"In his eyes, yes," Samuel replied. "His criteria are rather different, to say the least. He is determined to not pursue a large-eared woman."

A line between Esther's brows appeared. "A large-eared woman?" she repeated. "Are there very many of them in high Society?"

"I suppose he doesn't want to take that chance."

"I'm afraid to ask what his other requirements are for a perfect bride."

Samuel opened the back door of the townhouse and stood to the side to allow Esther entry. "The rest of the list is equally ridiculous," he explained as he followed her inside.

"What if we were to help him create a new list, a more realistic list?" Esther asked.

"I fear that my friend is past hope when it comes to the ladies."

As they walked down the corridor, Esther asked, "Does he want to marry this Season?"

"He does, well, at least he claims he does."

"You aren't sure?"

Samuel hesitated before saying, "I have my doubts. Mr. Whitmore is a great friend, but he tends to be a lover of all the ladies. I don't see him committing to just one."

"Cavorting with the ladies seems to be encouraged for gentlemen before they are wed, but that doesn't mean they won't be faithful afterwards."

Samuel chuckled. "I daresay that your opinion might change when you meet Mr. Whitmore."

"I doubt it."

"All right, I shall bring him by tomorrow when I come to call," Samuel said. "You shall see for yourself that he is past hope when it comes to the ladies."

Esther stopped in the entry hall and turned to face him. "I shall look forward to proving you wrong."

"Until tomorrow, then."

Her eyes shone with a mischievous glint as a smile played on her lips. "Until tomorrow," she repeated.

He stared at her for a moment longer than what was considered proper before he headed towards the main door. For some reason, he found it amusing that she thought she could help Mr. Whitmore. But at the same time, he found it oddly endearing, as well.

Chapter Six

The sound of her bedchamber door opening woke Esther up, but she didn't want to open her eyes. It was far too early to wake up. Most likely, it was her lady's maid going about her tasks and she would leave shortly, leaving her to return to her restful slumber.

Her stepmother's exasperated voice came from next to the bed. "Good heavens, do you intend to sleep the entire day away?"

Esther peeked through one eye and replied, "Is that an option?"

"It is time for you to rise and prepare for the day."

With a quick glance at the window, she saw that the sun was high in the sky and was casting an enormous amount of light into her bedchamber. How had she slept so late? But she already knew that answer. She'd had a restless night of sleep. She couldn't seem to calm her racing mind enough to sleep as she considered what prospects she had for her future. Frankly, it looked rather grim.

She grabbed her pillow and placed it over her head. With any luck, her stepmother would leave her in peace.

But she was not so lucky.

Susanna sighed. "Do you intend to make your callers wait for you to ready yourself?"

"I have no callers," she said, her voice muffled from the pillow.

"Is Mr. Moore not calling on you today?"

Esther removed the pillow from her face and sat up in bed. She wouldn't mind a visit from him. "He did say that he would come and bring a friend with him."

"More the reason for you to get out of bed." Susanna gave her a disapproving look. "Your hair looks like a rat's nest, despite the cap on your head."

She was in no mood to be insulted by her stepmother. "May I ask why you troubled yourself to come to the other wing to wake me?"

Susanna grew solemn. "I was hoping we could talk."

Esther resisted the urge to groan. What now? What fresh torment did her stepmother plan to inflict upon her? Was she going to make her sleep in the attic now? Or the stables?

Coming to sit on the end of her bed, Susanna said, "I am worried about you."

"You have no reason to be worried about me," Esther said in a harsh tone.

Susanna pressed her lips together before saying, "I just feel—"

Esther cut her off. "You don't get a say in my life. You are not my mother."

"I am not trying to replace your mother," Susanna attempted. "I want to be your friend."

With a disbelieving huff, Esther replied, "Our friendship ended the moment you married my father."

"Why?"

"Surely you can't be that daft?" Esther asked. She knew she was being rude, but she wanted Susanna to know how she truly felt. "You have been trying to control me ever since you got married."

"I have not."

Esther lifted her brow. "You banished me to another wing of the townhouse just so you could get rid of me."

"We did not banish you. We just needed your bedchamber for the baby."

"We have a nursery on the next level," Esther responded. "My parents thought it was sufficient enough for me to grow up in."

"I want my baby closer to me," Susanna said.

"Regardless, you tried to marry me off to Lord Warley," Esther stated.

"For your own good."

Esther frowned. "I doubt that."

"You seem to forget that I married your father, who is much older than me," Susanna said. "It allowed me to have my own household and have a baby."

"I am not you. I want more out of a marriage."

Susanna placed a hand on her stomach. "You and I are so similar…"

She huffed.

"… and we need the protection of a man's name. It is the only way to survive in this world."

Esther shook her head. "You and I may have been similar in the past, but not anymore," she argued. "We are on two very different paths."

"And that is what concerns me the most."

"I don't need a husband to be happy."

"No, but you need a husband to provide for you," Susanna contended. "For how else will you live? Unless you intend to be a drain on your father's finances."

Esther was tired of having the same argument with her stepmother. She didn't know what the future held for her, but whatever happened to her would be because she chose that path. She didn't want someone else to choose the path for her.

Susanna awkwardly rose. "I do not wish to be a naysayer,

but I wish you would accept the facts. If you don't land a husband this Season, you could very well become a spinster."

"I am not afraid of being a spinster."

"You should be," Susanna said. "It is a lonely existence. You will only have your cats to keep you company."

"I don't own a cat."

"You will."

"There is no shame in owning cats."

"It is when they are your only source of entertainment."

Esther now wanted a cat. Not because she wanted to be a spinster, but she wanted to irk her stepmother.

A knock came at the door, interrupting their conversation.

"Enter," Susanna ordered.

The door opened and Anne stepped into the room. "Mr. Daniel Fairchild has come to call, my lady," she announced.

"Daniel is here? To see me?" Esther asked.

Anne bobbed her head. "Yes, my lady."

Esther furrowed her brow. Her cousin would occasionally come to their townhouse, but it was to see her father. Daniel had never once sought her out, and if their paths did cross, they would only exchange the briefest of pleasantries.

Susanna seemed to share the same confusion as she did. "Do you have any business with Daniel?"

"I do not," Esther replied.

As she walked over to the door, Susanna said, "I will go down to speak to him while you prepare yourself for the day. With any luck, I can glean why he has come to call."

After Susanna departed from the room, Anne walked over to the wardrobe and pulled out a yellow gown with a square neckline. "Will this gown be sufficient?"

"I suppose so."

"You seem unsure," Anne said, holding the gown up.

Esther considered the gown before she explained, "I do not want to give the impression that I dressed up to see my cousin."

"Would you care for a more simple gown?" Anne asked as she went to put the gown back.

"I think that might be for the best," Esther said. "Regardless, I just hope that Daniel doesn't get the wrong impression."

"Would it be so bad if he did?"

She tossed off the covers and placed her legs over the side of the bed. "My cousin is a gambler and has a terrible reputation. He is not a man that I wish to associate with."

"But he is family."

"He is more of a distant cousin," Esther corrected. "It would appear that my family has a hard time producing boys."

Anne draped the gown over the back of the settee before she moved to the dressing table. She patted the back of the chair and encouraged, "Shall we style your hair?"

Esther removed her cap as she rose. "My stepmother says it looks like a 'rat's nest'."

With a laugh, Anne responded, "Your hair has seen better days, my lady."

It was sometime later before Esther departed from her bedchamber. Her hair was neatly coiffed and she opted to wear a blue gown. It was her most simple afternoon gown, but it still had enough embellishments to be more than respectable.

She gracefully descended the stairs and could hear her cousin's voice drifting out from the drawing room. Had he always been such a loud talker?

As she stepped into the room, Susanna's eyes lit up with relief when they landed on her. "Esther, you have arrived."

Daniel promptly rose from his seat and turned to face her. He wasn't an unattractive man with his square jaw, straight nose and deep-set eyes. But his words had always sounded less than genuine. It almost appeared as if he said what he thought the other person wanted him to say.

He bowed. "My lady," he greeted.

Esther curtsied. "Cousin."

Susanna waved her closer. "Come sit, Esther," she encouraged. "I do believe Daniel would benefit from a cup of tea."

With a bob of his head, Daniel said, "I would."

She crossed the room and sat next to her stepmother as she worked to keep the annoyance off her face. Why on earth Susanna hadn't already offered him a cup of tea was beyond her. Was she the only person that could pour tea in this household?

Leaning forward, Esther reached for the teapot and poured three cups of tea. Then she extended one towards their guest before collecting her own.

Daniel took a sip and looked at the cup in surprise. "This is delicious."

Susanna smiled. "Thank you," she responded. "I add honey to the tea. I think it gives a little sweetness to it."

"You would be right," Daniel readily agreed.

Esther sipped her tea and she hoped that they would continue to converse without her. She wasn't really in a mood to engage her cousin.

Unfortunately, her cousin did not feel the same. "Cousin…" he started. "I was hoping to take you on a carriage ride through Hyde Park during the fashionable hour."

Unable to stop herself, she blurted out, "Why would you wish to do that?"

He chuckled. "To spend time with you, of course," he replied. "I think it is about time that we got to know each other better. Don't you?"

Esther had no desire to get to know her cousin better, but she didn't wish to be rude. What would her father think of her spending time with Daniel? After all, he had such a low opinion of Daniel, already.

Fortunately, as she attempted to think of a reason to

politely decline him, Susanna spoke up. "I'm afraid that Esther is busy today. She has agreed to go shopping with me."

Esther blinked, surprised- but immensely grateful- that her stepmother had lied for her.

"Perhaps tomorrow then?" Daniel pressed.

"Tomorrow?" Susanna repeated with a side glance at her. No doubt that she was attempting to come up with another lie. "I'm afraid we are going to go to Gunter's for some lemon ice."

Daniel looked disappointed. "I understand," he said as he placed his teacup onto the tray. "I should be going."

"So soon?" Esther asked, hoping her words did not betray her relief.

Rising, Daniel replied, "I have a few things that I need to see to."

Esther assumed those "things" were betting at the horse races. Rather than accuse him of such a thing, she smiled. "I wish you a good day, Cousin."

"Likewise." He tipped his head at Susanna. "Lady Mather."

After her cousin departed from the room, Esther turned towards her stepmother and said, "Thank you." She hoped her words properly expressed her gratitude.

Susanna shrugged. "I suspected that your father would be upset if you had accepted Daniel's invitation, so I thought it was best to come up with an excuse."

"You are probably right," Esther responded.

Placing her teacup down, Susanna yawned. Her hand flew up to cover her mouth. "My apologies, I'm afraid I am in need of a rest."

Esther noticed for the first time how tired Susanna looked. There were dark circles under her eyes and her shoulders seemed to droop. "Are you well?" she asked.

Susanna gave her a brief smile. "Nothing that a nap won't

cure," she said. "Remain in the drawing room and I will have a maid sent in to act as a chaperone while I am resting."

As Susanna waddled out of the drawing room, Esther found herself in the unusual position of being grateful to her stepmother. She no more wanted to go on a carriage ride with Daniel than have a thorn in her boot. But that didn't change anything between them. Being at odds with Susanna was familiar, but maybe it was time to change that.

———————

The black coach came to a creaking stop along the pavement and Samuel waited only a moment before the door was opened, revealing Mr. Whitmore.

His friend stepped into the coach and sat across from him. "It is about time you arrived. I almost had to wait," he said good-naturedly.

Samuel smiled. "My apologies. That would have been awful for you."

"Your note was rather vague on why you needed my assistance," Mr. Whitmore said as he shifted in his seat. "I must assume this has to do with your manner of dress."

"What is wrong with how I dress?"

Mr. Whitmore perused the length of him, giving him a disapproving shake of his head. "If you don't know, you are worse off than I thought."

"I am fashionably dressed."

"Perhaps, but we have so much work to do to make you more presentable," Mr. Whitmore said. "We could revisit the conversation about your perpetual scowl."

"I do not scowl."

"You do, entirely too often."

Samuel heaved a sigh. "Why am I friends with you again?"

"That is easy," Mr. Whitmore started with a smirk, "I am the only person that can deal with you, day in and day out."

"I have other friends."

"Can anyone else see these friends or are you the only one?" Mr. Whitmore asked with a teasing lilt in his voice.

"They are not imaginary."

Mr. Whitmore put his hand up. "I did not mean to imply such. But, out of curiosity, have any of your other friends decided to join us in the coach?"

"You are an idiot."

His friend chuckled. "So you have said, repeatedly."

With a shake of his head, Samuel said, "I do need your help but not in the way you are thinking."

"Pity."

Samuel grew serious. "I told Lady Esther about your list and she wants to help you create a new, more realistic list."

"What is wrong with my list?" Mr. Whitmore asked with a blank stare.

"It is…" His words trailed off as he tried to think of the right word. "Unbelievable."

Mr. Whitmore bobbed his head. "That is a good word for it. It is 'unbelievably' good."

"Some of your items are unrealistic."

Reaching into his jacket pocket, Mr. Whitmore removed a piece of paper. He slowly unfolded it as he said, "I think it gives the ladies something to aspire to."

"Or it might scare some of them off," Samuel suggested.

"Good riddance, then. I wouldn't want a wife that is easily offended anyways." Mr. Whitmore glanced down at his list. "Or one that has a small head."

"A small head?" Samuel repeated.

"Yes, like a freakish, shrunken head that is not proportional to her body," Mr. Whitmore responded.

Samuel gave him a curious look. "How do you determine the lady's head is too small?"

"I would say that it is fairly obvious."

Casting his eyes heavenward, Samuel said, "You need a new list. One that is practical and not filled with idiotic requirements."

"I could not disagree with you more." Mr. Whitmore held up the paper. "This list is like a guide map for me with the ladies."

"Pray tell, have you found one lady that passes all your silly requirements yet?"

Mr. Whitmore lowered the paper and tucked it back into his jacket pocket. "Not yet, but that is only because I am looking for perfection. These things do take time, or at least I assume as much."

"There is no such thing as perfection when trying to find a young woman to court. I daresay that perfection, in and of itself, is imperfection."

"Now you are just spouting nonsense."

Samuel glanced out the window and saw that they were about to arrive at Lady Esther's townhouse. His friend's refusal to create a new list was not surprising and it would only prove his point to Lady Esther that Mr. Whitmore was past hope with the ladies.

Mr. Whitmore tilted his head. "May I ask why this is so important to you?"

"It's not," Samuel replied.

"I think it is," Mr. Whitmore said as he studied him. "You seem to care greatly about what Lady Esther thinks."

"That is the furthest thing from the truth."

Mr. Whitmore clucked his tongue. "Interesting."

Samuel was afraid to ask, but he decided to press his friend anyways. "What is interesting?"

"You." Mr. Whitmore paused. "And Lady Esther."

Not sure where this conversation was going, Samuel was relieved when the coach came to a stop in front of Lady

Esther's townhouse. He didn't bother to wait for the footman to exit his perch before he opened the door.

After he stepped out onto the pavement, Mr. Whitmore came to stand next to him. "Do not think I don't know what you are doing."

"What exactly am I doing?"

"I may be very, very handsome," Mr. Whitmore said as he brushed his hair to the side, "but I can be rather perceptive when the situation warrants it."

"And this situation warrants it?"

Mr. Whitmore waggled his eyebrows. "You suddenly start showing interest in Lady Esther, but only after you discover that Phoebe is about to announce her engagement."

Samuel should have known that his friend would piece this together. Mr. Whitmore was many things, but he was not a fool. "This is all true," he admitted.

"Which leads me to assume that you are only pursuing Lady Esther to prove to Phoebe that you have moved on."

Rather than attempt to deny it, he decided to ask, "Is it so obvious?"

"To me, perhaps," Mr. Whitmore replied, "but that is only because I am your closest friend."

Samuel lowered his voice. "Can I trust that you will be discrete on this?"

Mr. Whitmore placed a hand over his heart in his usual dramatic fashion. "You have my word," he declared.

"We should call on Lady Esther before we garner any more attention by standing on the pavement," Samuel suggested.

As they approached the three steps that led to the main door, Mr. Whitmore asked, "If you have no real interest in pursuing Lady Esther, can I have a go at her?"

Samuel came to an abrupt halt. "Pardon?"

"I'm not saying I want to pursue her, but she is handsome

enough to tempt me," Mr. Whitmore replied as he continued towards the door.

He wasn't quite sure why the thought of Mr. Whitmore showing interest in Lady Esther bothered him, but it did.

Mr. Whitmore went to knock on the door and Samuel walked to catch up to him.

The door opened and the butler greeted them. "May I help you?" he asked.

"Is Lady Esther receiving callers at this time?" Samuel asked.

"She is, Mr. Moore," the butler replied as he opened the door wide. "Please come in and I will announce you."

Samuel stepped into the entry hall and watched as the butler disappeared into the drawing room.

Mr. Whitmore's eyes roamed over the blue-papered walls and the mural that was painted on the ceiling. "This place is exquisite," he said.

The butler emerged from the drawing room and said, "Lady Esther will see you now."

"Thank you," Samuel acknowledged as he approached the drawing room.

Once he stepped inside, he saw Lady Esther standing in front of the settee and her eyes seemed to light up when she saw him. Or had he just imagined that?

Lady Esther curtsied. "Mr. Moore," she murmured.

Samuel bowed. "Lady Esther," he responded before gesturing towards Mr. Whitmore. "Allow me to introduce you to my friend, Mr. Matthew Whitmore."

She shifted her gaze towards Mr. Whitmore. "It is a pleasure to meet you, sir."

Mr. Whitmore approached her and reached for her hand. "Likewise." He kissed the air above her knuckles. "You take my breath away with your beauty."

"That is kind of you to say," Lady Esther said.

"There is nothing kind about it," Mr. Whitmore responded as he released her hand.

Samuel did not like how close Mr. Whitmore was standing to Lady Esther or how he looked at her. He was being entirely too familiar with her.

He glanced at the maid in the corner and hoped that she would say something about Mr. Whitmore's familiarity. But, unfortunately, she remained silent as she worked on her needlework.

Lady Esther lowered herself onto the settee and Mr. Whitmore sat next to her. She met Samuel's gaze and gestured towards the armchair near her. "Would you like to take a seat, sir?"

"Yes, thank you." Samuel lowered himself down to the proffered chair. "How are you faring?"

"I am well," Lady Esther replied. "And you, are you well?"

Samuel bobbed his head. "I am," he said as he held her gaze. Her blue eyes now held traces of green and he found it captivating, especially since he had never seen eyes like Esther's before. They were unique, just as she was.

Mr. Whitmore spoke up. "I am well, as well."

Lady Esther laughed. "Now that is resolved we can move on and have a cup of tea." She reached for the teapot. "Would anyone care for a cup?"

"I would," Mr. Whitmore replied.

Lady Esther poured him a cup and extended it towards him. "There you go, sir," she said.

"Thank you." Mr. Whitmore took a sip before saying, "You pour tea exquisitely."

Samuel resisted the urge to groan. Did his friend think that compliment would work on Lady Esther?

With an amused look, Lady Esther remarked, "I appreciate the compliment, but I do not think my tea pouring skills are praiseworthy."

"I disagree," Mr. Whitmore stated. "You clearly do not

give yourself enough credit, my lady. One does not simply just pour tea. It is an art, and dare I say, a calling."

A giggle escaped Lady Esther's lips. "That is the most ridiculous thing I have ever heard," she said.

Samuel was pleased by Lady Esther's reaction. She was able to see right through Mr. Whitmore's flattery and did not seem to be taken in by him.

Mr. Whitmore leaned forward and placed his teacup down onto the tray. "I was in earnest with my compliment."

"Were you?" Lady Esther asked. "I am curious to know if how a lady pours tea is on the list that Mr. Moore told me about?"

"If you must know, it is not. I was just trying to offer you a sincere compliment," Mr. Whitmore said, feigning disappointment.

"I hope I did not offend you," Lady Esther said.

Mr. Whitmore's smile reappeared, just as quickly as it had left. "A lady as beautiful as you could never offend me."

Lady Esther seemed to brush off his compliment and turned her attention towards Samuel. "Would you care for a cup of tea?" she asked.

"I would not," he replied. "But I must second my friend and say that you have excellent form when you pour tea." He winked to let her know that he was teasing.

Her lips twitched. "Thank you, sir."

Samuel felt himself smiling, knowing he could do little to stop it. And he didn't want to. He decided it would be best if he changed topics. "I am surprised that your stepmother is not receiving callers with you."

"She went to go rest, but she will be down shortly," Lady Esther revealed. "Until then, a maid will ensure I am properly chaperoned."

"I do hope Lady Mather is well," Mr. Whitmore said.

Lady Esther nodded. "She is, but she gets tired easily."

"That is to be expected," Samuel remarked.

Mr. Whitmore leaned back in his seat and addressed Lady Esther. "How many children would you care to have?"

Lady Esther's mouth dropped but she quickly recovered. "Forgive me, but I do not think we know each other well enough for me to answer that question."

Samuel let out a sigh. His friend was truly an idiot.

Chapter Seven

Esther knew precisely the type of man that Mr. Whitmore was. He was a man that used flattery to his advantage, and she had no intention of falling prey to his charms. Not that he wasn't attractive. His hair was a light shade of blond, and his jaw was strong and defined—it made him look like some sort of Greek deity. She assumed that he had taken advantage of his good looks to get what he desired.

Samuel spoke up, drawing her attention. "I apologize for my friend's bold question, but he was raised in a barn."

Esther smiled at his attempt at humor. "No harm done."

"I was not raised in a barn," Mr. Whitmore said. "I was just merely making conversation and it seemed like a straight-forward question."

"You do not ask a young woman how many children she would care for," Samuel chided.

Mr. Whitmore smiled, no doubt in an attempt to disarm her. "I assure you that I meant no offense," he said.

"None taken, sir," Esther responded graciously. "Perhaps we could discuss something much more pleasurable."

"Do you have any pets?" Mr. Whitmore asked.

"I have considered getting a cat," Esther replied.

"Why not a dog?"

Esther shrugged. "My stepmother says that I should prefer cats."

"That is an odd thing," Mr. Whitmore remarked. "Cats don't do anything but lay around all day. Dogs are a much more respectable pet for a lady of the house."

"I shall take that into consideration," Esther said. She had no desire to debate this with him, or anyone else. If she did take a pet, she would make the decision on what animal it would be. Perhaps she would get a bunny. A bunny seemed like a good pet.

Mr. Whitmore leaned forward and picked up his teacup. After he took a sip, he shared, "I have hunting dogs, but they are not pets. They serve a purpose."

"My father has hunting dogs, as well," Esther said. "I used to sneak treats to them, and I would always get into trouble."

"As well you should. Hunting dogs cannot become spoiled or they are of little use to their owner," Mr. Whitmore said.

"Everyone deserves to be a little spoiled every once in a while," Esther argued.

Samuel interjected, "I must agree with Lady Esther. Life is hard enough. It is good to enjoy the little things that bring us joy."

"Who am I to argue with such a poignant thought?" Mr. Whitmore said.

Esther shifted in her seat to face Mr. Whitmore. "I understand that you wish to be married this Season?"

A flirtatious smile came to his lips. "Are you interested in the position?"

"I am not, but I might be able to help."

His smile remained intact. "You have piqued my curiosity, my lady. How do you intend to help me?"

"What type of young woman are you looking for?" Esther asked.

"A beautiful one," came his quick reply.

"Are there any other attributes that are important to you?" Esther pressed.

Mr. Whitmore seemed to consider her question before saying, "I want a wife that has a pleasing disposition about her, but I do not want a jester."

"I can understand that."

"I also do not want a wife that has one leg that is shorter than the other," Mr. Whitmore said. "I don't want her hobbling to keep up with me."

Esther lifted her brow. "That is an odd request."

"Trust me, they get much odder," Samuel muttered under his breath.

Mr. Whitmore reached into his jacket pocket and removed a piece of paper. As he unfolded it, he said, "I think my list is fair, considering any young lady would be lucky to have me as a husband."

"May I ask why that is?" Esther asked.

He smiled smugly. "Isn't it obvious?" he asked. "I am incredibly handsome and any young woman would look good on my arm."

Did Mr. Whitmore truly believe that was the most important factor for women when selecting a husband? To some, perhaps. But not to her.

Esther didn't know what to address first so she attempted, "Be that as it may, you must want a woman that cares more about you than how she looks on your arm."

With a baffled look, Mr. Whitmore asked, "What else matters to women?"

Samuel gave her a look that seemed to imply "I told you so."

Esther refused to believe that Mr. Whitmore was past hope. "Do you not wish for love?" she asked.

Mr. Whitmore arched an eyebrow. "What does love have to do with marriage?"

"It has everything to do with marriage," she asserted.

"You speak of love as if it is magic; a cure all fix to any relationship. But love fades with time, leaving bitterness and remorse in its wake. It is best if you have mutual toleration for your spouse."

Esther's spine stiffened in response to his words. Why was he so eager to deny that love should be the cornerstone of matrimony?

"You are wrong," she contended. "Love takes time, but if cultivated correctly, it will continue to grow, even under the most difficult circumstances."

Mr. Whitmore chuckled. "Now you are spouting nonsense, much like my good friend, Mr. Moore, does," he said. "I have loved many women over the years, but I always love the woman that I am with the most."

Samuel cleared his throat. "I do apologize for my friend, but he seems to have left his manners at home."

Esther felt herself relax. "It is all right," she said. "I do not mind a lively debate."

Mr. Whitmore pointed at Samuel. "Take my friend, here," he stated. "Love did no favors for him. He is still angry with how he was treated by the woman that he loved."

"Whitmore," Samuel said in a low, warning voice.

"She stomped on his heart, leaving him a shell of the man that he once was," Mr. Whitmore shared. "Was that fair of her?"

"No, but that doesn't mean he should give up on the pursuit of love," Esther replied.

"The pursuit of love?" Mr. Whitmore repeated. "Why? So he could get his heart shattered all over again?"

Esther frowned. "You don't know that for certain."

"Do you?" Mr. Whitmore asked.

Samuel shot his friend a pointed look. "You have made your point. Leave her be."

Mr. Whitmore turned his attention towards his friend. "I

do not mean to be a naysayer, but love is fleeting. It is such a small thing you do with your life."

Esther was not ready to concede. "I contend it is the most important thing you do with your life. Is life worth living without love?"

"You have been reading far too many books with happily ever afters," Mr. Whitmore said. "Real life does not mimic story time."

Samuel gestured towards the teapot. "May I have some tea, please?"

Esther tipped her head and went to pour him a cup. As she extended it towards him, he leaned forward and said, "Do not give Mr. Whitmore much heed. He was kicked in the head by a horse when he was young."

A burst of giggles escaped from her lips and she brought her hand up to cover her mouth.

"I can hear you," Mr. Whitmore said.

"Good," Samuel responded as he leaned back in his seat. "Then perhaps you will stop arguing with our hostess and let us enjoy one another's company."

"We were having a debate," Mr. Whitmore said.

"A debate that you know nothing about," Samuel responded. "You speak of love as if you have experienced it, but I contend you have not. For once you have fallen in love, you feel it, body and soul. It is the only thing you can think about and you fear that you are going mad with want."

"That sounds awful," Mr. Whitmore muttered.

"Love will not consume you, but, rather, it will set you free," Samuel said.

Mr. Whitmore arched an eyebrow. "Did it set you free?"

Samuel grew silent. "Before I met Phoebe, I felt that I couldn't love anyone. But I was wrong. She filled the empty void of my heart," he said.

"It made you sappy," Mr. Whitmore joked.

"Perhaps, but I do not regret loving Phoebe," Samuel

shared. "Quite frankly, I think a part of me will always love her."

Esther could hear the pain in Samuel's voice and her heart ached for him. It was obvious that he still loved Phoebe very much, and the scars had not yet healed from her rejection. "I'm sorry," she said.

Samuel looked at her with a baffled expression. "What do you have to apologize for?"

"I am sorry that she hurt you," Esther replied.

"Love is a gamble, is it not?" Samuel asked with undeniable sadness in his voice.

"I think you are brave that you followed the dictates of your heart," Esther said.

"You think he is brave?" Mr. Whitmore asked with a smile. "You should see how he screams when he sees a rat scurry across the room."

"I was thirteen," Samuel defended. "And the rat's shadow made it look much bigger than it really was."

"He jumped up on the bed and started shrieking. His shrieks woke up the headmaster," Mr. Whitmore shared.

Samuel winced. "Yes, and I received a proper punishment the next day."

"After that, he never screamed at a rat again," Mr. Whitmore said. "That was a good thing, because Eton was full of them."

With a slight shudder, Esther responded, "That sounds awful."

"Boys would hide food in their quarters and the rats would sniff it out," Samuel explained. "Unfortunately, Whitmore was the worst culprit when it came to hiding food in our room."

"It wasn't my fault. I would get hungry at night," Mr. Whitmore stated.

Samuel placed his teacup down onto the tray. "I think we have taken enough of your time today, my lady."

"Must you go?" Esther asked. She wasn't just asking for courtesy's sake, but she truly enjoyed their company. It broke up the monotony of the day.

"I think it would be for the best since I don't want Whitmore to reveal all of my secrets and shortcomings," Samuel said, rising.

Esther rose, as well. "I have enjoyed our time immensely."

"As have I," Samuel said. "Will you be in attendance at Lady Amanda Strunk's ball this evening?"

"I intend to be," Esther replied.

"You must promise to save me the supper dance," Samuel said.

Her lips curled into a smile as she felt her heart soar with his request. "I would like that, very much."

Samuel held her gaze for a moment, and she was curious as to what he saw in her eyes. She was coming to realize that he saw more than he would dare to admit.

Mr. Whitmore bowed. "If you give up this love nonsense, I think we could be very happy together," he said with mirth in his eyes.

Esther laughed. "I somehow doubt that, but I wish you luck in finding the perfect woman."

He put his hands out in a dramatic fashion. "But, alas, she is standing before me, and she is glorious and beautiful."

Samuel groaned. "That was awful."

"Do you mind?" Mr. Whitmore asked under his breath. "You are ruining this moment for me and Lady Esther."

"You are ruining it for yourself," Samuel bantered back.

Esther let out another laugh. It felt good to laugh. "Good day, Mr. Whitmore," she said. "Mr. Moore."

As the men departed from the drawing room, Esther realized that she was still smiling.

Samuel sat in the coach as it jostled back and forth. His mother and father sat across from him, dressed in their finery, but both wearing the usual contempt they felt for one another on their faces. He couldn't remember a time when they weren't at odds.

His father's voice drew his attention. "Have you made any progress with Lady Esther?"

"These things take time," Samuel replied vaguely.

"Do not take too much time," his father advised. "The longer you take to secure your bride, the more people have time to speculate on your relationship."

His mother spoke up. "Leave him be. I trust that Samuel knows what he is doing." She smiled encouragingly. "Don't you, Son?"

Samuel went to speak but his father answered for him. "Lady Esther would make a fine bride for him and I do not want him to squander this opportunity."

"She is a lovely young lady, but that doesn't mean we force him into a marriage," his mother argued.

"Why must you always insist on contradicting me, Woman?" his father growled.

"It is only because you say the most stupid things," his mother responded.

Samuel let out a sigh. It was always the same with his parents. At least it was familiar. He was grateful when the coach came to a stop in front of a brownstone townhouse. There was a line of guests that led from their coaches to the main door.

He waited for his parents to exit first before he followed suit.

His father offered his arm to his mother and smiled at the guests passing by. In a low voice, he said, "Do try to avoid embarrassing me this evening."

"With any luck, I will spend as little time with you as possible," his mother whispered, her smile plastered on her face.

"We are in agreement, then," his father said as he placed his hand up to acknowledge someone further up in the line.

Samuel followed his parents through the receiving line, where they gave no indication of any discord between them. In public, they always behaved, appearing as a loving couple. It was an act that he had grown tired of. Why couldn't his parents just be civil to one another?

He continued into the ballroom, not bothering to wait for his parents. They would make an appearance in the ballroom before they went their separate ways. It was always the same. He never wanted a marriage where he couldn't stand the thought of being around his wife.

His eyes scanned the room and he saw Phoebe on Lord Leyburn's arm. He felt his jaw clench as he looked away. It was none of his business who she associated with. She could marry one of the princes for all that he cared.

But it was getting warm in the ballroom, nonetheless.

Samuel walked towards the rear of the ballroom, stopping only to pick up a flute of champagne. He stepped outside and felt the cool night air on his skin. It reminded him of the night that he had offered for Phoebe. The sky had been full of stars and he had been filled with such optimism for the future. But all his dreams and aspirations had been for nothing in the end.

Phoebe had chosen someone else. He hadn't been enough for her in the past and he certainly wasn't enough for her now. Was there ever a possibility that he would be enough for her?

He approached the iron railing that surrounded the veranda and leaned against it. These wretched memories. When would he be free of them? He needed to banish them, but he was unable to do so. The memories they shared were still too vivid.

He cast his eyes heavenward. The stars were magnificent, reminding him of Phoebe and what they almost had. They would have been great together. He was sure of that.

He heard a voice he knew all too well; one that still lingered in his dreams. "Hello, Samuel," Phoebe said, her voice soft, but there wasn't a hint of hesitancy in the words. She had always been purposeful in everything she did. It had been one of the things he had admired about her.

Samuel closed his eyes, wishing that he was anywhere but here. He didn't have the strength to face her, not here, not now.

He heard her soft steps on the stones as she approached him. "Will you not at least turn around and greet me properly?"

Taking a deep breath, he slowly turned around and tried to pretend that her mere presence didn't affect him so greatly. Her blonde hair was swept up into an elaborate hairstyle with curls framing her face. Her rich blue gown hugged her curves, making it nearly impossible to look away, and an ornate diamond necklace hung around her neck. Her eyes shone brightly, as if she had stolen some of the shimmer from the stars above.

He bowed. "Lady Bedlington."

She looked hurt by his formality, but he refused to yield. Frankly, he couldn't. "How are you?" she asked.

"I am well."

For the first time, he could see a slip in her mask and he saw uncertainty in her eyes. "Why are you out here by yourself?"

"I needed a moment alone," he replied.

"Oh," she murmured. "Would you care for me to leave?"

Yes! Couldn't she see that he was barely hanging on with her being so close to him?

He shook his head, not wanting to give her the power to hurt him even more than she already had. "You can do what you want," he replied, his tone much harsher than he had intended.

She watched him for a long moment before saying, "I have

been following your career and you have really made something of yourself."

"Thank you," he said, unsure of what else he could say. He was secretly pleased that she had followed his career. What did that mean, he wondered.

"You did a good thing for Lady Eugenie," Phoebe said.

"I only did my job," Samuel responded.

Phoebe took a step closer to him, but still managed to leave more than enough distance to be considered proper. "I was hoping we could talk."

Not liking where this conversation was heading, he said, "We are talking." Perhaps if he was dismissive enough she would leave him be.

"Yes, but I feel as if I owe you an explanation."

An explanation? She owed him more than that but he didn't want to say anything that would encourage this conversation. It was in the past, where he wanted it to remain. "That isn't necessary."

"I think it is." She hesitated before adding, "I want to."

As he dreaded what Phoebe would say next, he heard Esther's voice over the music in the ballroom. "There you are, my dear," she said as she approached him with a purposeful stride. "I have been looking all over for you."

Esther came to a stop next to him and her eyes seemed to implore him. She had come to rescue him. "Am I interrupting something?" she asked, glancing between him and Phoebe.

"No, nothing too important." Samuel reached for Esther's hand, needing her touch to bolster his courage. "Have you two been introduced?" He knew full well they hadn't, but he was trying to be polite.

"I haven't had the pleasure," Esther said. "It is Lady Bedlington, is it not?"

Phoebe smiled, but it didn't quite meet her eyes. "Yes, it is, and you must be Lady Esther. I have read so much about you."

"Do not believe everything you have read," Esther remarked lightly, turning to face him. "Shall we go back inside? My father is asking about you."

Samuel smiled. "I wouldn't want to keep Lord Mather waiting." He bowed at Phoebe. "Good evening, Lady Bedlington."

She dropped into a curtsy. "Mr. Moore."

He kept his head held high as he led Esther towards the ballroom and only when he was out of sight of Phoebe did he let out a sigh of relief. "Thank you," he said.

"I hope I did not overstep my bounds," Esther responded.

"No, your appearance was much appreciated."

Esther looked up at him with concern. "You didn't look very pleased to be speaking to Lady Bedlington."

"I wasn't," he admitted. "I thought we had nothing more left to say to one another."

"I was with Lord and Lady Brentwood when we saw Lady Bedlington follow you out onto the veranda," Esther shared. "Lord Brentwood was the one who encouraged me to go help you. He feared that Lady Bedlington might sink her claws into you again."

Samuel lifted his brow and she rushed to add, "Lord Brentwood's words, not mine."

"I should have known," Samuel said.

Esther leaned in closer as they stepped into the ballroom. "I told Lady Brentwood that I would return with you."

"Lovely," he muttered.

As he drew closer to Lord Brentwood, his friend's expression changed, shifting from a look of pity to one of compassion. He didn't want either one; pity or compassion.

Esther removed her hand as they came to a stop in front of Lord and Lady Brentwood. "I was able to retrieve Mr. Moore without any unforeseen complications."

"Well done," Lady Brentwood praised.

Lord Brentwood placed a hand on his shoulder. "What did Phoebe want?"

"She just wanted to talk," he replied.

"No good would come from that," Lord Brentwood said, removing his hand. "She is a shrew of the highest order."

"You have never liked her," Samuel asserted.

"That is true, but only because she is not a very nice person," Lord Brentwood said. "Look at what she did to you, without a hint of remorse."

Samuel didn't want to get into a fight with his friend about this again. Lord Brentwood had always had a less than favorable opinion of Phoebe. It had been a source of contention when he had been pursuing her, but they had let bygones be bygones after Phoebe rejected his offer.

"Would you care to dance?" Esther asked.

"I believe I asked for your supper dance," Samuel replied.

Esther bobbed her head. "You did, but Phoebe has not stopped looking at us since we returned to the ballroom. I thought we could give her a better look at us on the dance floor."

Samuel brought his gaze up until his eyes stopped on Phoebe. She smiled and tipped her head, not showing any sign of discomfort at being caught staring.

Placing her hand on his sleeve, Esther asked, "Are you all right, Samuel?"

"I will be," he said. "I just need a moment on the veranda."

"Would you like me to accompany you?"

It was on the tip of his tongue to say no, but he could see the kindness in her eyes, disarming him. She really did want to help him. But did he want her help? He didn't want anyone to see him in such a vulnerable state.

Esther must have understood his reluctance because she gave him a weak smile. "We don't even have to speak. We can just remain in one another's company."

"Very well, then," Samuel said as he offered his arm.

She accepted his arm and they walked towards the veranda. He didn't stop until he arrived at a bench and assisted Esther as she sat down.

Samuel didn't claim the seat next to her but remained standing. Why wouldn't the ache in his heart go away? He was miserable, and it was of his own making. He couldn't quite seem to banish Phoebe from his thoughts.

Esther's voice broke through the silence. "I think you are very brave."

Him? Brave? He didn't think so, but he decided to ask, "You do?"

"You still believe in love even though your heart has been broken."

Samuel couldn't disagree with her more. "That is not brave. It is stupidity."

"I disagree," Esther said, rising. "When I look into your eyes, I can see your struggles even though you do your best to hide them. I know you are hurting and your pain is deep. But you are not alone in this." She entwined her gloved hand with his. "I am here, and I will help you."

He looked down at their hands, a part of him disbelieving what he was seeing. "What can you do?" He knew he was being rude, but it slipped out before he could stop himself.

"What do you want?" Esther asked as her eyes searched his.

"Pardon?"

"Do you want to win Lady Bedlington's heart?" Esther pressed.

Samuel shook his head. "It is too late. She is nearly engaged to Lord Leyburn."

"Until she announces the engagement, hope is not lost," Esther said, a smile tugging at her lips. "You seem to forget that I was almost engaged, as well."

"It is different."

"How so?" Esther questioned.

He ran a hand through his hair. "I don't even know where to begin or if it is even possible." Did he even want a second chance with Phoebe? Was it worth the risk?

Esther released his hand and took a step back. "Then I propose you first decide what it is that you are fighting for," she started. "And when you do that, I will help you."

"You make it sound so simple."

"It is, but I can't make this decision for you," Esther said before she walked back into the ballroom.

Samuel stared at her retreating figure as his mind whirled. He didn't know what he wanted and that was the problem.

Chapter Eight

The sun shone brightly as Esther stepped out of the carriage in front of Gunter's Tea Shop and stood on the pavement waiting for Susanna to join her. In her stepmother's condition, everything seemed to take an enormous amount of time and effort.

Susanna came to stand next to her and placed a hand on her protruding belly. "I must admit that I am looking forward to the lemon ice."

"I think I shall try something different today," Esther said. "I might even try one of the cheese flavors."

Her stepmother made a face. "That sounds awful."

"It is all the rage nowadays."

"Just because something is popular doesn't make it right."

Esther had to admit that her stepmother did have a point. "Fair enough," she said. "But I still would like to try it."

"I just pray it doesn't have too strong of a smell."

"If it does, I will sit at a different table while we eat our ices."

Susanna waved her hand in front of her. "You don't have to do that on my account," she said. "I shall make do."

A footman opened the door into Gunter's for them. Once

they stepped inside, a myriad of smells filled the air and Susanna's hand flew to her mouth.

Esther noticed that her stepmother's face had grown pale. "Are you all right?" she asked with concern.

"I need a moment," Susanna declared before she fled from the shop.

As she watched her stepmother take a few deep breaths outside, a server from behind the counter asked, "Would you care to order, Miss?"

"Yes, I would," Esther replied. "May I get two lemon ices?" She thought it would be best to get something that wouldn't assault her stepmother's senses.

After she paid for the ices, she exited the store and approached her stepmother. "Are you feeling better?"

"I am," Susanna confirmed. "I daresay the smell of dry sweetmeat was too much for me."

Esther extended the glass towards her. "Would a lemon ice help you?"

"It most definitely would," Susanna replied as she accepted the treat. "Thank you."

She acknowledged her words with a smile. "Shall we sit down and enjoy our treats?"

"That would be lovely."

They sat down at a table that was shaded by the building. Neither of them spoke as they started eating.

It was a few moments later when Susanna placed her spoon down. "I was hoping to speak to you about something."

"What about?"

Susanna looked hesitant. "Your father and I were coming up with names for the baby and we settled on the name of Adam if it is a boy."

"That is a fine name."

"We believe so," Susanna agreed. "But if it is a girl, we were hoping to name it Hyacinth, after your mother."

Esther was taken aback by the heartfelt homage to her mother, inhaling sharply in surprise. "Are you in earnest?"

Susanna rushed to add, "I thought it was a fine tribute to your mother, but if you are opposed to it then we can pick another name."

"No, no, I love it," Esther assured her. "I think it is perfect."

Susanna let out a sigh of relief. "I am pleased to hear you say that. I didn't want you to be upset with the name we selected."

"Will it be awkward for you, though?"

"Your father said something similar, but if I wasn't sure then I wouldn't have suggested it."

Esther's brow lifted in surprise. "You suggested it, not Father?"

Susanna picked up her spoon and dipped it into the bowl. "I am trying, Esther. I don't want to be at odds with you anymore and I have no desire to be the evil stepmother."

"I never said you were 'evil'."

With a knowing smile, Susanna said, "You didn't have to." Her smile slipped. "Your cousin is approaching."

"He is?" she asked with dread in her voice. The last thing she wanted to do was engage in pleasantries with her cousin.

"Just smile and he should be on his way soon," Susanna advised.

Time seemed to tick by until Daniel came to stand next to her. "Lady Mather," he greeted. "Cousin."

Esther turned her head to look up at him. "Cousin, what a pleasant surprise," she said, hoping her words sounded cordial enough.

"I just happened upon you two and I thought I would say hello." Daniel gestured towards the empty chair next to her and asked, "May I?"

"You may," Esther replied.

Daniel pulled out a chair and sat down. "What has preoccupied you as of late?" he asked, directing his question towards her.

"Nothing in particular," Esther replied.

"I understand that Mr. Moore has been showing you favor."

"Yes, that is correct."

"Do you intend to marry him?"

Esther blinked. "I have not yet decided." Why was her cousin being so bold in his questioning? Furthermore, what did it matter to him who showed her favor?

Leaning back in his chair, Daniel brought a lazy smile to his lips. "You should lighten up, Cousin," he said. "I am just merely curious."

Susanna awkwardly rose. "I think it is time for us to depart."

Rising, Daniel glanced at her cup of lemon ice. "But you have hardly touched your treat. Did you not enjoy it?"

Her stepmother placed a hand on her stomach. "I'm afraid it does not agree with me."

"That is because you did not try the mint ice," Daniel said. "Allow me to correct this most grievous error."

"That isn't necessary—"

Daniel cut her off. "Trust me. It is delicious," he said.

Susanna nodded as she reluctantly returned to her seat. "Very well."

After Daniel walked into Gunter's, Esther turned her baffled gaze towards her stepmother. "What is he about?"

"I daresay that he is trying too hard to win our favor," Susanna said. "But hurry and eat your lemon ice so we can depart sooner rather than later."

Esther dipped her spoon into the bowl and started eating as fast as she could handle the cold sensation in her mouth. Her cousin wasn't a terrible person, but she found him to be quite vexing. It just seemed like he was always putting on an act when around them.

Her cousin emerged with two bowls and placed them down onto the table. "Go on, then, try them," he encouraged.

Esther reached for a bowl and tasted the mint ice. "It is rather minty."

Daniel looked amused by her analysis. "That is why it is called 'mint ice'."

"I am not quite sure if I like it."

After Susanna took a bite, she pushed the bowl away from her. "I do not like it at all. It is far too overpowering for my tastes."

"I wouldn't say it was overpowering," Esther said.

"Neither would I, but it is not for everyone." Daniel reached for Esther's bowl and took a bite. "I, for one, thoroughly enjoy this decadent flavor."

Esther thought she should chide Daniel on his familiar behavior but it would do no good. He had always done what he had wanted to. It had been that way since they were children.

Susanna's hand shot to the side of her stomach. "The baby is kicking."

Daniel looked horrified. "You can feel such a thing?"

"I can, and I rather enjoy it," Susanna revealed.

"It sounds like something out of a horror book," Daniel said as he continued eating from Esther's bowl.

Susanna didn't appear upset by Daniel's remark. "Feeling a baby move inside of you is a glorious feeling," she said. "It makes me rather anxious to meet this little one."

Daniel licked the spoon before placing it back into the bowl. "Have you selected a name for the chit?"

"My father is hoping for a boy," Esther responded.

"Yes, well, you turned out to be a girl, did you not?" Daniel remarked. "No doubt he was disappointed in that, as well."

Esther bit her sharp tongue, knowing no good would come from challenging her cousin in such a public place. She would just have to pretend that his words had no effect on her. But they had hit their mark. Her father had never told her that he was disappointed that she was born a girl, but she had long suspected that might be the case.

Susanna spoke up. "David is very proud of Esther."

"Yes, I did not mean to imply anything to the contrary." Daniel shifted in his seat to face her. "Please say that I did not offend you."

Esther felt his apology was a little too contrived. "You did not," she said, rising. "But it would be best if Susanna returned home and rested."

Daniel moved to rise. "Would you like me to escort you home?"

"No," Esther rushed out. "I mean, we do not want to impose on you. I'm sure you have much more important things to do."

"It is no imposition," Daniel attempted.

Susanna winced slightly. "I must admit that I am not feeling very well." She placed a hand on the table to steady herself.

Esther rushed to her stepmother's side. "Are you all right?" she asked.

"I will be, but I just need to lie down," Susanna replied.

Daniel came to stand next to Susanna and held his arm out. "Allow me to at least escort you to the coach," he said.

"Very well," Susanna agreed as she placed her hand on his arm.

As they walked towards the coach, Esther saw that Susanna was leaning into Daniel for support, causing her to grow alarmed.

A footman opened the door and Daniel assisted Susanna into the coach. He turned back to face her, his countenance marked with worry. "I think I should fetch the doctor."

"Do you mind?"

"It is the least I can do," Daniel said as he held his hand

out to assist her. "Take care of Lady Mather and I shall rush as fast as I can."

Esther gave him a grateful smile. "Thank you," she said.

Daniel released her hand and closed the coach door.

She turned her attention towards Susanna and saw that her stepmother's face had turned pale. "What can I do to help you?"

"Just hold my hand," Susanna said in a weak voice.

The coach jerked forward as Esther clutched her step-mother's hand, feeling completely, and utterly, useless.

———⁓———

Samuel sat at his desk in his office as he finished writing down a few notes for his upcoming trial. He had been in court all morning and he was grateful for a chance to be alone with his thoughts.

He had promised that he would call upon Esther today and take her on a ride through Hyde Park. He had no qualms with spending time with her. She was a delightful young woman who made him smile. It felt good to smile. He hadn't done much of that since he had been rejected by Phoebe.

Phoebe.

Why did his thoughts almost always turn towards her? He couldn't believe that she had the audacity to attempt to talk to him last night at the ball. Had she intended to put salt on the wounds that she had left with him? There would be no good from him talking to her again. He was sure of that.

But Esther... she had saved him. She knew that he was in distress and she came to help him. She was a remarkable young woman, and with every moment spent with her, their friendship was deepening.

A knock at the door drew his attention.

Samuel brought his head up and glanced at the desk in the

corner where his secretary usually sat. Mr. Allen was out running errands for him so he would be of little use to him.

Pushing back his chair, he rose and walked over to the door. He stopped and adjusted his cravat before opening the door.

To his surprise, Phoebe was standing on the other side of the threshold.

She smiled at him. "Samuel." It was the same blasted smile that he couldn't seem to banish from his mind.

"Lady Bedlington," he responded.

"I would prefer if you called me Phoebe."

"And I would prefer that you were not here, but we both can't have what we wish," Samuel said, gruffly.

Her smile dimmed. "May we talk?"

Samuel glanced over her shoulder. "Where is your companion?"

"I am a widow and I'm allowed a little more freedom," Phoebe replied.

Knowing he would come to regret this, Samuel opened the door wide. "Come in," he encouraged. "But I do not have long. I am taking Lady Esther on a carriage ride through Hyde Park."

Phoebe visibly tensed. "How delightful."

Samuel was pleased by her reaction. It almost seemed that she was jealous of Lady Esther. Good. Let her have a taste of what she had put him through.

He waited for her to be seated before he casually moved to sit behind his desk. He was grateful for some distance between them. He wasn't sure he could trust himself if he was within arm's length of her.

Phoebe situated herself on the chair before saying, "I apologize for coming to your place of business but I didn't know what else to do."

"Are you in need of something?"

Looking uncomfortable, Phoebe said, "I do not like how things were left between us and I hope to rectify that."

He put his hand up, hoping to still her words. "There is no need."

"Do you hate me?"

He shook his head. "No, I do not hate you." He had tried to hate her, but he could never quite seem to. He cared for her far too much.

"That is a relief," Phoebe said, looking visibly relieved. "I do not think I could stand it if you hated me."

Samuel picked up the quill and placed it next to the ink pot. "Did you come all this way to ask me that?"

"I did."

"May I ask why it matters so much to you?"

Phoebe fidgeted with the reticule that was around her right wrist. "You are a good man, and I feel terrible about the way I treated you."

Samuel leaned back in his chair and he considered Phoebe. She seemed remorseful but he wasn't about to open up and tell her how much she had hurt him.

"I just wanted you to know that I am sorry," Phoebe said, rising. "That is all that I wanted to say and I shall leave you be now."

He rose. "Are you engaged to Lord Leyburn?"

"Not yet, but I am hoping he will offer for me soon."

"Why?"

Phoebe gave him a baffled look. "Whatever do you mean?"

"He is old, just as your first husband was."

"I am not concerned about his age."

Samuel knew he should just let the matter drop but he couldn't seem to help himself. "Do you truly care so much for your place in Society that you would marry another decrepit man to achieve your goals?"

"Lord Leyburn is not decrepit."

"No? You could have fooled me."

Phoebe's eyes flashed with annoyance. "I did not come here to fight with you."

"No, you came here to soothe your own conscience."

"I came to apologize."

"Did you?" he asked. "Because I have yet to tell you if I have forgiven you."

Phoebe tilted her chin stubbornly. "It isn't very gentlemanly of you to refuse a woman's apology. I hadn't taken you for being so petty."

"I am not petty."

"I disagree."

Samuel gestured towards the door and said, "You may leave at any time. I am not keeping you here."

"Please, Samuel, why are you being so difficult?" Phoebe asked. "This is not you."

"How do you know what I am like anymore? You lost that right when you turned down my offer of marriage."

The moment his words left his mouth, she grew tense and her mouth formed a tight line. "It was for a good reason."

"I know precisely why you did it." Samuel came around his desk and approached her. "You wanted to secure your place in Society and my title was not lofty enough for you."

"You know not what you speak of."

"Please correct me if I am wrong," he said dryly.

"My father was pressuring me to wed and he did not want me to marry you," Phoebe said. "He signed a marriage contract with Lord Bedlington."

"You could have said no."

Phoebe reared back, as if she had never considered this option. "And risk my reputation?"

"There are worse things."

"Now you are just spouting nonsense," Phoebe said. "A woman's reputation is the most important thing in the world."

"So you agreed to a loveless marriage?"

Phoebe's eyes grew downcast. "Philip was good to me," she said. "I did not want for anything."

"Except for love."

Bringing her gaze up, she stated, "What is done, is done. I have secured my place in Society and my marriage served its purpose."

"Then why are you marrying Lord Leyburn?"

A disbelieving scoff escaped her lips as she took a deep breath. "I do not answer to you, Samuel," she spat out. "I can do as I please."

"I do not dispute that, but why are you going from one loveless marriage to another?"

With a slight shrug, she replied, "Lord Leyburn is good to me. I should be so lucky to be his wife."

Samuel couldn't seem to help himself and took a step closer to her. "If you are so eager to marry Lord Leyburn, why did you come to see me?"

"I already told you why."

One of the things Samuel excelled at was reading people, especially Phoebe. He had made it a point to know everything about her, and she was keeping something from him.

"Do you want to know what I think?" he asked.

"Not particularly."

He smirked. "I think you came here because you wanted to see me." He paused. "No, you *needed* to see me."

"No, I told you—"

Closing the distance between them, he asked, "Did you find the closure you were looking for?"

She looked up at him with her wide eyes and his resolve almost vanished. "I have not," she admitted.

"Good," he said as he brushed past her. He opened the door. "It is time for you to leave, Lady Bedlington."

Phoebe's eyes narrowed. "Why are you such an infuriating man?"

"I suppose you bring this side out of me."

"I would have you know that I do not need you in my life," Phoebe said as she slowly walked towards the door. "I thought we could part as friends."

"Why would you want me as a friend since I cannot help you in any way?"

Phoebe approached him and stopped in front of him. She reached up and adjusted his cravat, causing him to grow rigid. "It was crooked," she explained as she lowered her hands.

"Goodbye, my lady," Samuel said dismissively. He didn't want to tell her that her nearness was affecting him greatly. He could smell the sweet familiar scent of lavender perfume drift off from her person. If she didn't leave soon, he would pull her into his arms and never let her go.

Phoebe placed a hand on his chest. "Goodbye, Samuel." Her words were soft, resigned.

They remained there, staring at one another, until he heard footsteps in the hall. Phoebe must have heard them, too, because she took a step back.

A moment later, Mr. Allen appeared in the doorway, and he blinked. "My apologies," he said. "I hadn't realized you had a client."

"Lady Bedlington was just leaving," Samuel said.

Phoebe tipped her head. "Yes, I was," she replied. "Thank you for your time, Mr. Moore."

"You are welcome."

With a parting glance, Phoebe departed from his office and he almost breathed a sigh of relief. He hadn't made a fool of himself by confessing the true extent of his feelings for her.

Mr. Allen stepped into the office. "I have the documents that you requested. Shall I put them on your desk?"

"That would be for the best."

His secretary placed the documents down onto his desk before he asked, "Would you like me to transcribe the notes you took in court today?"

Samuel remained in the open doorway. "Yes," he replied. "While you work on that, I have an errand I need to see to."

"Is it anything that I can do for you, sir?"

Reaching for his hat on a hook on the wall, he responded, "No, this is something I must do for myself."

"Very well," his secretary said as he picked up a file on his desk.

Samuel placed the hat on his head and exited his office. He needed a moment to clear his head before he went to call on Esther. He didn't want to burden her with his problems. That wouldn't be fair of him. She had her own troubles.

As he started walking down the pavement, he found that he was eager to see Esther. The way she looked at him, she saw all of him. Not just the parts that he wanted her to see. And that was a wonderful feeling.

Chapter Nine

Esther stood outside of her stepmother's bedchamber as she waited for the doctor to complete his examination. It felt like it had been hours, but it probably had only been mere moments. The fear of not knowing caused her heart to pound. Frankly, it scared her. She had been here before, and the outcome had been dire.

The door opened and her father slipped out, closing the door behind him.

"How is she?" Esther asked, eagerly.

Her father had a solemn look on her face. "She is feeling better, but Dr. Ramsey is recommending leeches to help with her recovery."

"And the baby?"

"Dr. Ramsey does not believe the baby will have any adverse effects," her father shared, visibly relieved.

Esther clasped her hands together. "That is wonderful news."

"It is," he said. "Susanna is asking for you. Would you care to see her?"

The image of her mother covered in leeches came to her mind and she knew she couldn't see Susanna. Not when she had leeches on her. It would take her back to a place that she never wanted to go to again. The memories were too raw, too painful.

Taking a step back, Esther asked, "Will you inform her that I shall see her after the doctor departs?"

Her father looked at her with concern in his eyes. "I will tell her, but she could use your support right now."

"She has you."

"That she does," her father said, "but she is frightened."

Esther shook her head. "I can't. I'm sorry," she said before she hurried down the hall. She knew she was taking the easy way out, but she couldn't see Susanna in her current state. The doctor had continuously applied leeches to her mother, and her mother had died. The leeching had done little to help her, and Esther doubted it would help Susanna.

As she descended the stairs, a knock echoed throughout the main level.

Gibson crossed the entry hall and opened the door, revealing Samuel. He was dressed in a dark gray jacket, buff trousers and a blue waistcoat. She had to admit that seeing him was a welcome reprieve.

He stepped inside and watched her until she came to a stop a short distance away. "What is wrong?" he asked with a furrowed brow.

Esther gave him a look of surprise. "Why do you suppose something is wrong?"

"Because you wear your emotions on your sleeve," Samuel replied.

"Oh, I hadn't realized."

His expression softened. "I prefer that, actually. It makes things much simpler. I tire of people hiding behind a mask of their own making."

With a glance at the stairs, Esther revealed, "My step-mother is not feeling well and the doctor is with her now."

"I'm sorry to hear that."

"Dr. Ramsey is applying leeches to help cleanse her blood," Esther said.

"That is a common practice."

"It is, but I do not care for leeches," Esther shared. "I am of the mind that leeching doesn't work."

"Do not let the doctor hear you say that," Samuel joked.

"Susanna wanted to see me, but I couldn't go in there," Esther confessed.

Samuel took a step closer to her. "Why is that?"

"My mother..." Her voice trailed off. Could she really talk about her mother to him? She rarely spoke about her mother.

He prodded, "Your mother?"

She waved her hand dismissively in front of her. "Yes, my mother used leeches and they did little good for her. She died, slowly and in a great deal of pain." She rushed out her words, hoping he would not press her on it.

His eyes shone with compassion. "My condolences on your loss," he said.

Esther hadn't told him that story to elicit sympathy. Her mother died and that was the end of it. No matter how much Esther grieved for her, she was not coming back. So why dwell on such an unpleasant topic?

Samuel came closer and placed a hand on her sleeve. "I did not know your mother, but if she was anything like you, she must have been extraordinary."

"She was," Esther admitted. "She was the best of mothers and I..." She paused. "I miss her, every moment of every day."

"That is to be expected."

"Is it?" she asked. "Because I feel like I am the only one that still mourns her."

"I am sorry to say but you will grieve forever. Grieving is a journey, not a destination," Samuel said.

Esther clenched her jaw and tried not to cry, feeling the tears welling up in her eyes. "Why does it still hurt so bad?"

"Because that is how you know your mother's life was worth celebrating."

Standing there, with his comforting hand on her arm, Esther didn't feel as alone. He was truly listening to her, and she felt understood. He wasn't trying to deny the validity of her emotions but was encouraging her to embrace them. For the first time in a long time, she felt heard.

"Thank you," Esther said.

He removed his hand but remained close. "I hope something in my vain attempt to comfort you helped."

"It did, more than you know."

Samuel smiled. "I must admit that I try to solve people's problems. It is much easier than trying to solve my own."

"I agree, wholeheartedly."

"Do you have any more problems that need to be solved?" Samuel asked, holding his hands out wide. "I am more than happy to help."

Esther laughed, feeling freer than she had in a long time. "I cannot think of any at the moment."

"You have the most beautiful laugh."

"I believe it is like most laughs, sir."

Samuel held her gaze as he replied, "When you laugh, the world stops for a moment. It is free of any pain."

"Then I have fooled you into believing so."

"Perhaps it is you that does not understand the power of your laughter," Samuel responded.

The intensity of his gaze made her blush and she averted her eyes. "You flatter me."

"That was not my intention. I only meant to tell you the truth."

Her father's voice came from the top of the stairs. "Mr. Moore, what an unexpected surprise," he said, his words curt.

Samuel moved to create more distance between them. He bowed. "Lord Mather," he greeted.

Her father descended the stairs as he said, "You will have to excuse us but I'm afraid Lady Mather is not feeling well."

"Lady Esther told me as much," Samuel responded. "I do hope that Lady Mather will have a quick recovery."

"The doctor is optimistic. He believes she is just under the weather," her father informed him.

"That is good," Samuel said.

Her father glanced between them with a furrowed brow before he met her gaze. "I'm afraid I must leave for the House of Lords. Will you go sit with Susanna?"

Esther opened her mouth to protest, but her father continued. "It shall only be until I get back. I just need to cast my vote."

"I don't know if that is wise, Father," Esther said.

"Why?"

Esther pursed her lips together, knowing it was time to admit the truth to her father. "I can't stand the thought of looking at the leeches on her body. They remind me of what Mother had to endure."

Her father's eyes grew sad. "Your mother was dying. No number of leeches would have helped her in her condition," he said. "Susanna just needs to have her blood cleansed and she will be back to her old self."

"What if she isn't?"

"I have buried one wife, and I refuse to do it again." Her father's eyes grew moist. "Susanna has to get better."

Esther could hear the pain in her father's voice and knew that he meant it. How could she deny his simple request? She may be uncomfortable around leeches, but she had to sympathize with how Susanna was feeling at the moment.

Gathering up all her strength, she said, "If it means so much to you, I will go sit with Susanna."

Her father gave her an approving nod. "Thank you, Esther."

After her father departed from the townhouse, Esther

LAURA BEERS

looked over at Samuel and asked, "Why did I agree to sit with Susanna?"

"Because you are good and kind," he replied.

"Or I am just a glutton for punishment."

Samuel gave her an encouraging look. "You can handle whatever comes your way, and if not, you can always try to climb a tree and run away."

"I like that option the best right now."

He studied her before asking, "What would you have done if you had managed to climb over that tree and escaped over the wall?"

"To be honest, I hadn't thought that far," she admitted.

"That is surprising," he teased.

Esther grinned, as she found their verbal sparring to be her new favorite thing. "Pray tell, what would you have done, given the circumstances?"

"Well, that is simple," Samuel replied. "I would have become a pirate and ruled the high seas with my cutlass."

"A pirate?" she repeated. "You would be an awful pirate."

Samuel looked amused. "Why is that?"

"A pirate does not fix people's problems, but rather is the cause of most of them."

"I shall be a pirate unlike any other pirate," Samuel said, puffing out his chest. "I will be known as 'Samuel the Wise'."

"Would you plunder villages?"

"No, but I would build them back up so they could become more prosperous."

Esther giggled. "I find it alarming how little you know about pirates and their way of life."

"Am I to assume that you are an expert on pirates?"

"More so than you," Esther replied.

Samuel chuckled. "We shall have to agree to disagree, my lady, because I think I would make a fine pirate."

"What about being a barrister?"

128

"I could be a barrister pirate and solve all their problems through a right proper debate."

"I do not think pirates care to debate."

"That is a shame."

A maid's hesitant voice came from next to her. "I apologize for interrupting, but Lady Mather is asking for you... again."

Esther had been so preoccupied with her conversation with Samuel that she'd failed to notice the maid's arrival. "Inform Lady Mather that I shall be up in a moment."

The maid tipped her head. "Yes, my lady," she responded before she left to do her bidding.

"I should go," Esther said. "I'm sorry that we aren't able to go on a carriage ride through Hyde Park like we had planned."

"There is always tomorrow."

"Yes, tomorrow," Esther said. "I shall be looking forward to it."

Samuel stepped forward and reached for her hand. He brought it up to his lips and kissed the air above it. "I daresay it is impossible for you to understand your own strength until you are forced to face an unbearable situation."

"I am not strong."

"You are stronger than you give yourself credit for." He released her hand and took a step back. "I am not wrong on this."

Esther watched as he departed from the townhouse and she wished that she could tarry just a little longer in his presence. He buoyed her up and she so desperately wanted to be the person he thought she was.

But whatever happened between them, she knew that his heart was not in it. He loved Phoebe, and he always would. She was just a distraction. Hadn't he told her as much on their first meeting? So why was she beginning to hope for things she knew she could never have?

Esther stepped into the bedchamber and her eyes were immediately drawn to the four leeches that were slithering on each of her stepmother's arms. She froze and couldn't seem to walk any further into the room.

Susanna's eyes were tightly closed, looking deucedly uncomfortable.

The doctor glanced up from his chair and pushed back the spectacles that hung low on his nose. "Ah, Lady Esther," he started, "you have come to keep Lady Mather company."

Susanna's eyes opened and Esther could see the anguish that was hiding within. "Esther, you came," she said, her voice shaky.

Mustering up all the courage she could, Esther started to put one foot ahead of the other until she found the chair sitting next to the bed. She sat down with a rigid back and attempted to ignore the little blood suckers. But it was proving to be an impossible task.

She wanted to run from the room, but she couldn't do that to Susanna. Her stepmother needed her, and it was time for her to be strong. Samuel thought she was strong, and she wanted to prove to herself that he hadn't misjudged her.

An image of her mother came to her mind and she was taken back to when she had sat by her bedside, holding her hand, as the leeches covered her arms. She remembered how she felt that day. Scared. Alone. She had prayed for a miracle, but none had come.

Susanna spoke up, drawing her attention back to the present. "I know how hard it must be for you to be back in this room, under these circumstances," she said.

"This situation is not ideal," Esther admitted.

"I know, but I am scared. I could use a friend," Susanna

said, her words betraying her emotion. "I know that we have drifted apart but can we just put that aside for now? Please."

Esther offered her a comforting smile. "I think that is a good idea."

Susanna glanced down at the leeches and made a face. "They are hideous little things, are they not?"

"They are," Esther agreed.

"I feel weak. So weak."

The doctor cleared his throat. "That is most likely caused by the leeches but you should be good as new soon enough."

Esther saw a book was on the nightstand and went to pick it up. It might be just the distraction that they both needed. "Would you like for me to read to you?"

"I would," Susanna replied.

She picked up the green cloth-bound book and read the title- *Pride and Prejudice*. This book was all the rage among the *ton*, but she had yet to secure a copy of the book. Her father had expressed his disapproval over her reading it and she didn't dare disobey him.

"Did you know that this book was written by 'A Lady'?" Esther asked in a low voice.

Susanna nodded. "That is why I bought it."

The doctor huffed. "A woman author. What rubbish."

"And why is it rubbish, Doctor?" Susanna asked in a tight voice.

He pushed the spectacles up further on his nose. "I meant no disrespect, but women should not dabble in men's professions."

"Is that what you think 'A Lady' is doing, dabbling in a man's profession?" Susanna asked.

"I can't presume to know what she is doing since she didn't use her real name," the doctor replied.

Esther met the doctor's gaze. "I think she is brave."

"As do I," Susanna said.

The doctor brushed aside their remarks and picked up a

glass jar. "It is time that I remove the leeches," he said. "I should warn you that it can be rather uncomfortable."

"More so than when they suck your blood?" Susanna asked.

"Much worse, I'm afraid," the doctor said as he went to remove the first leech.

Susanna let out a gasp of pain as he pulled it off her skin.

Esther sat forward in her chair and reached for her step-mother's hand. "It will be all right," she encouraged.

"How? The doctor just pulled off one leech and there are seven more to go," Susanna stated. "I have never tolerated pain well."

She knew she needed to distract Susanna so she said the first thing that came to her mind. "Do you remember when you broke your arm when we were looking for truffles?"

"How could I forget that?" she asked. "My parents were furious that we went into the woodlands, unescorted."

"But we brought back a basket full of truffles."

"True, but my parents wouldn't let me play outside for weeks until my arm healed," Susanna pointed out.

"Yes, but we feasted on truffles."

Susanna laughed, just as Esther had intended. "You and your truffles."

"They are delicious, and my mother loved them, too."

"Your mother was a good woman," Susanna said, the humor leaving her face. "I can never compete with her."

Esther cocked her head. "Why would you wish to compete with her?"

"I hear how your father speaks of her. It is almost in a tone of reverence," Susanna replied. "The only thing I can offer him is bearing him a son."

The doctor cleared his throat. "I am done." He rose with the jar of leeches in his hand. "I shall return tomorrow to see how you are faring."

"Thank you, Doctor," Susanna said. "Alice will show you out."

The maid walked over to the door and held it open.

After the doctor departed from the bedchamber, Susanna looked down at the red spots on her arms from where the leeches had been. "I hate bloodletting," she muttered as she dropped her head back onto her pillows.

Esther knew that her stepmother was hurting, and not just from the bloodletting. "You are wrong," she said. "You have more to offer my father than just bearing him a son."

"What else can I offer him? He is still in love with your mother and I am just an afterthought."

"You are giving him companionship."

Susanna sighed. "Companionship? Yes, I suppose I am. I was naive to think that he might start to care for me as he did his first wife."

"My father does care for you," Esther said. She knew that much was true.

"I appreciate what you are trying to do, but I made my choice and I must accept the things that I cannot change." Tears came to Susanna's eyes and she blinked them back. "I am tired. I think I will rest now."

"Susanna…" she started.

Her stepmother spoke over her. "I will be all right," she said. "I just need to close my eyes for a moment."

Esther rose. "I shall come back and check on you later."

With her eyes closed, Susanna murmured, "Thank you, Esther… for everything."

Knowing nothing would be resolved at this moment, Esther departed the bedchamber with a heavy heart. She had never once thought how deeply Susanna was affected by the love that her mother and father had shared. But what could she do? She couldn't very well force her father to love Susanna.

Alice approached her in the hall and announced, "Miss

Bolingbroke has come to call, my lady."

"Thank you," she replied.

She always welcomed a visit from Anette. She never quite knew what her friend would say or do, and it never failed to bring a smile to her face.

As she stepped into the drawing room, she saw Anette was sitting on a settee with her hands clasped in her lap.

"Anette, what a pleasant surprise," Esther greeted.

Anette smiled up at her. "I haven't spoken to you in days and I was worried you might have been mauled by a bear."

"Good gracious, there are no bears in London, or England, for that matter," Esther said.

"One might have escaped from the traveling circus."

"I have not visited the circus."

"That is a shame," Anette said. "We must remedy that at once."

Esther gave her friend a knowing look. "Traveling circuses are showcased at fairs and I doubt your mother would let you anywhere near one."

Anette looked put out. "You are right, of course, but it would be great research for my book."

"Have you started writing your book yet?"

"Not yet, but the ideas keep coming to me," Anette replied. "I just need to sit down and start writing it."

"Have you read the book by 'A Lady'?"

Anette nodded. "Yes, it is brilliant."

"My father expressed his disapproval for the book, but I was just in my stepmother's bedchamber and she had managed to purchase one."

Reaching for a biscuit on the tray, Anette asked, "How is your evil stepmother?"

"She isn't evil," Esther rushed to reply. "And I am starting to think I misjudged her."

Anette arched an eyebrow. "Are you feeling all right?"

"I am, and I know it sounds utterly ridiculous, but I don't

think she is as calculating as I have led myself to believe."

"Have you recently hit your head?" Anette asked, leaning closer to her. "Blink if you are in distress."

Esther laughed. "I assure you that I am in my right mind."

Anette didn't look convinced. "Why the sudden transformation when it comes to your stepmother?"

"She feels her entire worth is tied up in providing my father with a son," Esther shared. "If she fails, then what does she have to offer him?"

"That is unfortunate, but that doesn't excuse her behavior towards you."

"No, but I am starting to understand it a little more. She is pining after my father, but he is still in love with my mother."

Anette wiped the crumbs off her hands. "She did try to force you into an arranged marriage, or did you forget that?"

"I believe she thought she was doing what was best for me, albeit misguided."

"All right, you win," Anette said, placing her hands up. "I will stop referring to Susanna as the 'evil stepmother'."

"Thank you."

Anette leaned closer and lowered her voice. "I want to know how your pretend attachment with Mr. Moore is going."

"It is going well," she replied vaguely.

"I have read in the newssheets that he has called upon you multiple times," Anette shared. "Are you two growing close?"

"As friends, yes."

Anette studied her for a long moment and Esther was afraid of what she was seeing. Her friend had always been too inquisitive for her own good. "You like him, don't you?"

Esther dropped her mouth, feigning disbelief. "Of course not, this attachment is just for show."

"Mr. Moore is very handsome."

"Is he?" Esther asked. "I haven't noticed."

Anette smirked. "I doubt that very much."

Esther reached for the teapot and held it up. "Would you

care for some tea?" she asked, hoping to distract her friend from her interrogation.

But she was not so lucky.

"There is no shame if you did start developing feelings for Mr. Moore," Anette said. "You could easily turn this pretend attachment into a real one."

Esther shook her head. "I'm afraid it is not that simple. Mr. Moore is in love with another. I am merely a distraction for him."

"He told this to you?"

"He did," she admitted.

Anette moved to sit back in her seat. "That is rather disappointing."

Placing the teapot back down onto the tray, Esther said, "I disagree. Furthermore, it has given me a chance to get to know Mr. Moore better. He is a delightful man."

"A delightful man?" Anette replied. "Men and women cannot just be friends. One is almost always pining after the other."

"That is not true."

Anette pressed her lips together before saying, "I just don't want to see you hurt by this arrangement."

"I'm fine. Just fine." But even as she said her words, she knew she was in trouble. For she had started developing feelings for Mr. Moore- feelings that would never be reciprocated.

"If you are sure…"

"I am," Esther said firmly.

Anette bobbed her head. "Then I could use a cup of tea while I regale you with my mother's latest antics to encourage my brother to get married."

Esther breathed a sigh of relief as she poured a cup of tea for her friend. She suspected Anette wanted to press her on Mr. Moore, but thankfully, she dropped it. How could she adequately express what she was feeling when she didn't even know herself?

Chapter Ten

Samuel walked down the pavement as he headed towards White's. He needed a moment alone to sort through his thoughts and a drink would help, as well.

His mind kept replaying the conversation that he had with Phoebe. Had he done the right thing by being so rude and unaccommodating? Her words sounded sincere enough, but he couldn't bring himself to accept her apology. She had hurt him, destroyed him, really. How could they move on and part as friends?

Friends. Is that what he wanted to be with Phoebe? He could hardly stand to be around her. But he couldn't go on hating her. No, he didn't hate her. His emotions were so conflicted that he didn't know what to feel.

Why couldn't everything be as easy as his friendship with Esther? She was a rare jewel, indeed. A single word from her could bring a grin to his face, and her voice had a way of touching his heart. She might not recognize her own brilliance, but he did.

A liveried footman opened the door to White's and stood to the side to allow him entry. He stepped inside and heard his name being called out.

He turned his attention towards the rear of the room and saw Mr. Whitmore and Lord Brentwood sitting at a table.

Botheration. He had wanted to be alone, but he couldn't dismiss his friends so easily.

Samuel skirted the tables and approached his friends. As he sat down, a server approached him and took his drink order.

Mr. Whitmore smiled broadly. "I have the most brilliant news."

"Do you now?" Samuel asked.

"I have found my match."

Samuel's brow shot up. "You have?" he asked. "Pray tell, who is the unlucky lady?"

Brentwood chuckled. "I said something similar."

Mr. Whitmore continued, ignoring their remarks. "Her name is Miss Keene and she is the eldest daughter of Lord Southampton."

"I am not familiar with Miss Keene," Samuel said.

"This is her first Season and she is an heiress," Mr. Whitmore revealed.

"Besides being an heiress, what are her other qualities that you admire?" Samuel asked.

With a shrug, Mr. Whitmore responded, "What else matters? She is rich."

Samuel exchanged a concerned glance with Brentwood before saying, "Surely there is some other deciding factor on why you selected her."

"No, she is rich. That is all I need to know," Mr. Whitmore said. "Although, if you must know, she is handsome and has small hands."

"Small hands?" Brentwood inquired. "Do I even want to know?"

Mr. Whitmore bobbed his head. "Yes, you know what they say about a woman with big hands."

"No, I don't, but I am afraid to ask," Brentwood

responded.

"The bigger the hands, the bigger the brain," Mr. Whitmore stated. "And I refuse to marry a bluestocking."

"There are worse things," Samuel pointed out.

"I disagree. A bluestocking thinks entirely too much and then she starts questioning everything. That is not a good combination in a woman," Mr. Whitmore said. "A woman should be docile."

Brentwood gave his friend a look of disbelief. "You want a woman that doesn't have an opinion?"

"Precisely," Mr. Whitmore declared.

"You are a fool," Brentwood muttered as he brought his glass up to his lips.

Mr. Whitmore straightened in his chair, feigning outrage. "You offend me, my lord," he said. "Besides, you initially pursued your wife because she was an heiress."

"You are right, but I thankfully came to my senses and fell in love with her," Brentwood replied. "Rosamond saved me in more ways than one."

"I do not need saving. I just want her dowry," Mr. Whitmore remarked.

Samuel leaned to the side as a server placed a drink in front of him. "How romantic," he said, picking the glass up.

"You are just jealous that I have found my Juliet," Mr. Whitmore said.

"Didn't Romeo and Juliet die in the end?" Brentwood asked. "That is not the couple that I would want to emulate."

Mr. Whitmore picked up his empty glass and frowned. "I need another before I have the courage to go call on Miss Keene."

"Are you sure you are not rushing into this?" Samuel questioned.

"I just do not want another gentleman to swoop in and offer for her," Mr. Whitmore replied.

Samuel knew he was going to regret this but he decided to

ask it in spite of his reservations. "Lady Esther and I are going on a carriage ride through Hyde Park tomorrow during the fashionable hour. Why don't you and Miss Keene join us?"

"That sounds like a fine idea," Mr. Whitmore agreed. "It will give me an opportunity to see how well-behaved Miss Keene is around others."

"What makes you think that Miss Keene would be interested in you?" Brentwood asked.

Mr. Whitmore paused, as if he hadn't considered that as a possibility. "Why wouldn't she be interested in me?"

"You are shallow, pig-headed, utterly ridiculous… shall I go on?" Brentwood inquired.

"Only a true friend would be that honest with me," Mr. Whitmore said, appearing unaffected by Brentwood's remarks.

Brentwood huffed. "You are hopeless."

"Hopelessly in love," Mr. Whitmore rushed out.

"You love Miss Keene?" Samuel asked.

"I think so," Mr. Whitmore said. "The thought of marrying Miss Keene doesn't terrify me, and she comes from a respectable family."

"I thought you were opposed to love?" Samuel pressed.

"My thoughts changed on the matter when I realized how rich Miss Keene was," Mr. Whitmore said.

Samuel resisted the urge to groan. His friend had no idea what it was like being in love. You didn't "think" you were in love. You knew. It was all you could think of and nothing would put you out of your misery.

Brentwood grew solemn. "Love makes you a better person and brings out the best in you. It is all-encompassing. There is no greater joy than being with someone that loves you in return."

"I am already the best version of myself," Mr. Whitmore said as he tugged down on the lapels of his jacket. "You can't fix perfection."

"It is frightening that you believe such a thing, and I am

done talking in circles with you." Brentwood turned his attention towards Samuel. "How is Lady Esther?"

"She is well," Samuel admitted. "Lady Esther is a most agreeable young woman. I have enjoyed my time with her immensely."

"Hopefully you are not enjoying her company too much," Brentwood remarked with a stern look. "My wife considers Esther a dear friend and I will not tolerate it if you dishonor her."

"Nothing untoward has happened," Samuel assured his friend. "We have become friends."

Brentwood smirked. "Friendship can be the foundation for love."

"Love?" Samuel repeated. "No, Esther and I are just friends. Nothing more."

"Forget I said anything," Brentwood said.

Mr. Whitmore accepted a drink from the server before saying, "Besides, Samuel is still in love with Phoebe. I doubt he would even notice another woman."

Samuel decided to be honest with his friends, and hoped he didn't regret it. "Phoebe came to my office today."

Now he had the attention of both his friends, and by the shocked looks on their faces, they didn't believe her brazenness either.

Brentwood recovered first and asked, "What did she want?"

"To apologize so we could part as friends," Samuel revealed.

Scoffing, Brentwood said, "I hope you kicked her out of your office and sent her on her way."

"I did," he hesitated, "but only after we spoke for a moment."

"You cannot trust a word that comes out of that woman's mouth," Brentwood stated, his voice rising. "She will say anything to get her way."

Mr. Whitmore interjected, "What did you say to her?"

"I told her that I didn't hate her," Samuel replied. "I did ask her why she intended to marry Lord Leyburn."

"We already know why. She is a money-grabbing lady that will do anything to secure her place in Society," Brentwood grumbled.

"I accused her of that, but I said it in a nicer way," Samuel said.

"You are nicer than I am," Brentwood declared.

Mr. Whitmore leaned back in his chair and gave Brentwood a curious glance. "You seem to hate Phoebe a great deal."

"To hate her implies I feel something for her at all, which I don't," Brentwood said. "But I know the type of person Lady Bedlington truly is. She may wear a mask, but it has slipped on occasion."

Samuel pushed his empty glass to the center of the table. "Regardless, I have no intention of being friends with Phoebe."

"Good," Brentwood said. "You should focus on your friendship with Esther. She is worth pursuing."

"I am, but not in the way you are implying."

Brentwood looked the epitome of innocence. "I know not what you mean," he said, rising. "I do believe it is time I depart. I miss my wife."

"That is not natural," Mr. Whitmore remarked. "Women just sit around their homes and wait for us to return home so they can spoil us."

"I pity your future wife," Brentwood said with a shake of his head.

Samuel rose. "I will walk you out since I have work that I need to see to."

"Not et tu?" Mr. Whitmore asked. "Who shall I drink with?"

"You could always go home," Samuel suggested.

An Amiable Alliance

"Then I would have to speak to my parents." Mr. Whitmore shuddered. "I think it is better if I stay here."

Samuel tipped his hat. "Good day, then. I shall see you and Miss Keene tomorrow," he said before he followed Brentwood out of White's.

Once they were on the pavement, Brentwood asked, "Do you think Whitmore will marry Miss Keene?"

"I don't rightly know. He seems intent on marrying this Season," Samuel replied.

"I hope he realizes that getting married is a decision that he shouldn't take lightly, and I wish that he would burn that list of his."

Samuel grinned. "It is quite the list, even Esther thinks so."

"Lady Esther knows about the list?" Brentwood asked.

"Yes, Whitmore and I called upon her. She didn't want to believe that Whitmore was past hope when it came to love."

"What does she believe now?"

Samuel took a moment to consider his question before saying, "She probably still believes it because she seems to think the best of people."

"That is a fine quality to have."

"It is," Samuel agreed.

Brentwood came to a stop in front of his black coach and a footman rushed to open his door. "Would you care for a ride?"

"No, a walk will do me good."

"Very well," Brentwood said as he stepped into his coach.

As the coach merged into traffic, Samuel started walking down the pavement. It wasn't very gentlemanly of him to be walking but he found he enjoyed these private moments. It gave him peace, even if it was just for a short time.

Esther stepped into the dining room and saw her father sitting at the head of the table, reading the newssheets.

He rose when he saw her. "Good morning, Esther," he greeted.

She waved him back down and responded in kind. A footman pulled out her chair and she sat down to the right of her father.

"Is there anything of note in the newssheets?" she asked as she unfolded her napkin and placed it on her lap.

"Not particularly, but even if there was something, I would not tell you," her father said, placing the newssheets onto the table. "It is unsavory for a young woman to be well-versed in politics."

A footman placed a cup of chocolate in front of her and she reached for it. "Mother used to read from the newssheets to me."

Her father frowned. "That was wrong of her to do."

After she took a sip, she returned the cup to the saucer and asked, "How is Susanna feeling?"

"She is much better, but I encouraged her to spend the day in bed," her father replied. "We can't take any chances, considering how far along she is with the baby."

Esther knew that she shouldn't pry into her father and stepmother's relationship, but she had a few questions that kept pestering her. Taking a deep breath, she asked, "Did you marry Susanna because you cared for her or because she could give you a son?"

Her father furrowed his brow. "Why are you asking such things?"

She didn't want to break her confidence with Susanna, but her father needed to know that his wife was hurting. "It just seems that you care more about the baby than Susanna herself."

"What an absurd thing to say!" he exclaimed. "I care for Susanna."

"But you don't love her?" She knew she was being brazen but she needed to know the extent of her father's feelings.

Her father leaned back in his chair and stared at her. "Where is this coming from, young lady?"

There it was- young lady. He was starting to get mad at her, but she didn't care. She needed answers and only he could provide them.

"I know you loved Mother, but it is all right if you did fall in love with Susanna," Esther said.

"I didn't realize I needed your permission," her father remarked dryly.

"You don't, but I am just trying to help."

Her father huffed. "How, exactly? By prying into someone else's business?"

"Father…" she started.

He put his hand up, stilling her words. "My relationship with Susanna is not something that you get to have an opinion on."

"I did not mean to upset you, but Susanna is hurting," Esther revealed. "She wants to give you a son, desperately, but at what cost to her?"

"If this child is a girl, then we shall try again."

"And what if she only bears you females?"

Her father visibly stiffened in his seat and she knew that she had struck a chord with him. "Susanna knew what I expected from her when we wed."

"That is unfair of you since Susanna can't force herself to bear you a son," Esther said. "You are putting undue pressure on her."

Reaching for his white linen napkin on his lap, he tossed it onto his plate and shoved back his chair. "I will not stay here and have you preach to me."

"That was not my intention."

"You are trying to stir up problems in my relationship with Susanna. I didn't think you would stoop so low."

Esther held her father's gaze, having no desire to back down. "If you don't believe me, ask your wife how she is feeling."

"It is not a good time since she is so emotional about the bloodletting."

"You should have stayed with her yesterday when the doctor was tending to her."

"I had to record my vote at the House of Lords," he defended. "Besides, you were with her. What could I have done?"

With a sigh, she said, "Susanna was miserable during the bloodletting process."

"That is no surprise since she has despised leeches since she almost died when she was younger," he revealed.

"I hadn't realized that."

"When she was a child, she got pneumonia and it damaged her lungs. The doctor thought bloodletting would help heal her lungs but it just caused her to grow weaker. She nearly died before her father insisted they stop with the leeches," her father shared.

"No wonder she reacted so poorly to the bloodletting."

Rising, her father said, "My presence would not have made a difference, but my vote did."

Esther didn't think her father could be so insensitive, but she couldn't believe what he had just said. "You are wrong."

"Pardon?"

Knowing that she was risking her father's ire, she replied, "It would have made a difference if you had stayed with Susanna."

"But my vote was of utmost importance."

"As is your wife."

Her father scoffed. "My relationship with Susanna is none of your business. I would ask you to stay out of it." His tone brooked no argument.

Esther decided it would be best to bite her tongue and not

say what she was really thinking. Her father was so focused on himself that he failed to see that his wife was suffering in silence. When would he open his eyes and see the extent of the situation that he had created?

After her father departed from the dining room, she picked up her fork and knife and started eating from the plate of food that had been placed in front of her.

Gibson stepped into the room. "Mr. Daniel Fairchild has come to call, my lady. Shall I have him wait for you in the drawing room?"

"Yes, please," Esther replied. "Inform him that I will be there in just a moment."

"Very good," Gibson said before he went to do her bidding.

Esther wiped the sides of her mouth with the linen napkin and placed it onto her plate. She rose and headed towards the drawing room.

As she stepped into the room, she saw her cousin was pacing back and forth in front of the window. He stopped when he saw her and he asked, "Is Lady Mather all right?" The concern was etched onto his features, leaving little doubt to the distress he was feeling.

"She is well," Esther replied. "She is just resting now."

"And the baby?"

"The doctor said there should be no adverse effects to the baby."

Daniel heaved a sigh of relief. "I am relieved to hear that. I have been so worried since I left you both at Gunter's."

Esther found herself touched by the level that he cared for her stepmother. She didn't think he was capable of such emotion. "Had I known you were so upset I would have sent word to you about her condition."

"You had more important things to worry about."

Gesturing towards the settees, she asked, "Would you care to sit and have a cup of tea?"

"I would like that very much."

Esther sat down on the settee and Daniel sat across from her. She reached for the teapot and poured him a cup of tea. She extended it to him and asked, "Would you care for some cream?"

"No, thank you," he replied as he accepted the cup.

She poured a cup for herself and placed the teapot back onto the tray. Then she picked up her cup and took a sip of tea.

Daniel lowered his cup and saucer to his lap. "I am glad for this opportunity to speak to you, especially since it has been some time since we have spent time together."

"I have been rather busy," she attempted.

"We both have," he graciously replied.

Esther gave him a weak smile. "How is your mother?"

"She is in robust health and is constantly reminding me that she is in need of grandchildren before she leaves this earth."

"Are you courting someone?"

Daniel shifted in his seat before replying, "I have someone in mind."

"Wonderful," Esther said. "I bet that has made your mother very happy."

"It would if the young woman agrees to my courtship."

Leaning forward, Esther placed her cup onto the tray. "Well, I wish you luck with your endeavors."

"Thank you." Daniel took a sip of his tea. "How is your Mr. Moore?"

Esther pressed her lips together. "He is not 'my' Mr. Moore."

"At least, not yet, but I have heard that things are progressing nicely between you two."

"We are taking our time and seeing where it goes."

Daniel looked amused by her response. "It has been

reported that he has called upon you every day. Is that your definition of taking your time?"

"We are enjoying one another's company." There. That was the truth. She enjoyed every moment she spent with Samuel, but she didn't know if he felt the same.

"There is talk that you will be getting engaged soon."

"That is just gossip and I would not give it much heed."

Daniel ran his finger over the rim of his teacup. "Does that mean you are open to other suitors?"

Was she? It wouldn't hurt if someone else started to show her favor. If anything, it would be easier to break things off with Samuel. But she wouldn't want just anyone to be a suitor.

"I suppose it depends on the suitor," she replied honestly.

A smile came to Daniel's lips. "I am pleased to hear that because I was hoping that you would consider me as a suitor."

"But you are my cousin."

"Second cousin," Daniel rushed to correct. "And it is perfectly acceptable for us to wed."

Esther had no intention of taking Daniel on as a suitor but she didn't want to be rude. It would be best if she proceeded cautiously. "I am flattered, but I do not think it is a good idea."

Daniel moved to sit on the edge of his seat. "Whyever not?" he asked. "When I assume your father's title, I will be in a position to provide for you as you are accustomed to."

"That is assuming that Susanna does not bear any boys."

With a frown, Daniel asked, "Yes, well, we can't predict the future, can we?" His words growing hard.

"Regardless, that does not change my mind," Esther said. "I do not think we would suit."

Daniel placed his cup down onto the table and pressed his suit. "Even with just your dowry, we would be comfortable."

So that is what this was about. Her dowry. She doubted that he even cared for her. "I'm sorry, Daniel, but my mind is made up."

She expected him to get angry, to raise his voice, but instead, he just smiled. The most vexing of smiles. "We shall see, Cousin. I am not one to give up so easily."

"I wish you would."

Rising, he tugged on his blue waistcoat. "I will call upon you tomorrow, and the day after that, and so on, until you realize that we belong with one another."

"Daniel..."

He stepped closer to her and leaned in to kiss her cheek. "Save your breath, my dear," he whispered. "My mind has been made up."

Esther grew rigid as he remained close. She didn't dare wish to do anything that would encourage him, especially since the kiss had stirred up no emotions. Not that she expected it would. She had never considered Daniel as anything but family.

Daniel must have taken her silence as acceptance because his smile only grew. "Until tomorrow, my lady," he said before he departed the room.

She let out a breath that she hadn't realized she had been holding. What nerve of her cousin! How dare he try to force his intentions on her. She would never accept his offer of courtship, even if he were the last man on Earth.

A maid stepped into the room and announced, "Lady Mather is hoping you will come read to her, my lady."

"Inform her I shall be right up," Esther said.

The maid tipped her head before departing.

Esther knew if she told her stepmother about Daniel's intentions, she would be furious. And that was the last thing that Susanna needed while she lay in bed. It would be best if she waited to tell her. With any luck, Daniel would give up on this silly notion that they would suit.

Chapter Eleven

The barouche came to a stop in front of Lady Esther's townhouse and Samuel exited the vehicle, not bothering to wait for the footman to come around. He found he was rather eager to see Lady Esther. For some reason, when he was with her, he felt as if he had found a kindred soul.

He approached the main door and it was opened by the butler. "Good afternoon, sir," he greeted as he stood to the side to grant him entry. "Allow me to show you to the drawing room."

Esther's voice came from the doorway of the drawing room. "There is no need, Gibson, but thank you."

Samuel found himself smiling as he admired Esther. She was dressed in a pale blue gown with an ornate overlay with embroidered flowers. A straw hat was tilted on her head and two curls framed her face. It seemed that with every interaction, she was becoming even more beautiful to him. How was that even possible?

Esther dropped into a curtsy. "Sir."

Remembering his manners, he bowed. "My lady," he responded. "Are you ready for our ride through Hyde Park?"

"I am," Esther said as she closed the distance between them.

He offered his arm. "Our carriage awaits."

"Wonderful," Esther responded.

As he led Esther out of the townhouse, he asked, "Did you receive my note about Mr. Whitmore and Miss Keene joining us?"

"I did, and I am rather curious about this Miss Keene."

"As am I," he admitted. "Mr. Whitmore has never shown favor to just one lady before."

"Your friend is very entertaining."

"That is one word for him," he joked.

Esther laughed, and it felt as if his heart danced on the sound. "I do hope that Mr. Whitmore finds the woman of his dreams."

Samuel assisted Esther into the barouche and sat across from her. "His attention does wane quite frequently."

"I would like to think that when you find your match you would move heaven and earth to be with that person."

"That is a nice sentiment, but not everyone feels as deeply as you."

"Don't you?"

"I do." He paused before adding, "But both people have to be committed to one another for it to work."

Esther smoothed down her dress as the driver urged the horses forward. "I agree. My parents were a fine example of that. They loved each other, fiercely."

"You are lucky, considering my parents loathe one another."

"Loathe is such a strong word."

"It is, but they can hardly be in the same room with one another without fighting."

"How awful," Esther murmured.

Samuel nodded. "I won't disagree with you there, but my

parents' marriage is no different than many others amongst the *ton*."

"This is precisely why I do not wish to marry unless it is a love match. I don't want to grow to despise anyone."

"Quite frankly, I don't think you are capable of despising anyone," he said. "You are much too kindhearted."

"I see that I have fooled you into believing something that I am not," she remarked lightly, no doubt in an attempt to brush the compliment aside.

Samuel gave her a knowing look. "I see things differently than most people. I must assume that people are lying or engaging in half-truths until they have proved otherwise."

"That is a sad way to live."

"I'm afraid it is a curse of my profession," he responded. "But you are different. I have never doubted your intentions or words from the moment I met you. It has been refreshing, to say the least."

"I feel the same way about you. Which is odd since we barely know one another."

"That may be true, but I already consider you a friend. I hope one day that you will feel the same way about me."

Esther met his gaze, her eyes lighting up an already bright day. "That day is now."

Samuel didn't know why he was so pleased that she considered him a friend, but he was. Esther was someone he wanted to be associated with- always. But what would happen once they ended this farce of an arrangement? He had no doubt that Esther would go on to thrive. Would she select a suitor?

That thought did not sit well with him.

Esther's voice drew back his attention. "It is a lovely day we are having, is it not?"

"It is," he replied. "But I would prefer if we did not talk about the weather."

"What would you care to talk about?"

Before Samuel thought his words through, he replied, "Phoebe came to visit me at my office yesterday."

Her brow shot up. "That was brazen of her. What did she want?"

"She wanted to ensure that I didn't hate her."

"What did you say?"

Samuel adjusted the top hat on his head as he replied, "I told her that I didn't hate her."

"Why do you suppose that matters to her?"

With a shrug of his shoulders, he said, "I'm not entirely sure."

Esther fell silent for a long moment before saying, "It might mean that she still has feelings for you."

"That is impossible."

"Why, exactly?" Esther asked. "After all, it is entirely possible that she retained feelings for you even though she married another."

Samuel shook his head. "If she did have feelings for me, it wouldn't matter. I want nothing to do with her."

"But a part of you still loves her."

"A small part," Samuel asserted.

"Is that part still not worth exploring?"

Samuel was astonished. Could Phoebe still have feelings for him, even after everything that had happened between them? Did he want her to have feelings for him? He had tried so hard to push her out of his mind, only to fail, over and over.

He had pretended to have an attachment to Esther to make Phoebe believe that he had moved on from her. Perhaps even make her jealous. So why would he go back to the one woman who broke his heart?

"If there is any doubt in your mind, you might at least try. You don't want to live with any regrets." Esther spoke her words with conviction, but there was a sadness to them that he couldn't quite decipher.

"I already have too many regrets," he admitted.

"Then you best not add another one to your list."

"No, I suppose not."

Esther smiled, but it didn't reach her eyes. "It is settled, then," she said, her words lacking any emotion.

Why had his words caused such a reaction from her?

Before he could press her, the barouche came to a stop in front of Miss Keene's three-level, whitewashed townhouse. Samuel had just moved to exit the vehicle when the door opened and Mr. Whitmore escorted Miss Keene down the stairs.

Miss Keene was of average height with blonde hair and fair skin. She was attractive, but not remarkably so. Frankly, she appeared to be no different than the other debutantes this Season.

Samuel moved next to Esther as Mr. Whitmore assisted Miss Keene into the barouche. Then he claimed the seat next to her.

The barouche merged into traffic and headed towards Hyde Park. It wasn't long before they arrived at Rotten Row, joining the long line of carriages.

After they provided introductions to one another, Esther addressed Miss Keene. "Are you enjoying yourself this Season?"

A bright smile came to Miss Keene's face as she gushed, "I am. Everyone has been so nice to me."

Mr. Whitmore interjected, "You are an easy person to be nice to."

Miss Keene ducked her head in a shy fashion. "Thank you, sir."

Shifting on the bench to face her, Mr. Whitmore asked, "Have you been to Hyde Park before?"

"Lots of times," Miss Keene replied. "But I have since learned to be leery of the squirrels."

"Did you say 'squirrels'?" Samuel asked, fearing he'd

misheard her. He looked to Mr. Whitmore and saw him shaking his head, urging him to stay silent.

Miss Keene huffed loudly. "They are nasty little things and they have stolen my reticule twice now."

"This happened more than once?" Samuel pressed.

"Yes, and I do believe the squirrels are conspiring against me," Miss Keene declared.

Samuel had so many questions for Miss Keene but he wasn't quite sure where to begin. He saw Esther had her gloved hand up to her lips to hide a growing smile. Apparently, she found this situation humorous, as well.

"You need not fear. I will protect you from the squirrels," Mr. Whitmore declared with a swipe of his hand.

Samuel raised his eyebrows in response to his friend's words, observing the usual spark of amusement in Mr. Whitmore's eyes.

"Thank you, but I have found a way to outwit them." Miss Keene held up the blue and gold reticule that was around her right wrist. "I have put rocks in my reticule."

"Isn't it heavy?" Esther asked.

"Oh, yes, but I refuse to let those creatures steal another one of my reticules," Miss Keene said. "You put it down for one minute and they pounce on it."

Esther compressed her lips tightly, as if she were trying to contain a giggle. "That is awful," she remarked.

"Isn't it, though?" Miss Keene asked. "I tried to convince my brother to shoot every last one of them, but he refused to do so."

"That seems a little harsh for them stealing your reticule," Samuel said.

"Twice!" Miss Keene exclaimed. "It takes me days to knit a reticule, and I refuse to let them snatch another one."

Samuel decided to ask the most obvious question. "Why do you remove your reticule off your wrist if you don't want the squirrels to steal it?"

Miss Keene pouted. "My wrist gets tired of carrying so much."

"May I be so bold as to ask what you carry in your reticule?" Esther asked.

"Just the necessities, I suppose," Miss Keene replied. "A fan, scent bottle, handkerchief, and lots of sweets."

"Sweets?" Esther repeated. "Do you not think that encourages the squirrels to take your reticule?"

"Squirrels don't eat sweets," Miss Keene said.

Samuel exchanged an amused look with Esther before asking, "What do you think squirrels eat?"

"Squirrel food, such as nuts and berries," Miss Keene promptly replied.

"Yes, but could they not be tempted to eat something sweet?" Samuel questioned.

Miss Keene sat back in her seat with a baffled look on her face. "But the squirrel could get fat," she said, as if this thought was unimaginable.

Mr. Whitmore interrupted, "I must side with Miss Keene on this one. Why would a squirrel wish to get fat?"

Samuel knew it would be impolite to laugh, but he was finding it nearly impossible to do so. He had never met someone who had such a disdain for squirrels and their thieving ways.

***

Esther found the whole conversation about squirrels to be utterly ridiculous. The squirrels were taking Miss Keene's reticule because of the sweets that were tucked within. Fortunately, it appeared that Samuel thought as she did on the subject based upon his questions.

She decided it would be best if she moved the conversation past the devious squirrels. "It is a lovely day, is it not?"

She knew it was a lame attempt at making conversation, but it was the only thing that she could think of at the moment.

Miss Keene glanced up at the sky. "It is quite nice," she said. "I see a cloud that has a resemblance to an elephant."

"Not a squirrel," Samuel muttered under his breath.

Esther nudged his arm with her elbow to indicate he should keep his comments to himself.

In response, Samuel winked at her, causing a blush to form on her cheeks. How did such an innocent gesture on his part cause such a reaction in her? She just needed to remind herself that he was in love with another. Not her. She was foolish to develop feelings for him, no matter how small they were.

What had she been thinking when she had advised him to pursue his feelings for Lady Bedlington? But it had been the right thing to do. She suspected that Lady Bedlington still harbored feelings for Samuel, and it wouldn't be fair of her to not point that out.

Miss Keene kept staring at the sky as she held the side of her straw hat. Esther couldn't understand what was so fascinating about looking at the clouds. The sky was blue, the clouds were white... what else did one have to decipher?

Samuel spoke up. "Do you see any clouds that interest you?"

"I do not."

He pointed at a cloud and said, "That one looks like a boat."

Esther strained her eyes but all she saw was a big, white blob of nothingness. "I do not see it, but I am not one to analyze clouds."

"You have never laid in a field and stared up at the clouds?" Samuel asked.

"I can think of nothing more boring," she admitted.

Samuel grinned. "I think I finally found a flaw in you."

"It is not a flaw to have better things to do than to make up things that you see in the clouds," Esther defended.

"Just try it," Samuel encouraged.

Not wishing to disappoint him, Esther put her hand above her eyes to shield them from the sun and looked up at the sky.

He leaned closer to her and pointed at a cloud. "That one looks like a heart, does it not?"

Samuel was so close to her that she could smell the scent of his shaving soap on his skin. She was trying not to become distracted by his nearness but it was proving to be impossible.

"It almost looks like it has a crack in it," Samuel said. "Look in the middle."

Esther squinted and she could almost pretend that it looked like a heart. "I'm sorry. I just don't see it."

She turned her head towards Samuel and she was mortified to discover that their faces were only a few inches apart.

"My apologies," she murmured as she moved to create more distance between them.

Samuel appeared to be unaffected, and he continued to point out more clouds. However, her mind was on anything but.

A rider in the distance looked familiar as he approached their carriage. As he rode closer, she could see that it was her cousin- Daniel.

He tipped his head at her. "Cousin," he greeted. "What a fine day it is to have a carriage ride, is it not?"

"It is," Esther replied, knowing she had no choice but to play along.

Daniel turned his attention towards Miss Keene. "And who is this lovely creature?" he asked, his eyes perusing the length of her.

Esther knew the polite thing to do would be to introduce them to one another. "Miss Keene, allow me the privilege of introducing you to my cousin, Mr. Daniel Fairchild."

Miss Keene removed the fan from her reticule and opened it. "It is a pleasure to meet you, Mr. Fairchild."

"Likewise," Daniel said. "Are you enjoying yourself?"

"I am."

Daniel barely gave Mr. Whitmore or Mr. Moore any heed as he muttered, "Gentlemen." He returned his attention to Miss Keene. "Will you be attending Lady Danbury's ball this evening?"

"I have every intention of going," Miss Keene replied.

"You must save me the supper dance then," Daniel said.

Miss Keene brought the fan up to her face. "I would be delighted, sir," she said.

Mr. Whitmore cleared his throat, loudly. "Do not let us keep you, Fairchild." His words were unusually stern.

"It is no bother at all," Daniel said, his eyes not straying from Miss Keene.

Esther was confused. Had her cousin not declared his intentions for her only a few hours ago? Yet, here he was, blatantly flirting with Miss Keene. Not that she minded. It would be a good thing for him to become distracted by Miss Keene.

"Have I told you how breathtaking you look today?" Mr. Whitmore asked as he shifted to face Miss Keene.

"No, you have not," Miss Keene replied.

Daniel shifted the reins in his hands as he said, "That is a shame. A woman like you should be told often how beautiful you are."

Miss Keene smiled. "What a kind thing to say."

"If you will excuse me, I shall spend every moment anticipating our dance," Daniel said, reaching up to touch the brim of his hat. "Good day, Miss Keene."

"Good day," she replied.

Daniel hurried his goodbyes before he urged his horse forward.

Miss Keene's eyes remained on Daniel's retreating figure. "What a nice man."

"I should warn you that Mr. Fairchild is a known gambler and rake," Mr. Whitmore revealed.

"That is a shame," Miss Keene murmured with a crestfallen face.

"Rumor has it that he has spent his fortune gambling on horses at the track," Mr. Whitmore shared.

Miss Keene snapped her fan closed. "My father has specifically forbidden me from spending time with fortune hunters and rakes."

"That is some sound advice," Mr. Whitmore said. "You deserve far better than someone that just wants you for your dowry."

"I am rather rich, though," Miss Keene stated.

Esther's lips twitched at Miss Keene's declaration. What a thing to say out loud. Did she not stop and think about what she was about to say?

"I'm sorry Mr. Fairchild put you in such a difficult position by asking for your supper dance this evening. That was poorly done on his part, and he shouldn't have done so while you were on an outing with me," Mr. Whitmore said.

"No harm done." Miss Keene returned her fan to her reticule and removed a sweet. She plopped it into her mouth and chewed it before turning her attention towards Esther. "How many Seasons have you attended?"

"I am in my fourth Season," Esther replied.

"Are you not worried about becoming a spinster?" Miss Keene asked, aghast.

"There are much worse things."

Miss Keene didn't look convinced. "Such as?"

"Death. Dismemberment." Esther paused. "Do I need to go on?"

With a lift of her shoulder, Miss Keene replied, "A woman's greatest joy is to be a wife and a mother."

LAURA BEERS

"I agree, but not everyone falls in love."

Miss Keene pressed her lips together, clearly unimpressed by her remark. "My father told me that mutual toleration is the most that I should hope for when selecting a suitor."

Samuel interrupted, "I think Lady Esther should be praised for wanting a love match."

Esther offered him a brief smile as a sign of appreciation for what he had said.

Miss Keene's eyes darted to the trees that lined the woodlands. "Did you hear something?" she half-asked, half-demanded.

"I heard nothing," Esther responded.

"I thought I heard squeaking," Miss Keene said as she placed the reticule in her lap. "Those terrible creatures are plotting against me."

Samuel's lips quirked to one side. "I do not think the squirrels have nefarious intentions."

Miss Keene's eyes remained on the woodlands. "I know I must sound silly—"

Mr. Whitmore spoke over her. "Not to me," he said. "I have long disliked squirrels. They may look sweet and innocent, but their behavior suggests otherwise."

Esther wasn't sure if Mr. Whitmore was just trying to appease Miss Keene or if he really did believe what he was saying. But one thing was certain, Mr. Whitmore was trying hard to win Miss Keene's affection- perhaps too hard.

Miss Keene offered Mr. Whitmore a pleasing smile. "I am most grateful for your support, sir."

Mr. Whitmore reached for her hand and kissed the air above her knuckles. "I am but your humble servant."

Esther resisted the urge to roll her eyes. Surely Miss Keene would not be so gullible as to fall for such an overused line. However, her enamored face suggested that she believed Mr. Whitmore's words.

Samuel leaned closer and whispered, "First squirrels, then a show."

She giggled and her hand flew up to her mouth. "You are awful."

"They don't even notice us here," Samuel said. "They seem to be in their own world right now."

Esther saw that Mr. Whitmore and Miss Keene had their heads bent towards each other and they were speaking in hushed tones to one another.

Samuel shifted in his seat and asked, "What would you care to discuss?"

"I do believe we decided not to speak about the weather," Esther replied lightly.

"Heavens, no," Samuel said. "And the state of the gardens is out, as well."

Esther gave him a blank look. "What else is there to speak about?" she joked.

Samuel chuckled. "How is your stepmother feeling?"

"She is much better now," she replied. "The sickness came on fast, but it left just as quickly. The doctor was pleased with her progress."

"That is wonderful news."

"It is," Esther agreed. "For so long, I have held animosity for my stepmother, but I am thinking I was wrong to do so. She is trying to mend our relationship."

"Do you think she is being genuine?"

"I do."

Samuel gave her an encouraging look. "Then you should trust your instincts."

"Is that it?" Esther asked. "That is your advice- to trust myself?"

"What is wrong with my advice?"

Esther smirked, feeling a need to tease him. "You are a barrister. I would have thought your advice would have been more profound."

"Sometimes the best advice is obvious, and sometimes it is not. Be humble enough to take advice from other people but take from it what feels right for you."

"That was better. I feel that you truly dug deep for that advice."

Samuel's eyes held amusement as he said, "You are a minx."

Miss Keene's shrill voice reached her ears. "You saw a minx?" she asked, looking towards the woodlands in a panic. "Where?"

Samuel put his hand up. "No, I called Lady Esther a minx, but I was just teasing her."

"Really, sir," Miss Keene huffed. "You should not go around shouting 'minx.' It is not becoming of you."

"I wasn't shouting," Samuel said.

"What if there was a minx?" Miss Keene asked with pursed lips. "Would the carriage be able to outrun it?"

"You are safe in here," Mr. Whitmore replied. "A minx could not jump high enough to enter the barouche."

"That is a relief." Miss Keene strained her neck as she looked at the carriages in front of them. "How much longer do you suppose we will be here?"

"It could be hours," Mr. Whitmore replied.

"Goodness, I hope not," Miss Keene sighed. "I require a nap before I attend the ball this evening."

"The driver is moving as fast as he can," Mr. Whitmore assured her.

Esther had to admit that she didn't mind the long carriage ride. She found Miss Keene to be an interesting person, but she was just young. She would learn. Everyone was forced to grow up at some point, and some faster than others.

Samuel glanced over at her and smiled. It was such a simple gesture, but just like that, everything seemed right in the world.

Chapter Twelve

The late morning sun was streaming in through the lone window as Samuel sat at his desk in his office. He had made a decent dent in the pile of work that he had to accomplish. It felt like a never-ending task but he was grateful for the work that he did have. He felt immense pride to be one of the top barristers in London, but he knew that could change at any moment. His winning record was all that mattered to his clients; it was all that mattered to him.

Mr. Allen pushed back his chair and rose from his desk. "Can you sign this, sir?" he asked as he placed the paper in front of Samuel.

Samuel took a moment to review the document before he signed his name. He blew on the ink as he handed it back to his secretary.

"I shall deliver this to Sir Walter Chenard at once," Mr. Allen said, rolling up the document. "Hopefully, he will agree with your argument for dismissal of the Walker case."

"He will," Samuel responded. "The reasonings are sound and there is no reason why this case should go to trial."

Mr. Allen tipped his head. "I will return shortly."

As he opened the door to depart, Mr. Whitmore stepped

into the room with his arms out wide. "I am wholly and emphatically in love!"

"Did we not already establish this?" Samuel asked as he placed the quill next to the ink pot. His friend was entirely too cheerful for this early hour.

"I can't help myself," Mr. Whitmore said. "I want to sing it from the rooftops."

"Please don't. You have a terrible voice."

Mr. Whitmore grinned. "Yours is not much better." He approached the desk and sat down in an upholstered armchair. "What did you think of Miss Keene? And be honest."

Samuel wasn't quite sure what to make of Miss Keene. He decided to keep his response vague, but truthful. "I found her to be an interesting young woman."

"Yes, she is very interesting," Mr. Whitmore readily agreed. "I can never quite anticipate what will come out of her mouth."

"Is that a good thing?" He preferred predictability so that would be an awful thing for him.

Mr. Whitmore nodded. "It is," he replied. "She always finds a way to make me laugh."

Samuel decided to use some tact as he knew this was going to be a most difficult conversation. "I just want to make sure you are pursuing Miss Keene for the right reasons."

"I am," Mr. Whitmore said. "She is beautiful, agreeable and rich."

"Are you sure you are not blinded by her being rich?"

Mr. Whitmore leaned back in his seat and stretched out his legs in front of him. "At first I was, but it has all changed as I got to know her. I have never met someone quite like her before."

Samuel could not agree with his friend more. Miss Keene was unique, but she had some interesting quirks. "Do you not take an issue with her aversion to squirrels?"

"They did steal her reticule- twice!" his friend exclaimed, clearly siding with Miss Keene. "They are sneaky little devils."

"If you are sure, then…" His voice trailed off.

"I am," Mr. Whitmore responded. "Now I just have to flatter Miss Keene so profusely that she will allow me to court her."

Samuel closed the ledger in front of him. "I would imagine your mother is thrilled with the attention you are giving Miss Keene."

"She is. My parents just want me to settle down with the right girl," Mr. Whitmore said. "Besides, I need to marry an heiress since I am a younger son of a baron."

"A rich baron," Samuel corrected.

"Yes, but my father only intends to leave me a small inheritance, and the rest will be entailed to my older brother."

Samuel took his hand and rubbed the ache that was in the back of his neck. He had been hunched over this desk for far too long. "Shall we go to White's for a drink?"

"That is a brilliant idea," Mr. Whitmore said as he rose.

Rising, Samuel took the time to push in his chair. "I need a break from all this work," he admitted.

"You work too hard."

"I have to, because if I fail, it is on me. I have no one else to blame."

Mr. Whitmore opened the door. "You are your father's heir. There would be no shame in closing up shop and working alongside your father."

"That sounds miserable. My father and I would not work well together since we hardly see eye to eye."

"Being a barrister is for younger sons, not heirs," Mr. Whitmore said.

Samuel started to walk down the corridor. "Yes, but it is my passion."

"Passion does not pay the bills."

"In this case, I make a decent income," Samuel

contended.

Mr. Whitmore gave him a knowing look. "Is it anything compared to the income you make on your estate?"

Samuel knew that his friend had a point, albeit reluctantly. It would be better for him to work with his father and help manage the estate. But he didn't want to give up being a barrister until he had little choice in the matter. He wanted to help as many people as possible. It was the least he could do to atone for what he had done. One small mistake had jeopardized his peace of mind.

He should never have let his friend get onto that horse that fateful night. Charles was drunk and wasn't in his right mind. If he had been, he never would have raced through the streets and caused chaos in his wake.

Mr. Whitmore held open the door as Samuel stepped out of the building. His eyes held compassion as he asked, "Are you thinking about Charles?"

"I am," Samuel replied, seeing no reason to deny it.

"What happened was not your fault," Mr. Whitmore attempted. "You need to stop blaming yourself."

"How, exactly?"

Mr. Whitmore matched his stride as they walked along the pavement. "Charles was drunk and made a poor choice."

"I should have stopped him."

"You, and what army?" Mr. Whitmore asked. "Charles wasn't exactly known as a reasonable drunk."

"I should have made a more valiant effort."

"You did the best you could."

"It wasn't good enough," Samuel asserted. "It is my fault that girl died."

Mr. Whitmore placed his hand on Samuel's sleeve and turned to face him. "No, it was Charles' fault. His horse trampled her. You had nothing to do with his mistake."

"But I witnessed it," Samuel said. "Charles rode off, as if nothing had happened."

With a solemn gaze, Mr. Whitmore responded, "You were the one that stopped and consoled a dying girl. That is admirable. Do not discount what you did."

Samuel brushed off Mr. Whitmore's arm. "I did nothing more than what my conscience dictated." He didn't dare admit to his friend that he still had nightmares about what had happened that night. He would wake up drenched in sweat, knowing his actions helped cause that girl's death.

Mr. Whitmore opened his mouth, no doubt to press his point, but Samuel didn't want to hear about it. He couldn't. He knew what he had done and talking about it would do no good.

Samuel resumed walking down the street and it only took a few moments before his friend matched his stride.

"You are stubborn," Mr. Whitmore said.

"I would prefer if we talked about something else."

An obnoxious smile came to Mr. Whitmore's lips. "We could discuss Miss Keene. I daresay that she is my favorite thing to talk about."

He didn't want to talk about Miss Keene, but then again, he wasn't in the mood to discuss anything of importance.

Mr. Whitmore opened his arms out wide. "Miss Keene is the most beautiful of women," he declared. "She would make a fine bride for me."

"I wish you luck with Miss Keene."

As his words left his mouth, he saw Phoebe walking towards him and she was engaged in conversation with her companion. It appeared she had not seen him based upon the smile that was on her face.

Samuel felt the slightest twinge of guilt over how he had treated her the last time they had spoken. He shouldn't have been so harsh with her, especially since she was trying to mend their fractured relationship. Was Esther right about Phoebe still harboring feelings for him? But more importantly, did he want her to?

Mr. Whitmore lowered his voice and asked, "Do you want to step into a shop and hide?"

"No, I need to learn to be civil around her."

"Are you sure now is the time to do so?" Mr. Whitmore asked.

"I am."

Phoebe turned her head and he saw the moment she recognized him. The smile left her face, and her expression turned to one of wariness. He didn't blame her for her reaction. He hadn't given her any reason to be pleased to see him.

He came to a stop in front of her and bowed. "Lady Bedlington," he greeted politely.

She curtsied. "Mr. Moore. Mr. Whitmore." She gestured towards her companion. "Are you acquainted with Mrs. Stevens?"

Samuel tipped his head. "I have not had the pleasure."

Mrs. Stevens beamed up at him. "Mr. Moore, it is a pleasure to be meeting you. What you did for Lady Eugenie was nothing short of extraordinary."

"Thank you, ma'am," Samuel said. "But I do not deserve all the praise. I did have help in exonerating her."

"It was fascinating to read in the newssheets about how you discovered that her own sister killed her lover and conspired with his wife," Mrs. Stevens continued on.

"Again, I didn't go about it alone," he said. "Lord Rushcliffe played a vital part in the investigation."

"I, for one, did not care for the late Lord Rushcliffe," Mrs. Stevens stated with a wave of her hand. "He was far too fond of the ladies but I did not wish him dead. He just—"

Phoebe spoke over her friend. "Well, good day, Mr. Moore," she abruptly said. "We don't wish to keep you from whatever it is that you are doing."

"We were just heading to White's for a drink," Samuel revealed.

Looping arms with her companion, Phoebe said, "I hope

you enjoy your drink." Her words had barely left her mouth before she started walking down the pavement.

Mr. Whitmore watched Phoebe's retreating figure as he muttered, "That went well."

"It went better than expected," Samuel admitted.

"You have low expectations then," Mr. Whitmore joked. "Phoebe couldn't wait to leave us or should I say you."

Samuel continued down the pavement. "It is not proper to stand on the pavement, especially at this hour."

"If you wanted Phoebe to hate you, then I must say that you have succeeded."

"I do not want her to hate me."

"What do you want?" Mr. Whitmore asked.

Samuel wasn't quite sure how to answer that question. When he had last spoken to Esther, he had decided to explore his feelings for Phoebe. But was that a mistake to do so? He had already been down this road before with Phoebe and she had rejected him. Was it worth taking the risk... again?

Esther sat in the drawing room as she tended to her needlework. She was biding her time until Samuel came to call. He may not look forward to seeing her, but she always looked forward to his visits. These pesky feelings would do her no good. Samuel's heart belonged to another. She was just a distraction.

So why could she not stop thinking about him?

Her stepmother's voice broke through her musings. "What is wrong?"

"Nothing," Esther attempted.

"You were frowning," Susanna said.

"Was I?" she asked, lowering the needlework to her lap. She didn't think it was prudent to reveal her feelings to

Susanna. No doubt, she would feel obligated to offer some advice, and that was the last thing she wanted. No, it was best to suffer in silence.

Susanna gave her a curious look. "Something is upsetting you."

"I can't seem to think of a thing."

"I see that you have no intention of telling me, but if you change your mind, I am willing to listen."

Esther placed her needlework on a table and reached for her cup of tea. "How are you feeling?"

"Much better," Susanna said. "I don't know what came over me, but I am glad that bout of sickness is gone. The doctor believes I just got overheated, which is fairly common in my condition."

"I forgot to tell you, but Daniel came to see how you were faring. I thought that was rather sweet of him."

Susanna did not seem impressed. "Yes, and that doesn't sound at all like him."

"Perhaps he has changed."

"Your father doesn't believe so," Susanna said with a shake of her head. "His opinion of Daniel is rather poor, I'm afraid."

"He might be trying to change. Should we not give him the benefit of the doubt?"

Susanna placed her hand on her stomach. "I suppose you are right."

Esther decided it would be best if she didn't mention that Daniel had asked to pursue her, especially since he had showered attention upon Miss Keene the day before. He might have decided to give up on her due to her lackluster response.

Gibson stepped into the room and announced, "Lady Oxley and her daughter, Miss Bolingbroke, have come to call. Shall I show them in?"

"Yes, please," Susanna replied.

It was only a moment later Lady Oxley and Anette

stepped into the room. Lady Oxley had her blonde hair carefully arranged and looked regal in her dark blue gown. Whereas Anette's brown hair was loosely tied with curls framing her face and she was dressed in a jonquil gown. The two couldn't appear more different.

Susanna gestured towards the settee. "Would you care to have a seat?"

Lady Oxley glided over and sat down. She patted the seat next to her and ordered, "Come have a seat, Dear."

Anette blew at a curl before saying, "As you wish, Mother."

After Anette was situated, Lady Oxley turned her attention towards Susanna. "How are you feeling?"

"Large," Susanna replied. "I just keep getting bigger and bigger."

"You will until it is finally time to deliver the baby," Lady Oxley said. "I may have broken a chair or two when I was pregnant with Caleb. It was a mortifying experience."

"That sounds awful," Susanna acknowledged.

Lady Oxley waved her hand in front of her. "I may have indulged in far too many sweets but when else do we not have to worry about our figures?"

Esther spoke up. "Would either of you care for a cup of tea?"

"I would," Lady Oxley replied. "As would Anette."

She went about pouring the cups of tea and extended them to the ladies.

Anette accepted the cup and offered her a grateful smile. "How is Mr. Moore?" she asked.

Lady Oxley gave a disapproving shake of her head. "Anette," she started, "we do not ask such personal questions. It is not proper to do so."

"It is all right," Esther said, coming to her friend's defense. "I have spoken of Mr. Moore to Anette in the past."

"Very well," Lady Oxley said, taking a sip of her tea.

Esther addressed her friend. "Mr. Moore is doing well. We went on a carriage ride through Hyde Park yesterday."

"Yes, I read about it in the newssheets," Anette said. "Apparently, you were accompanied by Miss Keene."

"That we were," Esther confirmed. "It was a pleasant afternoon."

Anette looked as if she had more on the subject that she wanted to say but she snuck a glance at her mother. "That sounds delightful."

Esther wondered why Anette was acting so reserved around her mother. Usually, she was much more forthcoming with her thoughts.

Lady Oxley took a sip before asking, "Have you prepared the nursery for the baby?"

"I have," Susanna replied. "Would you care to see it?"

"I would love to," Lady Oxley said, placing her teacup down onto the tray.

Susanna awkwardly rose and they started walking towards the door. Once they were out of sight, Anette let out a ladylike groan and dropped back in her seat.

"Thank heavens, she is gone," her friend said.

"Who?" Esther asked.

"My mother," Anette replied. "She has decided that I act too much like a hoyden and wants me to act like a proper lady."

"Do you even know how to act like a proper lady?" Esther teased.

Anette rolled her eyes. "I can pretend, just as well as anyone," she said. "But we have been calling upon people all morning. It is exhausting. I do not think I can stand one more cup of tea."

Esther held up the plate of biscuits. "Would you like a biscuit?"

"Yes, please," Anette said, reaching for one. "My mother is determined to turn me into her."

"Why would she wish to do that?"

Anette waved the hand with the biscuit in the air. "Because she was a diamond of the first water and I am not. I am just Anette. A lady with no prospects."

"I do believe you are selling yourself short."

"At least you are pretending to have an attachment with someone," Anette said. "I have nothing."

Esther put a finger up to her lips. "Keep quiet. Someone might hear you."

Anette gave her a repentant look. "My apologies." She lowered her voice. "How is the very handsome Mr. Moore?"

"He is well," Esther said.

"That is all you wish to tell me?" Anette asked, looking disappointed. "Surely you have more details than that."

Esther didn't dare wish to admit her true feelings. She needed to sort them out, on her own. "He is charming, as well."

Anette nibbled on her biscuit while her eyes remained intently fixed on the subject of her regard. "I know you have fallen for him," she said. "I have known you for years and you are terrible at hiding your emotions."

"Mr. Moore says the same thing."

Anette moved to sit next to her on the settee. "What else does Mr. Moore say?" she asked. "Does he whisper sweet nothings in your ear?"

"It isn't like that," Esther replied.

"Whyever not?" Anette asked. "You like him, he likes you…"

Esther spoke over her. "I do not presume to know his feelings."

"Regardless, there is nothing wrong with turning a pretend relationship into a real one," Anette said.

"Unfortunately, it is not that simple," Esther admitted. "His heart lies with another."

"Who?"

"Lady Bedlington," Esther said.

Anette stared at her for a moment. "Isn't she supposed to be getting engaged to Lord Leyburn?"

Esther nodded. "She is, but I fear she still has feelings for Mr. Moore," she replied. "She even visited him at his office."

"Oh, to have the freedom of being a widow," Anette muttered. "If I dared to call upon a gentleman, I would be ruined."

"Do you wish to call upon a gentleman?"

Anette shrugged her shoulders. "I would at least like the option to."

"Regardless, I encouraged Mr. Moore to explore his feelings for Lady Bedlington."

"Why would you do that?"

"It was the right thing to do."

With a disbelieving huff, Anette said, "Sometimes in love and war, you must not play by the rules."

"I never said I loved Mr. Moore."

"It is merely an expression," Anette said. "Are you sure that Mr. Moore still loves Lady Bedlington?"

"I believe so, yes."

"Then we need you to turn his eye and save him the embarrassment when Lady Bedlington accepts Lord Leyburn's proposal."

Esther bit her lower lip. "I doubt his affection can be weaned so easily."

"Men are nothing if not predictable," Anette said. "I have read many books that have confirmed this to me."

"I don't know…"

"Trust me," Anette said, jumping up from her seat. "Have you tried batting your eyelashes at him?"

"I did, and it ended poorly."

Anette placed a hand on her hip and started sashaying across the room. "You need to walk in such a fashion that he notices your nice, childbearing hips."

"You look ridiculous," Esther said, holding back laughter.

"It is all the rage to walk this way," Anette responded as she continued around the room in an overexaggerated motion. "Come, try it with me."

"I will not."

Anette stopped and turned to face her. "From now on, you will laugh at all his jokes. Men like it when you find them amusing."

"I don't know if that will work."

"Why? Is Mr. Moore not amusing?" Anette asked. "I hope not, because you cannot be with someone that is a bore."

Esther felt a smile forming on her lips. "He is very droll."

"Good," Anette said. "Now we must practice your flirting. Go on, say something flirtatious."

Now Esther just felt ridiculous. She had never been good at flirting and she wasn't going to start now. "What is wrong with just being myself?"

"That is a good start, but you need to grab his attention," Anette said. "For example, you could say to your Mr. Moore- 'You are a pippin'."

"I could say no such thing."

"Why? It just means that you think very highly of him."

"I know what it means, but that would be much too brazen of me to do so," Esther said. "I might as well call him a 'cowfyne'."

Anette snapped her fingers. "That would work."

"I am joking," Esther said. "I could never be so bold as to call him such a term of endearment."

"That is a shame."

Esther reached for her cup of tea. "Mr. Moore has no interest in me and I have no intention of embarrassing myself in front of him."

"I'm just trying to help," Anette said as she returned to her seat.

"I knew what I was getting into when Mr. Moore and I

devised our plan," Esther said. "I just need to ignore these feelings and they will go away."

"I don't think that is how feelings work."

Taking a sip of her tea, Esther said, "It is just how it will have to be."

Anette leaned back in the settee and let out a sigh. "I think that is a mistake."

"If so, it is my mistake and not yours."

Lady Oxley's chiding voice came from the doorway. "Sit up straight, Anette," she ordered. "It is never appropriate to slouch when calling upon someone."

Anette sat up and clasped her hands in her lap. "Yes, Mother," she murmured.

Susanna followed Lady Oxley into the room and said, "I hope you both found something to occupy your time while we were looking at the nursery."

"We did," Esther confirmed.

Lady Oxley turned her attention towards her daughter. "What did you discuss?"

A mischievous look came into Anette's eyes as she replied, "We were just discussing the Napoleonic War and how it is affecting politics in England and abroad."

Now, that was the Anette that she was familiar with, Esther thought.

With a frown, Lady Oxley replied, "I certainly hope not. Those topics are hardly appropriate for young women to discuss."

"You are right, Mother," Anette said. "We were just discussing the art of flirting."

Lady Oxley's frown deepened, clearly not amused by her daughter's antics. "I think it is time that we depart."

"Very well," Anette muttered, rising.

Esther resisted the urge to smile at Anette. Her friend was a constant source of entertainment, even if she was unable to take her advice.

Chapter Thirteen

Samuel stood in front of Phoebe's townhouse and hoped that he was making the right choice. He had no idea how this conversation would go, but he knew it needed to happen. It was the only way he would be able to get closure. Is that what he wanted- closure? Or did he want another opportunity to win her heart? He was conflicted, and that was the problem. He didn't quite know what he wanted. He just wanted this aching in his heart to go away.

He approached the main door and used the knocker to announce his presence. He adjusted his white cravat and waited.

It was a long moment before the old, white-haired butler opened the door. "May I help you, sir?"

Samuel went to retrieve a calling card from his waistcoat pocket. "Will you inform Lady Bedlington that I would like to speak to her?" he asked, extending the card.

The butler accepted the card and looked down at it. "Please come in, sir," he said, opening the door wide. "I will see if Lady Bedlington is taking callers."

Samuel stepped into the entry hall and took a moment to

admire the red-papered walls and fine tapestries that ran the length of the hall.

The butler disappeared into a room off the entry hall but it wasn't long before he reemerged. "Lady Bedlington will see you now," he said, gesturing towards the open door.

He didn't need to be told twice. He headed into the drawing room and saw Phoebe standing in front of a camel-back settee. She was dressed in an alluring dark green gown, her blonde hair was neatly coiffed and a diamond necklace hung around her neck.

Phoebe dropped into a curtsy. "Mr. Moore," she said.

"It is Samuel, if you don't mind," he responded.

A smile came to Phoebe's face. "Samuel," she murmured. "I must admit that I was surprised to hear your name being announced."

He walked further into the room and decided it would be best if he started with an apology. "I came to apologize for how I have been treating you."

"You had every right to treat me as you did."

"No, I didn't," Samuel contested. "You came to make amends and I reacted harshly to you. It was unfair of me."

"I forgive you," Phoebe said. "Dare I hope that you have accepted my apology? It has been weighing heavily on my conscience ever since that night…"

"You rejected me," he said, finishing her thought. "I think it is best if we put all that behind us and move forward."

"I would like that very much." Phoebe gestured towards an upholstered armchair next to her and asked, "Would you care to sit?"

Samuel waited until Phoebe returned to her seat before he went to sit in the armchair. He had to admit that he enjoyed being in Phoebe's presence again, without all the fighting. They had too much of a past together to just ignore.

Phoebe gave him a nervous smile as she asked, "Where do we go from here?"

"I know not," he replied.

"We could always pick up where we left off."

Samuel was unsure of her meaning. "What are you suggesting?"

"Surely you must know that I never stopped caring about you, and I am hoping that you feel the same," Phoebe said. "We could always become lovers."

He could not have been more surprised by her bold request. "Do you still intend to marry Lord Leyburn?"

"I do," Phoebe said. "We would have to be discreet, and I am sure that Lord Leyburn would look the other way."

"I could never do something so dishonorable."

Phoebe sighed. "I should have assumed as much. You have always been much too honorable for your own good."

Samuel decided to propose a different idea. "What if we courted?"

"That is not a good idea."

"Why?"

Phoebe looked crestfallen as she replied, "You are only a son of a viscount. That has always been the problem."

"My title isn't grand enough for you? Is that what you are saying?" he asked, his voice rising.

Phoebe lowered her gaze. "I meant no disrespect, but it is true. It doesn't change my feelings for you. I am willing to overlook that so we can be together."

Samuel felt like he had been punched in his gut. She may care for him, but not enough to let him court her. She cared more about her place in high Society than him. It was just as he had always thought. He just didn't think it would hurt so bad when she confirmed it.

He refused to take her as his mistress. His honor was at stake and that was more important than succumbing to his desires.

In a voice that was far calmer than the emotions that were

whirling inside of him, he said, "I'm sorry, but we cannot be together."

"Why?"

"I have seen firsthand how my father's indiscretions have affected his relationship with my mother, and I won't put my wife through that."

Phoebe's shoulders slumped slightly. "Do you intend to marry Lady Esther?"

It was on the tip of his tongue to deny it, but instead he replied, "I haven't decided, but she was the one that encouraged me to sort out my feelings for you."

"You told her about me?"

"I did," Samuel replied. "And she responded as graciously as I have come to expect from her."

Phoebe did not look pleased by what he had revealed. "She sounds like a blasted saint," she muttered.

"She is not a saint, but she is a remarkable young woman," Samuel admitted. "I always enjoy spending time with her."

A young maid entered the room carrying a silver tray with a tea service on it. She stumbled over the edge of the carpet, causing one of the teacups and saucers to slip off the tray and shatter on the floor. They split into several large fragments.

Phoebe jumped up. "You clumsy oaf!" she shouted. "How did you manage to blunder such a simple task?"

The young maid was visibly shaking. "I'm sorry, my lady."

Samuel rose and walked over to the maid. "May I?" he asked as he took the tray out of her hands and placed it down on the table.

Swiping her hand in front of her, Phoebe ordered, "Clean up the broken teacup and leave us. But be sure that the cost of that setting will be deducted from your pay."

With tears in her eyes, the maid dropped to the floor and picked up the pieces of the teacup and saucer from the floor. She rose with the broken pieces in her hands and hurried out of the room.

Samuel felt bad for the young maid. It was evident that she was in distress and it didn't help that Phoebe had reacted so rudely to her.

Phoebe sat down. "Good help is so hard to come by," she declared in a haughty fashion.

"You handled that poorly."

"That was my grandmother's tea set that she had commissioned on her wedding day," Phoebe explained. "It is the only thing I have left of her and I will not allow incompetence to take that from me."

"But the maid is so young."

"How else will she learn?" Phoebe asked. "You are fortunate not to have to run a household. It needs to be done with a firm hand or else the servants will do as they please."

That wasn't entirely true, but Samuel didn't wish to contradict her. If he was unwed when he inherited his father's title, he would run a household and he knew in his heart that he would never treat the servants in such a disagreeable manner.

Phoebe picked up the teapot. "Would you care for a cup of tea?" she asked, her voice sweet and unassuming.

Samuel had the strangest desire to leave, and never return. But where had that thought even come from? He and Phoebe still had much to discuss. "Yes, I would," he replied as he returned to his seat.

As Phoebe poured him a cup of tea, she asked, "How long do you intend to work as a barrister?"

"As long as I am able," he replied.

"I have never understood your desire to be a barrister, considering you are your father's heir," she said. "You should be learning how to manage your estate."

"I can do both."

"It is beneath you to work as a barrister," Phoebe said, placing the teapot down. Then she extended him a cup of tea.

Samuel accepted the teacup and took a sip. It wasn't as

sweet as the tea that Lady Esther served and he found it to be rather disappointing.

"Is something wrong with your tea?" Phoebe asked.

"I was just thinking about how Lady Mather puts some honey on her tea leaves and it makes the tea that much sweeter."

Phoebe looked unimpressed. "I do not enjoy honey."

"It isn't for everyone," he said, taking a sip.

The room filled with an uncomfortable stillness as the moments passed by. He wasn't quite sure what to say, which was unlike him.

Fortunately, Phoebe spoke up. "What have you decided about us?"

"Us?" he repeated with a shake of his head. "I'm afraid there can be no 'us.' You are determined to marry Lord Leyburn and I won't take you on as a mistress."

"You and your principles," Phoebe grumbled.

The butler stepped into the room and announced, "Lord Leyburn has arrived. Would you care for me to show him in?"

Phoebe leaned forward and placed her teacup onto the table. "Yes, please send him in," she said as she smoothed back her hair.

It was only a moment later that the tall, silver-haired marquess stepped into the room. His eyes narrowed on Samuel and he looked displeased by his presence.

Samuel tipped his head. "Lord Leyburn," he greeted.

"I didn't expect you to be here, Mr. Moore," Lord Leyburn said with contempt in his voice.

Phoebe spoke up. "Mr. Moore is an old friend and we were just catching up. But he was just leaving, weren't you?" she asked, her eyes imploring him to go along with what she was saying.

Samuel rose. "Yes, we have reminisced enough about our past. It is time that we move forward now."

Lord Leyburn walked over to Phoebe and kissed her

cheek. "I'm afraid you just took me by surprise since I hadn't realized you were acquainted with Mr. Moore."

"Our families had neighboring estates when we were young," Phoebe said. "Mr. Moore and I were even known to climb a tree or two together."

"Climbing trees is dangerous. I do hope our children won't behave so hoydenish," Lord Leyburn remarked.

"Of course not," Phoebe said.

Samuel knew it was time to leave, especially since he was now an interloper. He bowed. "Thank you for the cup of tea, Lady Bedlington."

She smiled, but it appeared strained. "I wish you luck with Lady Esther."

"That is right," Lord Leyburn said with almost a note of relief in his voice. "You are pursuing the lovely Lady Esther. I take it that it is going well."

Samuel nodded. "It is," he replied.

"I had considered her as a wife for me, but she is in her fourth Season. I worried there was a reason why she wasn't married yet," Lord Leyburn revealed.

"I assure you that Lady Esther is a delight," Samuel said. "Good day."

After Samuel departed from the townhouse, he shouted up to the driver, "Lady Esther's townhouse."

He found after his conversation with Phoebe that he needed to see Esther.

━━━━━━━━━━━━━━━ ⌇ ━━━━━━━━━━━━━━━

Esther sat in the drawing room as she worked on the reticule that she was knitting. She thought about the squirrels in Hyde Park and how they stole Miss Keene's reticules. What an amusing story.

Her stepmother's voice broke through the silence. "You are smiling."

"Am I?" she asked. "I was just thinking about what a squirrel would do with a reticule."

With a furrowed brow, Susanna said, "You woolgather about the most interesting things."

"It was a story that Miss Keene shared with us," Esther explained. "The squirrels stole two of her reticules because she had sweets in them, so she resorted to putting rocks in it."

"Wasn't it heavy?"

"She didn't seem to care as long as she kept the squirrels away from it. But she still kept sweets in the reticule."

Her stepmother laughed. "Dear heavens, she isn't very bright, is she?"

"She is just young. She will learn."

"You always manage to think the best of others," Susanna said. "I admire that about you."

Esther lowered the reticule to her lap. "Thank you."

"I was thinking…" Susanna started. "What if you returned to your old room?"

"But it is already prepared for the new baby."

Susanna nodded. "I know, but perhaps I was too hasty in making you switch bedchambers. After all, you will be here after the baby is born and I could use your help."

"You want my help?"

"I do," Susanna said, placing her hand on her stomach. "This child will be your brother or sister and I want them to know you."

Esther smiled, touched by her stepmother's thoughtful gesture. "I would be happy to help, but I do not want to switch bedchambers. I think my old one is perfect for your baby."

"That is kind of you."

"I have never tended to a baby before," Esther admitted.

With a swipe of her hand, Susanna said, "It won't be too hard. After all, we have two nursemaids to care for our son."

"What if it is a girl?"

Susanna's eyes grew downcast and Esther realized that she had struck a chord. "Your father will be very disappointed in me."

"It is hardly your fault if it is a girl," Esther said, "and I would love to have a sister."

"I just hope it is a boy, for your father's sake."

Esther could hear the aching in her stepmother's voice and couldn't imagine the pressure she was facing to produce an heir. Her father had talked of little else since she had started increasing. How would he react if it was a girl? Would he shun her?

Her old father wouldn't. She was sure of that. But he had changed since her mother had died. He was almost obsessed with the idea of having a boy.

Hoping she sounded convincing enough, Esther said, "It will be all right. Whatever happens, happens, and we must accept that."

"That is easy for you to say, but I can't stand the thought of letting down your father."

"You have hardly let him down," Esther said. "You are having his child and you have loved him."

Tears came into Susanna's eyes and she blinked them back. "But he will never love me, not how he loved your mother."

Esther wasn't sure what she could say to comfort her stepmother since she could tell that the woman was hurting.

Gibson stepped into the room and met Esther's gaze. "Mr. Moore has come to call, my lady. Shall I show him in?"

Esther glanced at her stepmother for permission, who was wiping her eyes.

In a shaky voice, Susanna said, "Send him in."

Gibson tipped his head. "Yes, my lady."

A moment later, Samuel stepped into the room and Esther

admired his handsome face. Just seeing him lifted her spirits and she felt a smile spread across her face.

Samuel stopped in the center of the room and bowed. "Lady Mather," he said. "Lady Esther."

"Mr. Moore," Esther greeted. "Please have a seat."

He didn't move but instead said, "I was hoping to speak to you privately. Perhaps we could tour your gardens?"

Susanna nodded her head in approval and Esther rose. "I think that is a grand idea."

Samuel held his arm out towards her. "Shall we?"

Esther placed her hand on his arm. She enjoyed being close to him, despite her heart always seeming to start racing at the most inopportune times. How she wished that he noticed her, truly noticed her. Not just as a friend, but as something much more.

They walked towards the rear of the townhouse and a footman opened the door. Once they started walking down a path, Esther admired the rows of rose bushes that were in bloom. The fragrant smell wafted in the wind, reminding her of a much simpler time.

Samuel didn't drop his arm and she saw no reason to remove her hand. She was content with him. Even if he didn't have feelings for her, she wanted him in her life. She would just need to accept the fact that they were friends, and nothing more.

He cleared his throat. "I just came from speaking to Phoebe."

"Oh," she said, unsure of what else to say. She didn't really want to talk about Phoebe, but knew it was inevitable.

"You were right. She still harbors feelings for me," Samuel said.

Esther tried not to let her displeasure show. She knew it was a possibility, but she had been hoping she had been wrong. Although, she was pleased for Samuel since he still loved her.

Samuel continued, unaware of her discomfort. "She still intends to wed Lord Leyburn but was hoping we would come to another type of arrangement."

Not sure what he was implying, she asked, "Such as?"

He clenched his jaw. "She wanted to become my mistress."

Esther stopped on the path and turned to face him. "What did you say?" she asked with dread in her voice. She knew he was an honorable man, but most men had their limits, especially when it came to being with the woman that they loved.

"I turned her down," Samuel informed her.

She let out the breath that she hadn't realized she had even been holding. "I'm sorry," she said, not knowing what else she could say in this moment.

"I would never do something so dishonorable," he declared. "Asking me to do so makes me wonder if Phoebe ever truly knew me."

Esther looked deep into his eyes, hoping that he could feel the truth of her next words. "You are a good man, Samuel."

"No, I am not," he replied. "In this instance, perhaps, but not always."

"I find that hard to believe."

Samuel dropped his arm and a look of anguish came to his expression. He looked miserable. "It was because of me that a little girl died."

Esther knew there had to be more to the story. Samuel was not the type of person to do anything dishonorable. She was sure of that. Taking a step closer to him, she placed her hand on his sleeve. "May I ask what happened?"

"I'm afraid if I tell you, you will look upon me differently," Samuel said.

"I assure you that will not be the case."

"Do not promise me something that you might be unable to honor."

Esther held his gaze for a moment before saying, "I know

precisely what I am promising, Samuel. I am not the only one that wears their emotions on their sleeves."

Samuel was always so strong, so sure of himself, but he just seemed different now. He was vulnerable and hurting.

Placing his hand over hers, he said, "My friend, Charles, and I went drinking at a tavern one afternoon. We got deep into our cups and made the mistake of not hailing a hackney when we departed. Instead, we got onto our horses and made our way through the streets."

Samuel continued. "Charles thought it was funny to ride on the pavement and force the street vendors out of his way. It wasn't until I heard screaming behind us that I stopped my horse and saw a young girl laying on the ground. She wasn't moving and her eyes were closed."

Esther could see that Samuel's eyes shone with tears, but she didn't dare interrupt him as he shared this harrowing moment.

"I turned my horse around and went back to the girl. She was almost gone. I held her in my arms and consoled her until she died," he said, hanging his head. "The worst part is that no one came forth to claim her. I paid to have her properly buried and hired a Bow Street Runner to find her family. But he was unable to do so."

"It was nice of you to ensure she had a proper burial," Esther said.

Samuel closed his eyes tightly. "Charles should have seen to that, but he was so upset by what he did that he took his own life."

Esther gasped. "How terrible," she murmured.

"I should never have let Charles get onto his horse that fateful day," Samuel declared. "If I hadn't been so drunk, I could have stopped him."

"You can't blame yourself for his actions," Esther attempted.

"It isn't that simple," he replied. "Every time I close my

eyes, I see their faces. They haunt my dreams and invade my senses."

She didn't know what to say that would alleviate the pain she could hear in his voice. She wanted to help him, but she was at a loss for words.

A tear slipped out of Samuel's eye and he reached up to swipe it away. "That is why I work as hard as I do as a barrister," he said. "If I can just help enough people, perhaps these feelings will go away."

Esther placed her hand on his cheek and waited until Samuel looked at her. "Helping people will make you feel better, but it won't take away the pain."

"What will?" he asked.

"You must forgive yourself for what happened," she encouraged.

"Forgive myself?" he asked in disbelief. "Never!"

Esther decided to try a different tactic. "Were you able to forgive Charles for what he did to that girl?"

"Yes, but that is entirely different—"

"Then why can't you forgive yourself?" she asked, speaking over him.

Samuel's eyes seemed to search hers as he said, "It is not that easy."

"No, it is not," she agreed. "At times, it can be more difficult to forgive ourselves than it is to forgive others. We tend to expect much more of ourselves than we do of others."

"I don't… I don't…" He stopped speaking as he tried to calm his breathing. "I don't think I am capable of forgiving myself."

"You are more than capable," she assured him.

"Why do you have so much faith in me?"

Esther smiled up at him. "Because you are a good man."

"You still believe so, even after what I just revealed?" he asked incredulously.

"When I say that you are a good man, I do not mean that

you are perfect, but you are a man who tries every single day to do the right thing," Esther said. "That, to me, is the definition of someone who is good."

Samuel stared at her, as if he could not believe what she said. "I don't know what I did to deserve you as a friend."

Friend.

That word cut her deep. But it didn't change how she felt about him. Every word that she had said was true and from her heart.

Esther withdrew her hand from his cheek and took a step back.

"Did I say something wrong?" Samuel asked, watching her closely.

"No, I just realized how familiar I was being," she said. "I shouldn't have been so bold in my speech or actions."

He took a step closer to her. "I am grateful for what you said. I do not share that story very often."

"I am glad that we are friends." *Friends?* Why had she just said that? Couldn't he see that she wanted to be so much more?

Samuel grinned. "As am I," he said. "I am pleased that I found you that day in the gardens, attempting to climb a tree. You have forever changed my life."

Esther glanced back at the townhouse and saw that her stepmother was approaching at a slow pace.

Susanna came to a stop in front of them and addressed Samuel. "I was just informed that our dinner will be served soon. I was hoping that you would be available to join us."

"I wouldn't want to be a bother," Samuel said.

"You could never be a bother, Mr. Moore," Susanna responded.

Samuel glanced at Esther before saying, "I would be honored to dine with all of you."

Susanna nodded in approval. "Very good," she replied.

"Shall we wait in the drawing room until the dinner bell is rung?"

Samuel stepped forward and offered his arm to Susanna. "Allow me to escort you back to the drawing room, my lady."

"Thank you, sir," Susanna said as she took his arm.

Esther trailed behind them and she had an immense desire to run and hide in her bedchamber. How was she supposed to endure a meal with Samuel when her heart was so conflicted? Why did she have to fall for a man that loved another?

Samuel would only ever see her as a friend. It was hopeless to assume any different.

Chapter Fourteen

Samuel escorted Lady Mather into the townhouse and he was acutely aware that Esther was trailing close behind. Why did her mere presence have such an effect on him?

She looked stunning in her pale-yellow gown and her hair was tied into a low chignon at the base of her neck. She was beautiful, but not like the other girls of the *ton*. It was the way that she always saw beauty in others that made her such a beautiful person.

For so long, he had suffered in silence for what had happened with Charles. But with one conversation with Esther, he felt lighter, as if the burdens he was carrying weren't so heavy anymore. She was right. He needed to forgive himself and move on, but that was much easier said than done. Although Esther believed that he could and that made all the difference.

Lord Mather met them in the entry hall. "Thank you for escorting my wife, Mr. Moore, but I shall take it from here."

Samuel dropped his arm and Lady Mather joined her husband. As they walked off, he turned back to face Esther.

She smiled at him, but it seemed contrived.

"What is troubling you?" he asked.

"Nothing," came her prompt reply. It was too prompt.

Now it was obvious that something was troubling her, but how could he get her to open up to him? He had just poured out his heart to her in the gardens and she had helped him immensely. He was hoping to return the favor. He didn't want her to feel an ounce of sadness.

He took a step closer to her and held her gaze. "How can I help you?" he asked.

"I do not need your assistance."

"I think you do."

"I do not," she said with a stubborn tilt of her chin.

Samuel thought it might be best to drop the matter. He didn't wish to anger her by his prodding. "Very well," he responded, taking a step back.

Her eyes flickered with relief. "Shall we adjourn to the dining room?"

Bringing his arm up, he replied, "Only if you allow me the privilege of escorting you."

"I suppose I will allow that," she said, placing her hand on his arm.

Samuel reached for her hand and moved it to the crook of his arm. "I would prefer to have you closer, my dear."

He watched as she blushed and lowered her gaze. It pleased him that she had such a reaction to his words. For the first time, he wished that their pretend attachment wasn't a ruse. He could see himself happily settled down with Esther. Good gads, where had that thought even come from? He wasn't ready to settle down with anyone.

Besides, his heart was too shattered to give her what she wanted- a love match. He was unworthy of Esther, in every way. And he wouldn't insult her by even suggesting a marriage of convenience.

Samuel led Esther into the dining room and pulled out her chair. Once she was situated, he claimed the seat next to her.

Lord Mather was sitting at the head of the table and his wife was seated to his right.

A footman stepped forward and poured wine into the glasses. As he finished filling Esther's, he inadvertently knocked it over, causing it to spill all over the table and onto her lap.

The footman's face grew pale as he rushed out, "My apologies, my lady. I am usually not so clumsy…"

Esther spoke over him. "It is all right." She retrieved her napkin and started dabbing at the wine on her gown.

"It is not all right, my lady," the footman remarked frantically. "I ruined your gown and I am terribly sorry."

Shifting in her chair to face the footman, Esther offered him a kind smile. "It is only a gown and I have many more of them. There is no reason to feel an ounce of distress."

"But your gown——" the footman started.

"Is just a gown, and I have no sentimental attachment to it," Esther assured him. "It was just an accident and I harbor no ill-will towards you."

The footman looked visibly relieved. "Thank you, my lady."

"But I do have a problem," Esther said.

"What is that?"

Esther reached for the glass and held it up. "May I get more wine?"

The footman cracked a smile, which was no doubt Esther's intention. "Of course," he said as he poured the wine into her glass.

As Esther took a sip of her drink, Samuel leaned closer to her and whispered, "That was most gracious of you."

"People are more important than possessions, in my humble opinion," she replied.

"Not everyone feels the same as you."

"Then they are wrong," Esther said with mirth in her eyes.

"I would rather stray on the side of kindness than anything else."

Samuel sat back in his seat as he recognized that Phoebe and Esther's reactions to their servants' mistakes could not be more different. Phoebe chided her maid for incompetence and Esther reacted in a kind fashion. He respected Esther more for her approach.

Lady Mather spoke up as the bowls of soup were being placed in front of them. "How is your mother faring?"

"She is well," Samuel said. "Thank you for asking."

"I know that my mother counted her as a dear friend before her passing," Lady Mather shared.

"My condolences on your loss, my lady," Samuel said.

Lady Mather reached for her spoon as she responded, "It was many years ago." Her words were light but there was pain associated with them.

Lord Mather interjected, his dark eyes assessing Samuel. "Are you still a Whig?"

"My beliefs do align more with the Whigs than the Tories," Samuel replied.

"That is absurd," Lord Mather declared. "King and Country are the most important things to abide by."

"Being a Whig does not mean I do not support King and Country," Samuel argued.

"You have radical views and want to bring down the monarchy."

"No, we believe the political power should ultimately belong to the people and the monarch is only in power because we allow him to be."

Lord Mather stiffened. "That is blasphemy."

"Change is coming, and we need to be prepared to accept that change when it does," Samuel said.

"The monarchy is going nowhere," Lord Mather stated.

"The Prince Regent is widely unpopular and his spending

habits are out of control," Samuel contended. "How long will it be before the people revolt?"

Lady Mather cleared her throat. "Perhaps you two can discuss the state of our government over a glass of port after dinner."

Lord Mather nodded. "You are right, my dear," he said, but not before giving Samuel a disapproving look.

Samuel glanced over at Esther as she ate her soup in silence. "Do you have any thoughts on the matter?" he asked her.

"I do, many, in fact," she replied. "But a woman does not speak about political matters, especially in front of a gentleman."

"The Duchess of Devonshire and the Duchess of Gordon have no such reservations," Samuel pointed out. "They are leading hostesses for the Whigs and Tories."

With a hesitant look, Esther asked, "Do you truly wish to know my thoughts?"

"That is why I asked."

Esther took a deep breath before saying, "I like the idea that the political power rests with the people and the monarchy is held responsible for their choices." She snuck at peek at her father before adding, "But I do not wish to be affiliated with any one party."

Lord Mather pursed his lips together. "Women do not understand the complexities of politics and it is unfair of you to ask my daughter such a question."

"Women understand more than we give them credit for, my lord," Samuel said, earning an approving look from Esther.

"Next you are going to encourage my daughter to read books that should be banned from any respectable library," Lord Mather grumbled.

"A woman who is well-versed in literature has an incredible strength that should not be underestimated," Samuel stated.

Lord Mather frowned. "Esther should be more focused on getting married than reading. Security is far more important than filling her mind with useless information."

Samuel leaned to the side as a footman came to collect his bowl. "I contend that she could be doing both."

"Well, I have put my foot down and I refuse to let her read anything that is written by a woman. They have no place in writing books," Lord Mather said.

Esther exchanged a look with Lady Mather before she reached for her wine glass.

Lady Mather wiped the edges of her mouth before saying, "I have recently read a book by 'A Lady,' and I found it to be quite exemplary."

With a disbelieving look, Lord Mather said, "I thought we both agreed that you would not read that book."

"No, *you* decided that I wouldn't read that book but I was able to obtain a copy," Lady Mather said. "I found I was most curious since it is all the rage of the *ton* right now."

"At least Esther hasn't read it yet," her father stated.

Lady Mather placed a hand on her stomach. "I gave her permission to do so," she revealed. "There is nothing in there that would be considered controversial."

"Other than it was written by a lady," Lord Mather grumbled.

Esther spoke up. "I think it is brilliant that more women are writing books. The more they do, the more it will become accepted as normal."

Lord Mather sighed and shook his head slowly. "I should have known that my wife and Esther would eventually team up against me."

Lady Mather reached for her husband's hand and encompassed it. "You should be pleased that Esther and I have put our differences aside for now."

"I am," Lord Mather said, bringing his wife's hand up to his lips.

A footman placed a tray in front of them that was filled with mutton. Lord Mather rose and started serving the ladies.

Once they all had food, a comfortable silence fell upon them as they ate. Samuel had to admit that this was nice. His parents would always fight over dinner or would glare relentlessly at each other. There never seemed to be a happy medium for them.

But Esther's family was different. They were able to debate points, but they held no hostility for one another. It was evident that there was love in this household.

Although, he did think Lord Mather held some archaic views. But he was no different than most gentlemen of the *ton*. Samuel would much rather have an educated wife than one that held no opinions.

Esther turned her head towards him and asked, "Are you not hungry?"

"I am, but I'm afraid I got distracted," he replied.

"You should eat because this mutton is delicious," she encouraged. "It is one of our cook's best dishes."

Samuel picked up his fork and knife and started eating. As he listened to the conversation around the table, he realized that this is what he had been searching for. A family that would inevitably have disagreements, but they were able to resolve them with kindness and a willingness to listen.

His family was dysfunctional, but that didn't mean he had to make the same mistakes as his parents. He could choose his own path. And he was beginning to think that path began and ended with Esther.

The rays of the sun seeped through the glass windows as

Esther sat in the drawing room. She was waiting for callers to arrive, but she doubted any would come. The only gentleman that called upon her anymore was Samuel, and she took no issue with that. But Susanna was adamant that they were available for anyone who cared to visit them.

Her thoughts strayed towards Samuel. After dinner, they had played card games well into the night. He was competitive, just as she was, and it was the most enjoyable evening. They had formed an easy friendship, much to her chagrin. She wanted so much more, but knew he wasn't capable of giving her what she sought. He was still in love with Lady Bedlington. She could hear it in his voice when he spoke of her.

Gibson stepped into the room and announced, "Miss Bolingbroke has come to call, my lady. Shall I send her in?"

Esther perked up from her seat on the settee. "Yes, please," she said eagerly. She always looked forward to seeing her friend.

After the butler departed from the room, Anette appeared in the doorway and smiled broadly. "Good morning, Friend."

"You are in a fine mood today," Esther said.

Glancing around the room, Anette asked, "Where is your stepmother?"

"She had to go speak to the cook about tonight's supper, but she will be back soon."

Anette sat down next to her. "I have been dying to ask," she started, "did my advice help you?"

"I didn't employ any of your advice on Mr. Moore."

"Whyever not?" Anette asked. "It was brilliant."

"Was it?" Esther asked with a smile.

Anette leaned back against the side of the settee. "I have read enough about flirting that I daresay that I am an expert on it."

"Yet you have not secured a husband."

"Why would I?" Anette asked. "I have no desire to marry. I will remain a bluestocking forever and be blissfully happy."

Esther gave her friend a knowing look. "Does your mother know that?"

"No, and you are not going to be the one who tells her," Anette replied.

"I promise I will not tell a soul."

Anette let out a dramatic sigh. "I have too many things that I want to do with my life and I don't want to be trapped by having a husband."

"Not everyone feels as you do."

"I know, but that is because they don't know any different," Anette declared. "They marry and then their hopes and dreams go up in smoke. But they convince themselves that is what they had wanted to begin with."

"You can still have hopes and dreams and be married," Esther contended.

"Assuming your husband will allow that."

Esther leaned forward and placed her needlework onto the table. "Mr. Moore isn't like that," she said. "He praises me for my opinions."

"Do you two have an understanding yet?"

Esther shook her head. "No, and we won't. You seem to forget that he is still in love with someone else."

"You can always turn his head by using my advice." Miss Bolingbroke batted her eyes and giggled.

With a laugh, she replied, "I think it would scare him off."

"You could always discuss the mating rituals of elephants with him," Anette suggested with a slight shrug of her shoulders.

"Pray tell, why would I do something so vulgar?"

Anette smirked. "You can see if he is a prude or not."

"I think I will refrain from discussing any mating rituals with Mr. Moore," she said. "We will stick to more appropriate topics."

"Like the weather?"

"Yes, the weather is always a safe, polite conversational topic."

"But it is so boring," Anette declared.

Esther reached for the plate of biscuits and held it up. "Would you care for a biscuit?"

"Obviously, I do," Anette said as she picked one up. "I thought it was rude of you not to offer me one until now."

As she placed the plate down, Esther asked, "How is your mother?"

Anette let out an unladylike groan. "She is upset with me because she caught me wearing trousers."

"Why would you want to wear trousers?"

"It is so much easier to ride a horse when wearing trousers," Anette shared.

"Where did you even get trousers?"

Anette dusted the crumbs off her hands before replying, "I had the modiste make me two pairs of trousers."

Esther knew her friend would often balk at tradition, but to be willing to wear gentlemen's clothing? That was brazen, even for Anette.

Her stepmother stepped into the room and Anette quickly moved to sit up straight.

Susanna smiled at Anette. "Miss Bolingbroke," she greeted. "What a pleasant surprise to see you here so early."

"I was just so eager to see my dear friend," Anette said.

"Or you came for the biscuits," Esther joked.

Anette reached for another biscuit off the plate. "Your cook makes the best biscuits. I need to get the recipe."

Susanna waddled across the room and sat awkwardly down on an upholstered armchair. "Did you come by yourself?"

"Yes, because I needed a break from my mother." Anette's hand shot up to cover her mouth. "I shouldn't have said that."

Susanna looked amused. "It is all right to admit such things, especially to friends."

"My mother just holds me to an impossible standard," Anette shared.

"I think it is a mother's job to teach her children to not have any need of her anymore. However, the hardest part for her is to accept that," Susanna said.

"Well, if you ask my mother, I am in desperate need of her help," Anette stated. "At times, she calls me hopeless."

"No one is hopeless," Susanna assured her.

"I might be," Anette admitted.

Gibson stepped into the room and announced, "Mr. Daniel Fairchild has come to call. May I show him in?"

Susanna bobbed her head. "Yes, thank you."

It was only a moment later that Daniel stepped into the room with a plate of biscuits in his hand. "I have come bearing gifts."

"You have brought biscuits?" Esther asked. That was odd. Her cousin had never brought them gifts before.

"Yes, but they are special biscuits," Daniel replied. "My cook has had this recipe in her family for generations."

Anette's eyes lit up. "May I try one?"

Daniel seemed pleased by her request. He walked the plate over to her and handed her one. "I hope you enjoy it, Miss Bolingbroke."

After she took a bite, Anette declared, "These are delicious. I have never had a mint biscuit before."

"Esther?" Daniel asked, extending her a biscuit. "Would you care for one?"

"I would," Esther said as she accepted his offering. She had no objection to mint but she was curious as to why Daniel would choose to bring these biscuits when Susanna had had such an unfavorable reaction to the mint ice at Gunter's.

Daniel turned towards Susanna and asked, "Can I tempt you, my lady?"

Susanna put her hand up. "No, thank you," she replied. "I am not particularly fond of mint."

With a disappointed look, Daniel said, "That is a shame. I had my cook make them especially for you."

Susanna pressed her lips together. "I suppose one biscuit wouldn't hurt." Her words were tight, as if it took everything she had to say those words.

Daniel selected a biscuit off the top and handed it to her. "You won't be disappointed," he said, looking pleased.

Her stepmother brought the biscuit up to her lips and took a bite. "The mint is rather strong, is it not?"

"I think it is the right amount of mint," Anette replied. "May I have another?"

"You may," Daniel said as he placed the plate down onto the tray. "I intend to leave the rest of the biscuits with you."

Esther finished the biscuit and gestured towards the teapot. "Can I offer you some tea, Cousin?"

"No, thank you," Daniel said, putting his hand up. "I just wanted to come by and deliver the biscuits."

"That was most thoughtful of you," Esther acknowledged. Her cousin wasn't known to be very thoughtful of others, but perhaps she was seeing a side that he had kept hidden.

Susanna had only taken a few bites before she placed the half-eaten biscuit down on the tray. "I agree with Esther. It was very kind of you to think of us."

Daniel's eyes strayed to Susanna's discarded biscuit. "Do you not want to finish the biscuit?" he asked.

"I have had enough for now," Susanna replied.

"Did you not care for it?" Daniel asked.

Susanna placed a hand on her stomach. "I am just not hungry at the moment."

With a tight smile, Daniel remarked, "I have never met anyone that did not love my cook's biscuits."

"I mean no disrespect," Susanna said.

Daniel's eyes darted up and his smile seemed to become

more genuine. "Of course not," he rushed to say. "I will just have my cook prepare another one of her biscuit recipes. Perhaps one that is not flavored with mint."

"That is kind of you," Susanna graciously murmured.

"It is my pleasure, my lady." He bowed. "If you ladies will excuse me, I have work I need to see to."

After her cousin departed, Esther turned her attention towards Susanna. "I take it that you did not like the biscuit."

"It was far too minty for my tastes," Susanna said.

Anette reached for another biscuit off the plate. "I find them to be scrumptious. I think I could eat this whole plate."

Esther gave her friend an amused look. "That isn't saying much. You would eat almost any biscuit that is placed in front of you."

"Not any biscuits. I do have standards," Anette said.

Susanna rose slowly. "I am going to rest now," she shared. "Please send word when Mr. Moore comes to call."

"That is assuming he intends to call upon me today," Esther said.

"He will," Susanna responded.

Esther arched an eyebrow. "How can you be so sure?"

Susanna smiled, as if privy to a secret. "Call it a lucky guess," she said before departing from the drawing room.

Anette leaned back in the settee and ate her biscuit. "You aren't getting rid of me as long as there are biscuits on that plate."

"You will hear no objections from me," Esther said.

Chapter Fifteen

A few hours later, Esther sat next to Susanna's bed. Her stepmother's face was pale, and a thin line of sweat appeared on her brow. She had taken ill shortly after Anette had departed. Not only was she terribly nauseous but she had stomach pains to add to her misery.

It didn't quite make sense to Esther. Her stepmother was not one to experience such bouts of illnesses and they seemed to come on so suddenly. The only correlation between the two illnesses was Susanna had eaten something that Daniel had offered her. Perhaps she was just having an adverse reaction to the mint. But Susanna had eaten mint before and hadn't gotten sick. Something wasn't adding up and that greatly concerned her.

A knock came at the door before it was opened, revealing Alice. "The doctor has arrived," she informed them, opening the door wide.

Dr. Ramsey stepped into the room and had a solemn look on his face. He approached the bed and placed his hand on Susanna's forehead. "You are feverish." He glanced at Esther. "I would like to examine Lady Mather before we start blood-letting."

In a weak voice, Susanna asked, "Is there no other way?"

"I'm afraid not," Dr. Ramsey replied as he placed his bag down onto a table. "We must not have cleansed your blood enough the last time. That is my only reasoning as to why you have taken ill again."

Susanna's complexion took on a ghostly pallor and Esther put a hand on hers. "It is all right. I will stay with you," she assured her.

"Thank you," Susanna said as she closed her eyes.

The door was thrown open and Esther's father rushed into the room. "Susanna," he said. "I just received word and I came home straightaway."

Esther released Susanna's hand and took a step back so her father could be closer to his wife.

"I am here. What can I do for you?" he asked, his voice frantic.

"The doctor wants to do bloodletting," Susanna revealed as she winced slightly.

Dr. Ramsey spoke up. "It is the only way, my lord."

Her father retrieved a chair and repositioned it next to the bed. "I will stay with you," he said. "You are not alone in this."

Esther was pleased by her father's reaction. It made her hope that he cared more for his wife than he realized. Susanna deserved to be loved, just as she loved her husband.

Dr. Ramsey pushed his glasses up higher on his nose. "I need to examine my patient," he said. "Lady Esther may stay outside in the hall until I finish my examination."

Knowing that Susanna was in good hands, Esther nodded. "Very well," she responded as she walked over to the door.

She had just stepped into the hall, being mindful of closing the door behind her, when the housekeeper, Mrs. Powers, approached her with an anxious expression.

Sensing that something was wrong, Esther asked, "Is everything all right?"

"Sarah has taken seriously ill and I was hoping that the doctor might examine her after he finishes with Lady Mather," Mrs. Powers said.

"What symptoms does she have?" Esther asked.

"Pain in her stomach, nausea, and vomiting," Mrs. Powers responded. "I do believe it is similar to what Lady Mather is experiencing."

Esther was baffled. The last time she had seen Sarah was when she had collected the tray from the drawing room and she had looked healthy. The only thing left on the tray was Susanna's discarded biscuit. Would Sarah have eaten that? If so, what would that mean?

"May I see Sarah?" Esther asked.

Mrs. Powers looked unsure. "You may, but she is rather sick. I should warn you that she isn't saying much right now."

"I understand, but it is important that I speak to her."

"Follow me, then," Mrs. Powers said, turning on her heel.

Esther followed the housekeeper to the narrow set of stairs that led her up to the upper level, where the female servants were housed.

Once they stepped into the hall, Esther saw Sarah was lying on her bed, her eyes were closed and her face was an alarming shade of white. She was surrounded by the other servants as they placed wet cloths onto her forehead.

The servants moved to make room for her by Sarah's bed. Esther reached for Sarah's hand and observed the young maid. She appeared to have taken much sicker than Susanna and that concerned her greatly.

"Sarah… can you hear me?" Esther asked.

When no response was forthcoming, Esther decided to try again, only with a different tactic. "If you can hear me, squeeze my hand."

It took a long moment, but she felt Sarah squeeze her hand, albeit weakly.

Esther took that as a victory. "Earlier, when you returned

the tray to the kitchen, did you eat the half-biscuit that was left on the plate?"

No response.

"It is fine if you did. I am not upset," Esther said. "I just need to know if you did eat the biscuit. It is important."

Sarah squeezed her hand.

Esther closed her eyes as realization washed over her. There was no way that this was a coincidence. It could only mean one thing- Daniel had poisoned that biscuit. Why would her cousin do something so devious?

"You did good, Sarah," Esther said as she released her hand. "The doctor will be here shortly to examine you."

Esther stepped back from the bed as her mind was whirling. She needed to speak to Anette and Lady Oxley at once. They both were knowledgeable about herbs and botany. Perhaps they could tell her how Daniel was poisoning her stepmother.

With a purposeful stride, she headed towards the main level and saw Gibson in the entry hall. "Will you ensure the doctor visits Sarah when he finishes with Lady Mather?"

Gibson tipped his head. "Yes, my lady."

Esther reached for a bonnet on a hook and said, "If my father inquires as to my whereabouts, inform him that I am visiting Miss Bolingbroke."

"Would you like me to bring the coach around?"

"There is no need," she replied. "I shall walk since it is only a block away."

Gibson looked unsure. "Will you not wait for a maid to accompany you?"

"I assure you that my visit is of the utmost importance, and I do not have time to wait," Esther said as she placed the bonnet on her head.

The butler moved to open the door for her. "I shall have the coach waiting for you outside Miss Bolingbroke's residence."

That was the least of her concerns, but she appreciated the butler's concern. "Thank you," she said as she exited the townhouse.

It wasn't long before she arrived at her friend's home. She walked up to the door and knocked.

The door opened and the butler gave her an odd look. "May I help you, my lady?"

"I need to speak to Miss Bolingbroke," she announced.

The butler glanced over her shoulder, no doubt looking for who had accompanied her. "Do come in," he encouraged.

Rather than wait for the butler to announce her, Esther walked towards the drawing room and stepped inside.

Anette was sitting on the settee and looked up at her in surprise. "Esther, is everything well?"

"No," she replied plainly.

Lady Oxley spoke up from her seat. "What is wrong?"

"Susanna has taken ill again and I suspect that my cousin is poisoning her," she said.

Anette gasped. "Why would you think such a thing?"

"Both times that Daniel has offered Susanna food, she has taken ill shortly thereafter," Esther explained. "I need your help on figuring out what he is poisoning her with."

Lady Oxley rose and approached her. "That is quite the accusation. Do you have any proof of what you are saying?"

"Susanna didn't finish the biscuit that Daniel had given her and a young maid ate it. She has since taken ill and her symptoms are very similar to Susanna's," Esther shared.

Anette had a baffled look on her face. "But we ate from the same plate of biscuits. Should we not have been poisoned as well?"

"I didn't notice it at the time but Daniel handed us the biscuits. He could have easily given us biscuits that weren't laced with the poison," Esther said.

Lady Oxley placed a hand on her shoulder. "Come have a seat and we can discuss this. Perhaps over a cup of tea."

"I don't want tea," Esther responded. "I just need your help so Daniel won't get away with this."

The viscountess must have sensed her determination because she dropped her hand and said, "I should warn you that there are many ways to poison someone. We might not be able to pinpoint the exact poison used."

Anette interjected, "Lady Mather did mention that her biscuit was too minty."

"Minty?" Lady Oxley repeated. "That rules out arsenic since it is odorless and tasteless when mixed with food." She paused. "I'm afraid there are many types of mint plants that are poisonous if taken- water mint and horsemint come to mind."

"What about dead nettle?" Anette asked.

Lady Oxley bobbed her head. "Yes, that would be one as well," she replied. "What are Susanna's symptoms?"

"Abdominal pain, vomiting and nausea," Esther responded. "The doctor intended to treat her by bloodletting."

"I would expect as much." Lady Oxley had a thoughtful look on her face. "What about pennyroyal?"

Anette's face lit up. "That might be it. What if he wasn't trying to kill Lady Mather with pennyroyal but was trying to get rid of the baby?"

Lady Oxley clasped her hands together. "Brilliant," she said. "Pennyroyal in high doses has been known to cause women to lose their babies, but most of the time the mothers die as a result to the damage that is caused to their livers."

"That would make sense since Daniel wouldn't inherit my father's estate if Susanna has a son," Esther mused.

"Do you think your cousin would be so cold-hearted as to do such a thing?" Anette asked.

"Any other time, I would have said no, but it surely can't be a coincidence that my stepmother is getting sick after

Daniel gives her food," Esther said. "Does pennyroyal have an antidote?"

"Unfortunately, there is no cure for pennyroyal," Lady Oxley said. "You will just need to wait and let the illness take its course."

Esther frowned. "I can't just sit around and do nothing."

"Go home, and tell your father your suspicions," Lady Oxley encouraged. "He will know what to do."

With a shake of her head, Esther said, "My father has a temper and might challenge Daniel to a duel."

"Could you go to the constable?" Anette asked.

"With what proof?" Lady Oxley asked. "It is only her word and people get sick all the time. Even if Susanna did die, pennyroyal is impossible to detect in the body."

Esther felt her shoulders droop. "I can't just stand by and do nothing."

"For starters, don't eat anything that your cousin offers you," Anette remarked. "If you want me to shoot him, I can."

Lady Oxley shot her daughter a warning look. "No one is shooting anyone."

"Pity," Anette muttered.

With an encouraging look, Lady Oxley said, "Go home and take care of Susanna. Let the poison run its course and with any luck, there won't be any long-term effects."

Esther refused to sit by and do nothing. "Surely there must be something else that I can do?"

"There is not much you can do, but do stay away from Daniel," Lady Oxley ordered. "If he is desperate enough to poison someone, who knows what he is capable of?"

With a dejected sigh, Esther said, "Very well."

She would go home and ensure Susanna and Sarah were properly cared for. Now that she was onto Daniel, she would ensure that he would never have the opportunity to poison anyone again.

The sun was starting to set as Samuel exited his coach and approached the main door of Esther's townhouse. He was hoping she would agree to a trip to Vauxhall Gardens with him. He found he wanted to spend as much time with her as possible and far away from the stuffiness- and the formalities- of the drawing room.

The door opened and the butler had a solemn look on his face. "May I help you?" he asked.

"I was hoping Lady Esther is available for callers," he said, seeing no need to produce a calling card.

The butler opened the door wide and stood to the side. "Come in and I shall see if Lady Esther is available."

"Thank you," he said as he stepped into the entry hall.

"You may wait for her in the drawing room," the butler encouraged, gesturing towards the open door off the entry hall.

Samuel headed into the drawing room and was surprised that neither Esther nor her stepmother were there to greet him. He approached the mantel over the hearth and admired the small vases that sat there.

It was a long moment before he heard Esther's voice greeting him from the doorway. "Samuel," she said. "I do apologize for not being here to greet you."

As he turned around to face her, he immediately knew that something was wrong by the troubled look in her eyes. "What has happened?"

"My stepmother has taken ill again," she revealed.

"Is it serious?"

Esther shook her head. "No, but the doctor just left moments ago and Susanna is resting now. He thinks the worst is over."

"That is good."

"It is, but I believe I have found the reason why my step-mother keeps falling ill." She glanced over her shoulder and lowered her voice. "She is being poisoned by my cousin."

Samuel reared back. "Poisoned?" he asked. "Are you sure?"

"Not at first, but then a young maid became ill after finishing off the biscuit that Daniel had intended for Susanna to eat," she replied. "The first time my stepmother had gotten sick was after Daniel had given her a mint ice. It is just too much of a coincidence to discount."

"That is suspect, but it would still be considered circum-stantial evidence," Samuel reluctantly shared. "No judge would bring this case to trial based upon those limited facts."

Esther tossed her hands up in the air. "What am I to do?" she asked. "Give up and let Daniel continue to poison my stepmother with pennyroyal?"

"Did you at least tell the doctor about your suspicions?"

She frowned. "I did, and he was less than impressed by my explanation," she replied. "But I am not surprised since he doesn't want to believe a woman figured out what was wrong with one of his patients."

"That is a shame that he didn't take you seriously."

"I am used to it by now, I'm afraid," Esther said.

Samuel closed the distance between them, stopping a proper distance away. "No man should discount you so easily."

"That is easy for you to say since you were born a man. Women are often overlooked."

"That doesn't make it right."

"Regardless, that is the way it has always been."

Samuel heard the sadness in her voice and it made his heart ache. "What do you want from me, Esther?"

She looked at him and replied, "I want you to believe me."

"I do," he replied.

Her eyes softened. "You do?" she asked. "But what about the circumstantial evidence?"

He took a step closer to her. "If you say that your cousin is poisoning your stepmother, then I will help you prove it."

"How can I prove it?" Esther asked. "I can't sit by and wait for it to happen again."

"I agree, and I know someone who can help us."

"Who?"

Samuel winced. "It is better if I don't tell you until he has agreed to help us."

"Us?"

Placing a hand on her sleeve, he replied, "I think it would be far easier to prove your cousin's nefarious actions if we teamed up. Don't you agree?"

Esther smiled and he had to admit that he had never seen anything so beautiful in his life. "I think that is a fine idea," she replied.

"I'm glad to hear that," he said, lowering his hand to the side. "Now, why would your cousin want to poison your stepmother?"

"I do not think he intends to kill her, but he wants her to lose her baby," Esther said. "If Susanna bears a son, then he is no longer my father's heir."

"Do you truly think he would stoop to hurting your step-mother and her child just to inherit your father's title and estate?"

Esther nodded. "Yes, I do."

"Have you told your father your suspicions?"

"No, because I fear what he would do," she admitted. "Until we can prove for certain that Daniel is poisoning Susanna, I don't want to get him involved."

"I think that is a mistake."

"Why?"

"What if your cousin tries again to poison Susanna when you are not home?" he asked.

Esther pressed her lips together in concentration. "I see your point, but what if my father goes off half-cocked on my cousin?"

Samuel had to admit that Esther wasn't entirely wrong. He had seen Lord Mather's temper flare up on occasion. "When we decide to tell your father, I think it would be best if I were there," he said.

"I would like that very much."

"Good. You will find that I can be quite useful."

With an amused look, she responded, "I am starting to see that."

"I was hoping that we could take a trip to Vauxhall Gardens this evening," he said.

"I'm afraid I wouldn't be very good company," she admitted. "I find that I am quite furious at my cousin for doing something so deceitful."

Samuel watched her cheeks flush with anger and he grew concerned. "Do not let anger consume you," he advised. "It is your kindness, your compassion, that makes you so uniquely remarkable."

"I just don't want Daniel to get away with hurting Susanna."

"He won't," he assured her. "Trust me."

Esther's eyes latched onto his, holding him transfixed. "I do trust you, wholeheartedly. I have from the moment we met under that tree."

Her admission touched him deeply and he found his lips curling into a smile. "I'm glad to hear that, because I find that I greatly want to win your approval."

"You already have it, Samuel," she said.

Samuel took a small step closer to her, causing her to tilt her head to look up at him. "You do not know what those words mean to me."

"I hope they flatter you."

He studied her face, admiring the loveliness of her eyes.

"They do flatter me, but it makes me think you see the real me."

Esther's voice was soft as she admitted, "It has been the same for me."

"I know, because you are terrible at hiding your emotions," Samuel teased. "You need to work on that."

"I have never had any complaints before."

Samuel leaned closer to her. "That is only because no one has been bold enough to tell you the truth before."

"And you think now is a good time to do so?"

"There are worse times," he joked.

Esther's lips twitched. "You, sir, are no gentleman."

Bringing his hand to cover his heart, he responded, "That hurts, my lady." Little did Esther know that his honor was hanging by a thread as he remained close to her. He could easily lean down and press his lips to hers, but she deserved more than a stolen kiss in the drawing room.

A clearing of a throat came from behind them, causing him to take a step back.

In the doorway, a lovely brown-haired young woman watched them with interest. She stepped further into the room and said, "Pardon the interruption, but I just came to see how Lady Mather is feeling."

Esther covered her cheeks with her hands, no doubt in an attempt to hide the blush that had formed there. "She is much better. Thank you."

Rather than wait for an introduction, the young woman walked up to Samuel and said, "You must be Mr. Moore."

"I am."

She grinned. "I am Miss Bolingbroke," she said. "I am Esther's dearest friend."

Esther spoke up. "Please excuse my friend. She has no patience for introductions."

"Why would I when it is so clear that this is your Mr. Moore?" Miss Bolingbroke asked.

"Mr. Moore is not mine," Esther responded.

Miss Bolingbroke glanced between them. "You could have fooled me," she said lightly. "Anyways, I did not mean to interrupt…" She hesitated. "Whatever it is that you two were doing."

In a rushed voice, Esther responded, "We were discussing Daniel and how he is poisoning my stepmother."

"Yes, that is exactly what it looked like to me," Miss Bolingbroke said with a knowing smile.

Samuel decided he needed tact to win Miss Bolingbroke over. "It is a pleasure to make your acquaintance. Any friend of Lady Esther's is most surely a friend of mine."

Miss Bolingbroke didn't speak for a moment. "How close of a friend are you to Lady Esther?" she asked.

He opened his mouth to speak, but Esther spoke first. "Honestly, Anette, you do not need to interrogate the poor man."

"Is he not a barrister?" Miss Bolingbroke asked. "I thought they learned how to debate in the womb."

Samuel chuckled. "Not that young, Miss Bolingbroke."

"That is a shame," she responded.

Esther gestured towards the tea service on the table. "Would anyone care for some tea?" she asked.

"None for me," Miss Bolingbroke said. "I have had far too much tea today for my liking."

Samuel thought it would be best if he departed and let Esther spend time with her friend. "I should be going."

"So soon?" Esther asked.

He met her gaze. "I need to meet with the person that I believe can help us stop your cousin for good."

"Very well."

Samuel noticed that Miss Bolingbroke was watching them both rather closely and he thought it would be a good idea if he kept his distance from Esther. Her friend seemed a little too astute for her own good and he was fearful of what she saw in him.

"Good day, ladies," he said with a slight bow.

As he walked out of the drawing room, he let out a deep breath and resisted the urge to steal another glance at Esther. What had come over him? He had almost kissed her. No good would have come from that. He was sure of it.

So why did he want to run back into the room, pull her into his arms and kiss her senseless?

Chapter Sixteen

Samuel stepped through the door of White's and his eyes roamed over the hall. He was looking for the one person that he knew would help him- Lord Rushcliffe.

His eyes landed on the former burly Bow Street Runner. He was having a drink with Lord Roswell Westlake and they appeared to be in good spirits. It was odd seeing Rushcliffe with a smile on his face since he had been a very private, solemn man before Enid came into his life.

As he approached their table, Rushcliffe noticed him first and the smile left his face. If he didn't know any better, it would appear that he was annoyed to see him, but that didn't deter him. Esther needed his help, and he had no intention of letting her down.

Lord Roswell raised his glass. "Mr. Moore," he said. "Come join us for a drink."

Samuel had no time for pleasantries. He was here to speak to Rushcliffe and then he would be on his way. "I need to speak to Rushcliffe."

Rushcliffe gestured towards a chair. "Have a seat, then. You have five minutes until I must depart."

Lord Roswell pushed back his chair and stood up. "I will

leave you two alone."

"You can stay," Samuel encouraged. Lord Roswell had proven himself useful before and, most importantly, Rushcliffe trusted him. That was enough for him.

After Lord Roswell returned to his seat, both men gave him an expectant look.

Samuel leaned forward in his seat and lowered his voice. "What I am about to tell you must remain between us."

"I assumed as much," Lord Rushcliffe said. "Does this have to do with one of your cases?"

"No, it has to do with Lady Esther," Samuel revealed.

A smirk came to Lord Rushcliffe's lips. "You have finally admitted your feelings for her, then?"

"What? No!" Samuel responded. "That is not what I want to talk to you about."

Lord Roswell spoke up. "But you do have feelings for Lady Esther?"

"That is neither here nor there," Samuel asserted. "I have a much more pressing matter that I need to discuss with you."

"I don't know what could be more important than acknowledging your feelings for Lady Esther," Roswell remarked.

"I agree," Rushcliffe said. "I used to think love was an inconvenience, but I was wrong."

"I am happy for you, but I do not have feelings for Esther," Samuel lied. He had developed feelings for her, but he hadn't been able to properly sort them out. It was unexpected, and messy.

Roswell shook his head. "You are in denial, I see."

"I am not," Samuel said. "I hardly know Lady Esther." Another lie. He was well acquainted with Esther. And the more he learned about her, the harder he was falling for her.

Lord Rushcliffe took a sip of his drink before saying, "I hope you are a smart enough man to recognize what you have right in front of you."

Samuel decided to be somewhat honest with his friends, but without revealing too much. "Lady Esther is a remarkable young woman." There. That was short and simple. There was no way either of his friends could read more into that.

But he was wrong.

Roswell chuckled. "Just marry the girl already and put yourself out of your misery."

"I said nothing about marriage," Samuel said.

"You didn't need to," Roswell claimed. "I can hear the affection you hold for Esther in your voice."

Was he so transparent? He hoped not. What if Esther knew of his feelings? Was that a good or bad thing, he wondered. He had almost kissed her earlier, but fortunately, he had his wits about him. If he had kissed her, it would have changed everything between them. And he wasn't sure if that was a good thing.

"Regardless, that is not what I wish to discuss with you," Samuel said.

Rushcliffe flicked his wrist. "Very well. What would you like to discuss?"

Samuel glanced over his shoulder to ensure their conversation remained private. "Esther believes that her cousin, Mr. Daniel Fairchild, has poisoned her stepmother on two occasions with pennyroyal."

In the blink of an eye, Rushcliffe grew serious. "Does she have any proof of this?" he asked.

"No, but Lady Mather grew ill shortly after Mr. Fairchild gave her a mint ice and a mint biscuit, on separate occasions," Samuel revealed. "And a maid went sick after eating half of the biscuit that she had discarded."

"Women that are increasing get sick all the time when they eat food that doesn't agree with them," Rushcliffe said. "I will admit that the maid getting sick gives me pause, but that isn't enough for a constable to open an investigation."

"What of a Bow Street Runner?" Samuel asked. "Surely they would take the case."

"Yes, but there is no need since I will help you," Rushcliffe said.

"I thought you retired."

Rushcliffe nodded. "I did, but my wife considers Lady Esther a dear friend. And she is an excellent judge of character."

Samuel sat back in his seat. "Thank you." He was grateful for his friend's assistance, but he knew recruiting him was just the beginning. Now they had to prove that Mr. Fairchild was guilty of poisoning Lady Mather.

Lord Roswell interjected, "How sure is Lady Esther that Mr. Fairchild is using pennyroyal?"

"She was pretty adamant about it," Samuel replied.

"Pennyroyal in large doses can kill a person, but in low doses it can mimic any number of illnesses," Lord Roswell said. "Furthermore, it is undetectable in a person, even after death."

With a questioning look, Samuel asked, "How do you know so much about pennyroyal?"

Lord Roswell shrugged his shoulders nonchalantly. "It has come in handy, on occasion," he shared.

Samuel decided not to press his friend since he needed to share one more crucial detail with them. "Esther believes that her cousin is giving Lady Mather enough pennyroyal to cause her to lose the baby."

"That is terrible," Rushcliffe said. "However, it is going to be nearly impossible to prove."

Samuel grimaced. "That is what I feared."

"But I have worked harder cases," Rushcliffe remarked smugly.

"As have I," Lord Roswell added.

Shifting in his seat to face Roswell, Samuel asked, "Pray tell, what kind of cases has a son of a marquess worked on?"

Lord Roswell's eyes flickered with something. Regret? Pain? He couldn't quite decipher it. In a calm, collected voice, he replied, "You wouldn't believe me if I told you." The way he spoke his words caused Samuel to pause. They were said with such conviction that he found he believed them. Which posed the question- how did his friend spend his free time?

Rushcliffe's voice drew back Samuel's attention. "I will investigate Mr. Fairchild and see what I come up with."

"Thank you," Samuel acknowledged.

Mr. Whitmore's jovial voice came from behind him. "Friends. Compadres," he greeted with his arms out wide. "Celebrate with me."

Samuel turned in his seat to face Mr. Whitmore and asked, "What are we celebrating?"

"Miss Keene has agreed to my courtship," Mr. Whitmore said. "The contracts will be signed tomorrow and it will be a done thing."

"How romantic," Lord Roswell teased.

"Marriage is nothing more than a transaction," Mr. Whitmore remarked as he pulled out a chair and sat down.

Rushcliffe frowned. "Do you at least like the girl?"

Mr. Whitmore placed a hand over his heart. "I am completely and utterly in love with her," he replied dramatically. "Her being rich and all just sweetens the deal."

"You are an idiot," Rushcliffe declared as he stood.

"I'm sensing tension between us," Mr. Whitmore said. "Please say that I am wrong. I would be heartbroken if you did not like me."

Rushcliffe pushed in his chair. "Save the theatrics. I think we both know that ship sailed long ago."

Mr. Whitmore looked the epitome of innocence. "Are you still harboring feelings over the time I beat you in a bout of fisticuffs at Eton?"

"I recall it very differently," Rushcliffe said. "You were on the ground, begging for mercy."

"I was winning."

"You and I have two different ideas of what winning is," Rushcliffe huffed.

Mr. Whitmore smirked. "I survived the ordeal, did I not?" He pointed at himself. "Winning."

Rushcliffe looked heavenward before saying, "Good day, gentlemen." He shifted his gaze to Mr. Whitmore. "Try not to make a complete fool of yourself today."

As Rushcliffe walked off, Mr. Whitmore watched his retreating figure. "It appears that Lord Rushcliffe will not be attending my wedding. Which is a shame. I would imagine he gives excellent gifts."

"I do not know why you insist on antagonizing him," Samuel said.

"It is like poking a bear. It is something that you cannot do just once." Mr. Whitmore held up three fingers to the passing server, indicating he wanted drinks. "The next round is on me."

Roswell shook his head. "I'm afraid I will have to pass. I have work that I must see to."

Mr. Whitmore looked amused. "You should do what I just did. Find an heiress to marry and spend your days exactly how you please."

"I'm afraid I want more than just a tenant in my home," Roswell said.

"As do I," Mr. Whitmore asserted. "That is why I made a list to find the most ideal wife for me. It helped me to focus on what was truly important."

With a curious look, Roswell asked, "Which was?"

Mr. Whitmore leaned forward and grew serious. "Money makes even the drabbest young woman appear like a diamond in the rough."

"I hope you are happy with Miss Keene," Roswell said.

"When are you going to settle down with the right girl?" Mr. Whitmore asked.

It appeared that Mr. Whitmore struck a chord with Roswell by the way he flinched slightly. "It will take much convincing on my part."

Samuel looked at his friend in surprise. "It almost sounds as if you have a specific young lady in mind."

"I have, but I'm afraid she wants nothing to do with me," Roswell revealed, his words holding a sadness to them.

He didn't know the details- or who the young woman even was- but he recognized when a man was in love. And Roswell was most definitely in love with this particular young woman.

"You must fight for her," Samuel encouraged.

"I'm not sure if it will do any good," Roswell admitted. "I had a chance, once, but I messed it up. Now I think she is lost to me."

Mr. Whitmore leaned towards Roswell and asked, "Is she rich?"

Roswell let out a heavy sigh as he rose. "And with that, I need to depart before it gets too late," he said as he pushed in his chair.

As Roswell walked off, Mr. Whitmore inquired, "What did I say wrong?"

"Everything out of your mouth is wrong," Samuel replied.

The server came and placed three drinks in the center of the table. "May I get you anything else, sir?"

"I feel like getting drunk this evening," Mr. Whitmore declared. "Keep bringing me drinks until I can no longer stand."

Samuel had no desire to watch his friend drink himself into oblivion. He had work that he needed to see to.

Rising, he said, "I'm afraid I need to cut this party short. I need to have a clear head for court tomorrow."

Mr. Whitmore held up a glass. "More for me then."

Esther stopped outside of her stepmother's bedchamber and knocked. The door was opened and Alice greeted her with a smile.

"Good morning, my lady," she said in a hushed voice. "Lady Mather is feeling much better but she just fell back to sleep."

"Will you inform me when she is awake?"

"Of course," Alice said before she closed the door.

Esther was relieved that her stepmother was feeling better. Now she had to ensure that Daniel went nowhere near her.

She headed towards the dining room on the main level and was surprised to see that her father wasn't sitting at the head of the long, rectangular table. He always ate breakfast at the same time, every day. It was like clockwork. So where was he?

Walking over to the buffet, she picked up a plate and piled her plate with food. She sat down and reached for the newssheets that sat untouched on the table. She opened the newssheets to the Society page and began to read the articles. There was nothing that sparked her attention so she placed the newssheets down and focused on her food.

Gibson stepped into the room. "Lady Bedlington has come to call, my lady. Are you available to receive her?"

Fearing she'd misheard him, she asked, "Pardon? Who has come to call?"

"Lady Bedlington," Gibson replied in a louder voice.

Esther stared at Gibson, unsure of what she should do. Yes, she was curious as to why Lady Bedlington was coming to call, but she truly did not want to speak to the woman that held Samuel's heart.

"My lady?" Gibson asked in a concerned voice. "What would you have me do?"

She forced a smile to her lips. "Please show Lady Bedlington to the drawing room and inform her that I will be there shortly."

"Very good."

After the butler left, she rose and walked over to the mirror that hung along the back wall. She smoothed back her blonde hair and wished she had done more to it than just have it pulled back into a loose chignon at the base of her neck. Furthermore, she was wearing a simple cotton gown because she hadn't anticipated callers at this hour. But it was too late for her to change now.

Esther walked out of the dining room and across the entry hall. She felt as if her feet were made of lead as she approached the drawing room. Why was Lady Bedlington here? They weren't friends. They weren't even in the same social circles. The only thing they had in common was Samuel.

Surely Lady Bedlington did not come to talk about him? But why else could she be here?

She stepped into the drawing room and saw Lady Bedlington standing in the center of the room. Her hair was neatly coiffed with pearls running throughout and she was dressed in a dark blue afternoon gown. A diamond necklace hung low around her neck.

Trying not to compare herself to the well-put-together Lady Bedlington, Esther greeted her guest. "Good morning," she said.

Lady Bedlington smiled, but it did not appear genuine. Her eyes perused the length of Esther and she saw she came up lacking. "Thank you for receiving me at this early hour," she responded, her words lacking any warmth.

Well, this was not going well.

Esther gestured towards the settees. "Would you care to sit and have a cup of tea?"

"I suppose one cup will not hurt," Lady Bedlington replied as she glided to sit on the proffered settee.

Once her guest was seated, Esther sat across from the

woman and poured two cups of tea. She placed the teapot down and extended a cup and saucer to Lady Bedlington.

They both began to sip their tea and neither one spoke. Esther had nothing to say to this woman and felt no need to attempt idle chit-chat.

Lady Bedlington cleared her throat as she lowered the cup to her lap. "You must be wondering why I am here."

"I have been," Esther admitted.

"You may not know this, but Samuel came to see me a couple days ago," Lady Bedlington started.

Esther arched an eyebrow. She didn't want to make this easy on her. "I assume this was when you asked to be his mistress."

Lady Bedlington looked displeased by her remark. "I see that he told you about our private conversation."

"He did."

"Samuel- at least, my Samuel- preferred discretion over anything else," Lady Bedlington said. "I am surprised that he is telling just anyone about what we discussed."

Esther's back grew rigid at that vaguely veiled insult. "I am not just 'anyone.'"

Lady Bedlington dismissively waved her hand in front of her. "Of course, you misunderstood me. It is early so I do not fault you."

She understood Lady Bedlington perfectly and had not misinterpreted the situation. This woman was trying to belittle her and she refused to be insulted in her own home.

"What is it that you want?" Esther asked.

Lady Bedlington nodded approvingly. "May I speak freely?"

"I would prefer it."

"Good, as would I," Lady Bedlington said. "You and Samuel are adorable, really, but you must know that it won't ever last. He is in love with me, and I am in love with him."

"Are you now?" Esther asked as she attempted to hide the

displeasure in her voice. "I only ask because you are practically engaged to Lord Leyburn."

"That is true, but it does not diminish my feelings for Samuel."

"Just so we are clear- you would rather enter a loveless marriage than marry Samuel?"

Lady Bedlington leaned forward and placed her cup and saucer onto the tray. "You are a smart girl. We must fight for our places in Society and I cannot do that from the bottom up."

"Samuel is hardly at the bottom."

"Once he inherits, he will only be a viscount," Lady Bedlington said. "That does not suit me or the life I have envisioned. But it is sweet that you are willing to take him as he is."

Esther tightened the hold on her saucer. "None of this explains why you are here," she said, her words tight.

Lady Bedlington's mouth smiled, but her face did not. It was not a smile that she trusted. "I was hoping we could come to an understanding."

"Meaning?"

"It is clear that Samuel has some affection for you and I encourage that, but his heart will never belong to you," Lady Bedlington said. "Quite frankly, you are not his type."

"His type?" she asked.

"There is no denying you are beautiful, in a nontraditional sense, but you will never be enough for him."

Esther pursed her lips together. "And you are?"

"I know Samuel, better than you do," Lady Bedlington replied. "I take no issue in your marrying him. But know this, I will never be far away."

"Samuel has said nothing about marriage to me," Esther said.

"No?" Lady Bedlington asked. "Well, if you agree to this agreement, then I will be happy to encourage him to offer for you. We could learn to coexist with one another. What do you say?"

Esther couldn't believe what Lady Bedlington was saying. The woman had some audacity to come into her home and say such ridiculous things. She placed the teacup down onto the table and rose. "It is time for you to go."

Rising, Lady Bedlington stuck her nose up at her. "I have seen the way you look at Samuel but you are wasting your time. He loves me, not you."

"I don't care who Samuel loves. I just want him to be happy."

Lady Bedlington let out a shrill laugh. "Happy?" she asked. "You have been reading far too many fairy tales. Life is to be endured, not enjoyed."

"I'm sorry you feel that way."

Taking a step closer to her, Lady Bedlington lowered her voice. "You may think you are better than me, but you have no idea what I have had to give up to get where I am."

Esther held her gaze with determination. "I don't think I am better than you but I do pity you."

"Pity me?" Lady Bedlington asked with a scoff. "Whatever for?"

"I will only marry a man who loves me and who I love in return. I won't settle for anything less than that."

"That is adorable that you think so, but that isn't real life. Surely, you are not that naïve?" Lady Bedlington mocked.

Esther kept her head held high, refusing to show any hint of vulnerability. "I would rather believe that love trumps all than live a lie with a man that I couldn't love."

Lady Bedlington narrowed her eyes. "I just want to be clear. Samuel is mine. He will always be mine, no matter what you say or do."

"If you really loved Samuel, you would have chosen him over status," Esther said, returning her ire. Two could play this game.

"I thought I would forget about him over time, but the longing in my heart has only increased tenfold," Lady Bedlington revealed. "I won't lose him."

"You can't lose what you don't have," Esther stated.

Lady Bedlington's face grew hard, and she knew her words had hit their mark. "Listen, you little chit—"

Anette's voice came from the doorway, interrupting their conversation. "I would choose your next words carefully or I will shoot you."

Esther turned her head to see Anette pointing a pistol at Lady Bedlington.

"Good heavens, put that down before someone gets shot," Lady Bedlington cried.

Anette's lips twitched. "That is what I am hoping will happen."

"Well, I never," Lady Bedlington declared. "I will go but heed my words, Lady Esther."

Esther watched as Lady Bedlington approached Anette and awkwardly moved around her to depart.

She moved to the window and watched as Lady Bedlington stepped into her coach. The driver flicked the reins and urged the team forward.

Anette brought the pistol to her side as she asked, "Are you all right, Esther?"

"Is she right?" she asked with dread in her voice. "Will Samuel always love her?"

"I wouldn't believe a word she said."

Esther turned to face her friend. "But it is true, isn't it?" she asked. "Samuel has loved her since he first met her. That kind of love does not just go away."

"I have seen the way Samuel looks at you. He cares for you."

"That is a far cry from love."

Walking further into the room, Anette said, "You mustn't

let Lady Bedlington get to you. She is a conniving woman who will say or do anything to get ahead."

Esther glanced down at the pistol. "Was a pistol truly necessary?"

"I thought it was called for, given the circumstances," Anette replied as she returned it to the reticule that hung around her wrist. "After all, she was threatening you."

Esther dropped down onto the settee. "Lady Bedlington is awful, just awful," she declared. "What does Samuel see in her?"

Anette shrugged. "I don't even find her that beautiful. She has a large nose."

"Her nose is perfectly proportional to her head."

"Then it must be her large head that I take issue with."

A giggle escaped Esther's lips. "That is terrible of you to say."

"I'm not wrong." Anette came to sit down next to her on the settee and asked, "What are you going to do?"

"I don't know what I can do," Esther replied. "Samuel loves Lady Bedlington and I must accept that. Even if he does offer for me, I refuse to go along with her proposed arrangement."

"So you are giving up?"

"Give up what?" she asked. "Samuel is not mine. He will never be mine, according to Lady Bedlington."

"Esther..." Anette attempted.

Esther shook her head, stilling her friend's words. "This is my fault for thinking I had a chance with him."

"You *do* have a chance," Anette asserted. "Yesterday, I walked in on you two almost kissing. I know that meant something."

Esther felt tears burn in the back of her eyes. "You must have been mistaken."

Alice stepped into the room and announced, "Lady Mather is awake and is asking for you, my lady."

She swiped at the tears that were threatening to fall. "Inform her that I will be up momentarily."

Alice looked unsure. "Are you well?"

"I will be," Esther assured her.

With a parting look that expressed concern, Alice left the drawing room.

Esther rose. "I should not keep Susanna waiting," she said, hoping her words sounded more confident than she felt. "Did I tell you that we are reading *Gulliver's Travels*?"

Rising, Anette reached out and placed her hand on Esther's sleeve. "You are worthy of being loved. I do not want you to think any differently."

"I know, but the person I love does not share my sentiment."

Anette's eyes widened in surprise. "You love him?"

"It hardly matters now if I do or not," Esther said as she took a step back. "Thank you for what you did with Lady Bedlington."

"If you want me to shoot her——"

Esther cut her off. "Absolutely not! No one deserves to be shot."

"What about Daniel?"

She thought about it for a moment. "I suppose he deserves to be shot but not in a place that would kill him."

"Understood," Anette said with a decisive bob of her head.

Esther gave her friend a pointed look. "I was joking."

"So was I," Anette responded in a less than convincing manner.

"Come, I will walk you out."

As they walked towards the main door, Anette glanced over and said, "I found the perfect name for the villain in my book. How does Lady Bedlington sound?"

She laughed. "It is perfect."

Chapter Seventeen

After a long morning in court, Samuel sat at his desk in his office as he attempted to complete all the tasks that required his immediate attention.

He put the quill down next to the ink pot and rubbed his eyes. He was tired, but nothing would keep him from calling on Lady Esther in a few short hours. She was starting to occupy entirely too much of his thoughts. Which was starting to pose a problem. He liked her, there was no denying that, and his feelings only intensified the more he spent time with her.

Botheration. It was a complicated mess that he found himself in. They were supposed to form a pretend arrangement, but he went and fell for her. It wouldn't be a problem if Esther considered him anything more than just a friend.

Mr. Allen spoke up from his desk in the corner. "Have you had a chance to review Larson's case files?"

Samuel reached for a file and opened it. "I will do so now."

The door to his office opened and Lord Rushcliffe stepped into the room. He was dressed in a tattered jacket and trousers, his hair was disheveled and he wore no top hat. It was a far cry from his usual appearance now that he had inherited his title.

Mr. Allen rose. "What is it that you want?" he asked, his words firm. It was evident by his tone that he did not realize he was addressing a lord.

Rather than take offense, Rushcliffe looked amused. "I have come to speak to Mr. Moore."

"Did you make an appointment?" Mr. Allen pressed.

"No."

Mr. Allen opened his mouth to no doubt turn Rushcliffe away but Samuel spoke first. "Lord Rushcliffe does not require an appointment to speak to me."

With wide eyes, Mr. Allen asked, "This is Lord Rushcliffe?"

"It is, and I would like some privacy when I speak to him," Samuel replied. "Would you mind stepping out for a moment?"

"Do you not want me to take notes?" Mr. Allen asked.

"That won't be necessary."

Mr. Allen bobbed his head. "Yes, sir." He picked up some files from his desk. "I will just have these delivered while you speak to Lord Rushcliffe."

After his secretary departed from the office, Samuel gave Rushcliffe an expectant look. "I must assume that you already have news for me."

Rushcliffe approached his desk and sat down on an upholstered armchair. "Mr. Fairchild is a rake and is heavily in debt."

"Define 'heavily,'" he said.

"If he wasn't the heir presumptive of Lord Mather, he would have been thrown into debtor's prison a long time ago."

"That would give him motive to want to rid Lady Mather of her baby."

Rushcliffe ran a hand through his hair. "There is more,"

he revealed. "Mr. Fairchild's mistress, Miss Watson, died under suspicious circumstances. She had just announced that she was increasing and she passed away the following week."

"Did the coroner open up an investigation?"

"He did, and he concluded that she had liver failure," Rushcliffe replied. "It makes me suspect that Lady Mather wasn't the first person he poisoned with pennyroyal."

Samuel leaned back in his seat as he considered Rushcliffe's words. It was entirely probable that Mr. Fairchild killed his mistress but they couldn't prove it.

"I know what you are thinking and we can't prove it… yet," Rushcliffe said. "Give me more time and I will see what I can come up with."

"It does appear as if Mr. Fairchild has no intention of killing Lady Mather, just her baby."

"Or perhaps Lady Mather didn't ingest enough of the plant," Rushcliffe remarked. "Regardless, we need to ensure that Lady Mather is protected from Mr. Fairchild."

"And Lady Esther."

Rushcliffe rose. "That goes without saying," he said. "If you will excuse me, I have things I need to see to."

"Thank you for what you've done."

"Don't thank me yet," Rushcliffe said. "I don't intend to stop until Mr. Fairchild is behind bars or transported."

"That is the outcome I desire as well."

Rushcliffe walked over to the door and stopped. He turned back around. "A bit of unsolicited advice," he started. "Don't overthink what you have with Lady Esther. Just trust your heart."

"My heart has been wrong before."

"No, it hasn't been. Because everything that you have experienced before, both good and bad, has prepared you for this precise moment."

Samuel decided to be honest with his friend. "We were

supposed to pretend that we formed an attachment. None of this was real."

If Rushcliffe was surprised by what Samuel had just revealed, he didn't show it. Instead, he said, "Some of the greatest moments in our lives often come because everything fell apart. That is when we pick ourselves back up and embrace what we have been given."

"You are rather good at giving advice."

Rushcliffe's eyes held compassion. "I have been where you are and I do not envy you. You have everything within your grasp but are too afraid of making a misstep."

"I have fallen in love before and it went horribly wrong."

"Your mistake was not falling in love but falling in love with the wrong person. Don't be too hard on yourself."

Samuel glanced at the large window that ran along the back wall before saying, "You are right. I don't want to make a misstep with Esther. I don't know what we have, but it is special."

Rushcliffe smirked. "I think the first step is stop pretending to pursue her and show her that you are worthy of her affection."

"You are right," Samuel said, rising. "I am going to tell her how I feel."

"Good," Rushcliffe praised.

Samuel stepped around his desk and reached for his top hat on the hook near the door. "This shouldn't be too difficult. I will just rationally explain why I should be her suitor."

Rushcliffe chuckled. "I see you do not speak from the heart very often. I should warn you that it leaves you tongue-tied."

"Need I remind you that I argue for a living?"

"My apologies," Rushcliffe said with a knowing smile. "I should never have doubted you."

After they departed from the office, Mr. Moore locked the door and followed Rushcliffe out of the building.

Samuel put his hand up to hail a hackney. "Want to share a hackney?"

Rushcliffe shoved his hands in his pockets. "No, I still need to investigate Mr. Fairchild further before I am satisfied," he replied before he started walking down the pavement.

The hackney came to a stop and Samuel shouted up the address to the driver. Then he stepped into the musty smelling coach. His boots stuck to the floor and the fabric on the bench was terribly worn.

He started rehearsing what he intended to say to Lady Esther and it wasn't long before he arrived at her townhouse.

After paying the driver, he approached the main door and knocked.

The door opened and the butler eyed him curiously. "May I help you?" he asked, as if he hadn't asked the same question every time he had called upon Lady Esther.

"Is Lady Esther available for callers?"

The butler looked hesitant but eventually opened the door. "Do come in and I will see if she is available."

Samuel stepped into the entry hall and waited as the butler disappeared into the drawing room, reemerging a moment later.

"Lady Esther will see you," the butler announced.

He didn't need to be told twice and he headed into the drawing room. He saw Lady Esther was sitting next to her stepmother, but it was the expression on her face that caused him to pause. It held sadness, pain. And he had the sudden desire to wipe it all away.

He bowed. "Lady Esther," he greeted. "Lady Mather."

Lady Mather offered him a polite smile. "Mr. Moore, what a pleasure to see you." She nudged Esther's arm. "Isn't it, Esther?"

Esther's eyes grew downcast. "It is a most pleasurable surprise." Her words lacked any real conviction.

Samuel wanted to demand that Esther tell him what was

wrong, but it wasn't his place to do so. He couldn't force her to confide in him. But he would still try.

"Would you have any objections to touring the gardens with me?" Samuel asked.

Esther's eyes shot up. "I do not think that is a good idea."

"May I ask why?"

She pressed her lips before saying, "It looks as if it is about to rain."

Samuel glanced at the window where the sun was streaming through. There was not even a cloud in the sky. "I think we could take our chances."

"What of the birds?" Esther asked. "They might attack us."

"Are the birds in your gardens usually aggressive?"

With a shake of her head, Esther replied, "No, but they might take issue since they are mating."

Samuel lifted his brow as Lady Mather declared, "What a ridiculous thing to say. Besides, we do not bring up mating around our callers."

"My apologies," Esther said, rising. "Allow me to go retrieve my bonnet. I will be back shortly."

She walked out of the room without sparing him a glance. What had happened between them? Was she upset that he had almost kissed her? If so, this did not bode well for him.

Lady Mather's voice drew back his attention. "I should warn you that Esther has been rather despondent since this morning."

"Is there a particular reason why?"

"I'm afraid she won't speak to me about it," Lady Mather said. "Perhaps you will have better luck than I did."

"I hope so," he responded.

Esther walked back into the room with a blue bonnet on her head. She met his gaze but quickly averted her eyes. This was definitely not going well.

He approached her and offered his arm. He could see the

hesitancy in her eyes but she eventually placed her hand onto his sleeve.

As he led her towards the rear of the townhouse, he leaned in and teased, "I hope your bonnet will protect you from any aggressive birds we encounter."

"I doubt it," she responded, looking away.

They exited the townhouse and started walking down one of the paths. She removed her hand and clasped it with the other in front of her.

"The weather is particularly lovely today, is it not?" he asked. He couldn't believe he was resorting to asking about the weather.

"It is."

Samuel couldn't take it any longer. Something was wrong and he needed to fix it. He didn't want an aloof Esther. That is not the lovely woman he was starting to fall in love with.

He placed a hand on her sleeve and turned her to face him. "Esther, please, tell me what I did wrong so I can apologize."

Esther's eyes remained on the lapels of his jacket. "You did nothing wrong," she murmured.

"Then what is it?"

Slowly, she brought her gaze up to meet his. Her eyes shone with tears as her quivering voice said, "I propose that we stop seeing one another."

Esther saw the confusion on Samuel's face as she fought with herself to even say those words. She didn't want to hurt him, but this was for the best. Just knowing that caused her heart to ache and she knew she would never love another as much as she loved him.

She loved him. How could she not? He believed in her,

supported her. But his heart would always belong to another. She couldn't stand the thought of seeing him every day, and not being able to tell him how she felt.

Lady Bedlington had managed to get into her head and she couldn't seem to convince herself that the wicked woman was wrong.

Esther expected Samuel to be angry, but what she didn't expect was him to reply with the simple word, "No."

She furrowed her brow. "No?" Could he just say that?

Samuel took a step closer to her. "I reject your proposal. I don't intend to stop seeing you."

"It is for the best," she attempted.

"Says who?"

Esther lowered her gaze and replied, "You are a good man, but…" Her words stilled when he put his finger under her chin, slowly lifting it until her eyes met his.

"Look me in the eyes and tell me that you don't want anything to do with me," he said. "If you do, I will obey and walk away."

Esther bit her lower lip as she tried to find the strength to say those words. She needed to say them, but she couldn't seem to do it. Not when he was looking at her like that. It was the way that every woman wanted to be looked at by a man.

A boyish grin came to his lips. "Do you want to know what I think?"

She nodded slowly. She very much wanted to know what he thought. Drats. Why did his opinion matter so much to her?

"I don't think you want to be rid of me," Samuel said. His words soft, intimate.

He was right. If she was smart, she would send him on his way. But she couldn't say those words. She wanted him in her life, however small.

Samuel's finger started to caress her chin and she was lost

in his touch. "But I don't want to force myself upon you. This needs to be your decision. Do you want me to go?"

Esther shook her head. "No, I want you to stay."

His smile grew. "Was that so hard to admit?"

He had no idea how hard it was for her to even formulate words when he was touching her like that.

Samuel remained close but dropped his hand. "Now, tell me, what has you so upset?"

Shifting her gaze away from him, she responded, "I don't want to talk about it."

"Very well," he said. "We can continue to discuss the weather. Or we can discuss the various flowers that are planted in the gardens."

Esther gave him an amused look. "Are you acquainted with the various types of flowers?"

"I am." Samuel pointed towards some flowers along the path and shared, "Those are beautiful delphiniums."

"Peach-leaved bellflowers," she corrected.

"My mistake," he said. "They look very similar."

Esther laughed. "No, they don't."

Samuel's face softened. "There is the laugh that I so enjoy hearing," he said. "You should laugh more often."

"I do, when the situation warrants it."

"And this particular situation warrants it?"

"It does when you confuse a delphinium with a peach-leaved bellflower."

"It is a common mistake."

Esther laughed again. "I assure you that it is not."

Samuel held her gaze, his eyes pleading with her. "I can't fix what is wrong if you don't confide in me."

"You can't fix this."

"Let me try, please," he said.

Esther knew it was only fair to tell him about Lady Bedlington. But how would he react? That is what she was afraid of. What if he sided with Lady Bedlington?

In a voice that was far from steady, she admitted, "Lady Bedlington came to visit me today."

"Phoebe visited you?" he asked. "For what purpose?"

She took a deep breath. This was it. She was about to find out how much or little she meant to him. "Lady Bedlington was mistakenly under the impression that we were to be married and she wanted to come to an understanding between us."

"An understanding? I don't understand."

"She wanted me to accept the fact that she would be your mistress, even after we were married."

Samuel's jaw clenched. "I see, and what did you say?"

"I told her that we had no intention of marrying and that you were free to do as you chose," Esther replied.

He took a step back before he turned around, muttering curse words under his breath. He didn't appear pleased, but who was he upset with? Her or Phoebe?

"Samuel?" Esther asked.

It was a long moment before he turned back to face her, holding a seriousness she had never seen before. "What Phoebe did was wrong, and I am sorry."

"You have no need to apologize for her."

"I feel as if I must," Samuel said. "She put you in an impossible situation and you handled it with grace and dignity."

With the slightest wince, she admitted, "That isn't true. I may have said some harsh words to her."

He grinned. "I'm glad to hear that. I do believe she could stand to hear more of them."

"So you aren't mad at me?"

"Why would I be mad at you?" he asked. "It is Phoebe that I am upset with. As I have told her, I would never take her as a mistress."

Esther let out a sigh of relief. "I am glad to hear that."

"For her to insult you in such a fashion is unforgiveable,"

Samuel said, his voice growing stern. "She had no right to make you feel inferior, in any way."

"She did no such thing. In fact, Miss Bolingbroke threatened her with a pistol when she refused to leave."

His brow shot up. "A pistol?"

"Anette carries one in her reticule," Esther explained. "I always thought it was foolish of her until today."

"I shall have to thank Miss Bolingbroke the next time I see her then." He paused. "But something you said did get me to thinking."

"What was that, because I have said many profound things today?" she joked.

Eyeing her closely, he asked, "What if we were to marry?"

Her mouth dropped but she quickly recovered. "I beg your pardon?" Did she dare hope that he did have feelings for her?

Placing his hands on her shoulders, he said, "Hear me out before you say no."

Unsure of where this was going, Esther decided to let him speak and hope she liked what he had to say.

Samuel appeared to be anxious, contrasting with his usual demeanor. "I care for you and I hope that you care for me," he started.

Feeling bold, she admitted, "I do care for you."

He looked relieved. "Wonderful. Since we both care for one another, it is only logical for us to get married."

"Logical?" Is that the type of marriage that he wanted-logical? She had seen the effects of a logical marriage with her father and stepmother. She wanted more- no, she *needed* more.

"Yes, we will figure out everything else as we go along," Samuel said. "I know it isn't the love match that you wanted, but with time, it might cultivate."

"Might?" How did that one simple word cause her heart to drop?

Samuel nodded. "Yes, you are a beautiful young woman

and I am in need of a wife." He stopped his speech and gave her a hopeful look.

Esther didn't quite know what to say. He admitted that he didn't love her, but he had said he cared for her. Could she marry him and hope that it turned into a love match? What if it didn't? Would she spend her days pining after a man, hoping to convince him to love her?

That was a risk that she was not willing to take.

Shrugging off his hands from her shoulders, Esther said, "I'm sorry, but I must turn down your offer."

"Why?" he asked.

"I have made no secret that I want a love match," Esther replied with a stubborn tilt of her chin. "A marriage of convenience does not tempt me."

As Samuel opened his mouth to respond, her father's voice came from behind them. "What is the meaning of this?"

Esther turned to face her father and saw that he had an irate look on his face. "What is wrong, Father?"

"You two are being entirely too familiar with one another," her father replied. "Do show some constraint or else I will insist you two are married by special license at once."

"Nothing untoward happened—" Samuel started.

Her father scoffed, stilling Samuel's words. "Come now, I know what I saw from the window of my study." He waved his hand at her. "Come along, young lady. If you two wish to finish this conversation, you may do so in the drawing room with Susanna as your chaperone."

Esther snuck a glance at Samuel before saying, "I do not think that will be necessary."

Samuel looked displeased by her words but he remained silent.

As they followed her father into the townhouse, she didn't speak as she retreated to her thoughts. What had Samuel been thinking when he had offered for her? It wasn't even a proper one. It seemed rushed and lacked any real conviction.

But she knew why. It was because he was still in love with Lady Bedlington. That had to be it. Although he had sounded sincere when he said that he wouldn't take her as a mistress. She wanted to believe him, but she was scared. No, she was wise to turn him down. She didn't want to spend the rest of her life being compared to Lady Bedlington.

Chapter Eighteen

Samuel was a fool. A complete and utter fool. He had blundered through his proposal to Esther and she had turned him down. Not that he blamed her. He had made a real mess of it. For someone who argued for a living, he had done a terrible job of convincing her that they would suit.

He knew he was already halfway in love with Esther, but he didn't dare admit that to anyone. He had been burned by love before and he was afraid to give his heart to another. He couldn't risk it. Hanging his head, he sighed. Why was he such a coward? He might have lost Esther due to his inability to properly express his feelings.

The coach came to a stop and Samuel opened the door. As he stepped onto the pavement, he stared up at Phoebe's townhouse and dreaded the upcoming conversation. It would be a difficult one, but it needed to be done. He hoped he could keep his anger in check long enough to say the words that needed to be said.

Samuel approached the main door and knocked.

It was a long moment before the door opened and the butler asked, "May I help you, Mr. Moore?"

"I have come to speak to Lady Bedlington," he answered.

With a look of regret, the butler said, "I'm sorry but she isn't taking any callers at the moment."

Samuel was not deterred by the butler's response but rather he buckled down. "Inform Lady Bedlington that I am here. I am sure that she will receive me."

The butler hesitated before tipping his head in acknowledgement. "Give me a moment, sir," he said before closing the door.

The sun was starting to set as he waited for the butler to return. The lack of clouds in the night sky made him think of Esther and how earlier she had tried to come up with the silliest reason not to be alone with him.

Good gads, he hoped he hadn't lost her. He needed her in his life, but it wasn't until now that he was beginning to see how much.

The butler opened the door and stood to the side to allow him entry. "Lady Bedlington will see you in the drawing room."

Samuel felt relieved. He was bound and determined to speak his piece to Phoebe tonight. Frankly, this conversation was long overdue.

He followed the butler into the drawing room and saw Phoebe was elegantly dressed in a silver gown and strands of pearls were draped around her neck. There was no doubt that she was beautiful, but her beauty seemed to pale in comparison to Esther.

He bowed. "Phoebe, thank you for seeing me."

Phoebe smiled. "I must admit that I am pleased that you are here," she said. "I do not have long though since I left dinner to speak to you."

"I assure you that this won't take long."

She sashayed towards him. "I hope this means you have reconsidered my offer."

Phoebe went to touch his cheek but he reached out and grabbed her hand. "My position has not changed."

While she withdrew her hand, she asked, "Then why are you here?" The displeasure was clearly written on her face.

"I understand that you had a conversation with Lady Esther."

"That conversation was meant to be private," Phoebe spat out. "That chit needs to learn some discretion."

Samuel frowned. Had she always been this disagreeable? Or perhaps he had been so blinded with his affection for her that he had failed to see what was right in front of him. "You were out of line and you had no right."

"I had every right," Phoebe declared. "I wanted Lady Esther to know what she was getting into. She deserved to know the truth."

"And, pray tell, what 'truth' was that?"

Phoebe brought her hand up and placed it over his heart. "I love you, Samuel, and I know that you still love me," she replied. "We are meant to be together."

"There was a time that I would have agreed with you, but that has all changed."

"You don't mean that," Phoebe said.

"I do," he replied. "Besides, you intend to marry Lord Leyburn."

"In name only," Phoebe purred. "You are the only man that I love. Lord Leyburn is just an old, boring man."

Samuel glanced down at her hand and responded, "I did love you, but I am not the same man that offered for you years ago."

"No, you are the same man," she asserted. "We can be happy together, if you just give it a chance."

"I'm sorry, but it is time that I let you go... for good this time," Samuel said, taking a step back.

Phoebe stared at him with a crestfallen look on her face as her hand dropped to her side. "Is this because I went to speak to Lady Esther?"

"No, this was a long time coming," he replied.

"Do you intend to marry Lady Esther?"

He nodded. "Yes, if she will have me."

Tears came into Phoebe's eyes. "What if I don't marry Lord Leyburn? We could run away and elope to Gretna Green. I would even be willing to overlook your lowly status."

Samuel shook his head. "There was a time I would have gladly taken you up on that offer, but not anymore. I want more. Frankly, I deserve better."

"But I love you," she whispered.

"You made your choice and now it is time that I made mine," Samuel said.

A deep, irate voice came from the doorway. "I have heard just about enough of this!" he shouted.

Samuel turned his head and saw Lord Leyburn approaching them, his nostrils flaring. He came to a stop next to Phoebe. "The engagement is off," he declared.

Phoebe looked at Lord Leyburn with wide eyes. "But, John—"

He swiped his hand in front of her, stilling her words. "You lied to me," he stated. "You told me that you had no feelings for Mr. Moore."

"I don't," she attempted. "We are just old friends."

"I heard what you said," Lord Leyburn said. "I am not a fool."

Phoebe went to touch the lord but he stepped out of her reach. "You must have misunderstood what I said," she attempted.

Lord Leyburn scoffed. "I will not tolerate dishonesty in a wife."

"This has all just been a big misunderstanding," Phoebe said with a nervous smile. "Give me a chance to explain."

"I don't think I will," Lord Leyburn responded.

Samuel thought it was best if he departed. He had no desire to listen to Phoebe try to weasel her way out of this situation. "I do not think my presence is necessary here any longer."

Lord Leyburn surprised him by saying, "Thank you for coming this evening. You have just saved me from making a terrible mistake."

"John," Phoebe cried out. "Surely you don't mean that?"

"I have never been so sure of anything, Lady Bedlington," Lord Leyburn said. "In fact, I will walk out with Mr. Moore."

Phoebe's face grew hard as she tossed up her arms and declared, "Fine. I don't need either one of you. I will be just fine on my own."

Samuel had heard just about enough and hurried to exit the townhouse. He went to step into his coach but he was stopped by Lord Leyburn's voice.

"Thank you, Mr. Moore," he said. "I wish you luck with Lady Esther."

He turned back to face the aged lord. "Thank you. I am going to need all the help I can get."

Lord Leyburn's eyes grew reflective. "When my wife died, I thought I would never love again, but that changed when I met Lady Bedlington. I fancied myself in love with her, but I am not sure that I ever was," he admitted. "I think I was just caught up by her beautiful face and I overlooked many things that I should have seen as warnings."

Samuel could see the anguish on the lord's face. "It sounds like you loved your wife very much."

"I did. I just wish I had one more day with her," Lord Leyburn said. "It is rather lonely when you have been fortunate enough to have experienced a great love story."

"I can only imagine."

Lord Leyburn gave him a sad smile. "Don't give up on your own love story. I can assure you it is worth everything that you must do to achieve it."

"I shall heed your advice."

"Goodnight, Mr. Moore," Lord Leyburn said before he started walking down the pavement.

Samuel watched his retreating figure and found himself feeling bad for the lord. Lord Leyburn had been tricked by Phoebe, just as he had been before.

As he began to step into his coach, he saw a burly shadowed figure sitting inside.

"Get into the coach," the familiar voice of Lord Rushcliffe ordered.

Samuel sat across from him and closed the door. "How did you know I would be here?"

Rushcliffe smirked. "Please, you are nothing if not predictable," he replied. "I could tell that you needed closure with Lady Bedlington before you offered for Lady Esther."

The coach jerked forward as Samuel revealed, "I already offered for Lady Esther and she turned me down."

"You must have done it wrong then."

"I blundered my way through it and I'm not entirely sure what I said."

Rushcliffe gave him a sympathetic look. "There is nothing more unnerving than offering for the woman you love."

Samuel put his hand up. "I do not love Lady Esther," he lied.

"My mistake," Rushcliffe said. "I just assumed you weren't still in denial."

Frowning, Samuel asked, "What is it that you want?"

Rushcliffe shifted in his seat before saying, "I visited Mr. Fairchild's residence and I found a few vials of what I believe to be pennyroyal."

"You 'visited'?"

"A window may have been left unlocked and I may have entered his home without his knowledge."

Samuel shook his head. "I don't want to know."

"Good, because that is the least of our worries," Rushcliffe said. "Even if we can convince a constable to open an investigation, there is little chance for a conviction without a confession."

"It has been my experience that people who willingly break the law do not like to confess to their crimes."

"Perhaps, but I am working on a plan."

"I hope it is a good one," Samuel said. "I have heard about the plan where you just went and knocked on the door."

"It worked, didn't it?"

Samuel gave him an expectant look. "Well, what is your plan?"

"I need to work out all the particulars, but I will come by later and discuss it with you. Until then, you need to go tell Lord and Lady Mather about Mr. Fairchild. They need to know the truth before he tries to strike again."

"I can do that, assuming I am allowed entry into their townhouse."

"Why wouldn't you?"

"Lady Esther and I didn't part on the best terms," he admitted. "You know, with the botched marriage proposal, and all."

"Just get it done." Rushcliffe took his fist and pounded on the ceiling. "This is where I will get out."

The coach came to a stop and Rushcliffe opened the door. He stepped onto the pavement and disappeared into the darkness of the night.

Samuel was grateful for Rushcliffe's help, but he couldn't help but wonder how many secrets his friend still kept.

Esther sat at the dining table as she picked at her food. She heard the conversation going on around her and she would respond at the appropriate times with a vague response, but she preferred retreating to her own thoughts.

Samuel wanted to marry her because it was "logical." But she didn't want a marriage based upon being the logical choice. She wanted a love match, and she had thought he had wanted the same. So why had he offered for her in the first place?

She was well aware that he loved Lady Bedlington, but she was done trying to earn his affection. He cared for her but that was a far cry from being in love.

Her stepmother's voice drew her attention. "Are you still with us, Esther?"

Without bothering to look up, she replied, "I am."

"It doesn't appear as if that is the case," Susanna said. "You seem like you are far away."

"I am just woolgathering."

"Anything you wish to share?"

Esther brought her head up and saw that Susanna was watching her with concern. "Not particularly," she replied.

Her father wiped his lips with a napkin. "Did Mr. Moore say anything that upset you earlier?"

She stiffened. "We just had a frank conversation." That much was true. She didn't want to reveal anything more than that. Frankly, it was embarrassing.

"You two appeared rather close before I arrived," her father remarked, giving her a pointed look.

"Looks can be deceiving," she muttered.

Susanna spoke up. "We can't help you if you do not tell us what is wrong."

"No one can help me," Esther said.

"Surely it is not as dire as you are making it," her father stated.

Esther decided that the time had come for her to tell her father the truth- the whole truth. It didn't matter anymore. "Mr. Moore and I just pretended to form an attachment. It was all a ruse so I wouldn't have to marry Lord Warley."

Her father's eyes crinkled around the edges. "I assumed as much."

"You knew, this whole time?" Esther asked.

He nodded. "I did, but I had hoped it would turn into something real, despite him being a Whig and all."

Esther placed her fork down onto the plate. "It doesn't matter now. He loves another, and I am just an afterthought."

"Do not sell yourself short," Susanna asserted. "I have seen the way he looks at you."

"He probably just had something in his eye," she said lightly.

Susanna smiled, just as she had intended. "That is not what I meant."

"I know what you meant, but you were wrong. I was wrong," Esther stated. "He may care for me but I want his heart- his whole heart."

"That is no less than you deserve," Susanna said.

Esther offered her stepmother a grateful smile. "Thank you."

Gibson stepped into the dining room with a solemn look on his face. He met her gaze. "I apologize for the interruption, but Mr. Moore has requested a moment of your time, my lady."

"I do not wish to see him. Send him on his way," Esther ordered.

"I tried, but he is rather insistent that he must speak to you," Gibson said.

Esther had no desire to speak to Samuel. He had broken her heart and she needed to learn to move on, without him.

As she opened her mouth, Susanna interjected, "Please send him in and set another plate at the table for him."

Esther stared at her stepmother in disbelief. Hadn't Susanna just been listening to what she had been saying only moments ago?

Susanna met her gaze and said, "Just trust me."

It was only a moment later that Samuel appeared in the doorway with his usual confident stride. Dear heavens, he was handsome. Would she always react that way when she saw him? She hoped not. It was rather inconvenient.

Samuel glanced her way and she realized that she had been caught staring. Drats. She wished that she was better at hiding her emotions. He probably saw right through her, just as he always did.

Susanna gestured towards the seat next to Esther. "Please join us for dinner."

"I don't wish to intrude," Samuel said.

"It is no intrusion," Susanna assured him.

A footman quickly went about preparing a plate setting for Samuel. Why did he have to sit next to her? There was enough room on the other side of the table.

Samuel came around the table and pulled out the chair. After he sat down, he said, "Thank you for allowing me to join you for dinner."

Her father's gruff voice spoke up. "You left us little choice in the matter. Now what is so important that you had to speak to Esther?"

Samuel leaned to the side as a footman served him food. "I do wish to speak to Esther, but I also needed to speak to you and Lady Mather."

"Whatever for?" her father asked. He wasn't going to make it easy on Samuel, and for that, she was grateful.

Shifting in his seat, Samuel leaned closer to her and asked in a hushed voice, "Do you want to tell them or me?"

"About what?" she asked, pretending his nearness wasn't affecting her.

"Daniel."

Esther pressed her lips together. "Are you sure that is wise?"

"I think it is time."

Her father interrupted, "Will someone just tell us what the blazes is going on?"

"Language, dear," Susanna chided.

"We are all adults here," her father responded.

Esther turned her head slightly and she was just inches away from Samuel. The familiar shaving soap that he wore wafted in the room and she realized that was her new favorite smell.

His eyes seemed to plead with her, but she wasn't sure what he was trying to tell her.

She had been so lost in his eyes that she barely heard her father say, "Esther. What did Daniel do now?"

Esther turned her head to meet her father's gaze. She thought it was best if they heard the truth from her. "I think Daniel has been poisoning Susanna with pennyroyal."

Her father's brow shot up. "Do you have any proof of this?"

She opened her mouth to respond but Samuel spoke first. "An investigator that I asked to look into it found some vials at Mr. Fairchild's residence that could be pennyroyal."

"Could be?" her father asked. "I do not like Daniel any more than you do, but that doesn't prove he tried to poison Susanna."

Esther shifted her gaze to Susanna. "You got ill shortly after Daniel gave you a mint ice and after he brought over the biscuits that his cook supposedly made."

"That is true, but it could have just been a coincidence," Susanna attempted.

"I didn't tell you, but Sarah ate the rest of your discarded biscuit and she grew very sick," Esther said. "She had the same symptoms as you."

Susanna pursed her lips. "That is most disconcerting."

"Lady Oxley told me that some people use pennyroyal as a way to lose a baby," Esther shared.

"You told Lady Oxley about your suspicions before you

told us?" Susanna asked as she rubbed her increasing stomach.

"I did, but only because she is proficient at botany. I thought she might be able to give me some insight on what poison Daniel is using," Esther defended.

Samuel cleared his throat. "There is more," he said.

"How could there be more?" her father asked.

"Daniel is heavily in debt and should be in debtor's prison," Samuel said. "The only leverage he has right now is that he is your heir presumptive."

Her father shoved back his chair and shouted, "Gibson! Retrieve my dueling pistols. This deceit will not go unpunished."

"Father, you cannot be serious!" Esther demanded. This was the precise outcome that she feared. Her father's temper was not one to be stoked.

The look in her father's eyes changed, becoming distant and unmoving, and she shuddered to think of what he might do next. "I have never been more serious."

In a calm voice, Samuel said, "If you die, then Daniel is one step closer to inheriting your estate. What if Susanna doesn't bear a son? Where would that leave all of you?"

Her father frowned. "You make a good point, but I refuse to let him get away with this," he said. "Should we send for the constable?"

"We might be able to get him arrested but a good barrister would argue that all the evidence is circumstantial. At least, that is what I would argue," Samuel explained. "We need to get him to confess."

"How do we do that?" Susanna asked.

"That is what we are trying to figure out right now," Samuel said.

Her father returned to his seat. "Who is 'we,' exactly?"

"It is best that you don't know, at least for the time being,"

Samuel replied. "The man I asked to help investigate is someone who values his privacy."

"And you expect us to trust this person blindly?"

Samuel bobbed his head. "I trust him, and if you value Susanna's life, you would, too."

Her father reached for his wife's hand and he responded, "All right. What would you have us do?"

"Do not let Daniel anywhere near Susanna and, this goes without saying, but do not accept any food from him," Samuel advised.

"Understood," her father said. "I should be surprised that Daniel would resort to such a dirty tactic, but I am not. He is not a very scrupulous man."

Susanna pushed back her chair and rose. "I need to go lie down for a moment. This is just too much for me to take in."

The men in the room promptly stood and Esther's father hurried to Susanna's side. "Allow me to help you," he said, putting his arm around her.

"Thank you," Susanna acknowledged.

As her father escorted his wife out of the room, he glanced over his shoulder and shared, "I will be just a moment. Do not make yourselves comfortable."

Her father had just departed from the dining room when Samuel shifted in his seat to face her. He stared at her with an intensity she had never seen before, and maybe, just maybe, it was longing?

"Esther," he started, "I want to apologize for what I said earlier. I did a terrible job of explaining everything."

"No, I think you stated it plainly enough," Esther said.

"I care for you and I never intended to hurt you."

There were those words again- "I care for you." There was no mention of love. She was trying to appear indifferent but her heart was shattering.

Esther pushed back her chair and went to rise. "I'm sorry, but I cannot... I will not... have this conversation again."

Samuel placed his hand on her sleeve, stilling her. "Will you not just hear me out?" he half-asked, half-pleaded.

"I believe I did so earlier today and you told me that you wanted to marry me because it was 'logical.'"

He had the decency to look ashamed. "I did, but I was wrong to do so."

Rising, Esther said, "At least we can agree on something." She wasn't ready to have this conversation with Samuel. Frankly, she wasn't sure if she would ever be ready. She was trying to be strong, but with every word that he uttered, her strength was waning.

Samuel moved to stand in front of her. He put his hands up as if he were going to touch her but stopped himself. "I went and saw Phoebe today."

That was the wrong thing to say. She had no desire to hear anything about Lady Bedlington. She turned to leave, but his next words stopped her.

"I told her I wanted nothing to do with her, ever again," he revealed. "What she said and did was wrong."

"How did she react to that?" The little she knew about Lady Bedlington made her assume that she did not respond favorably.

Samuel shrugged. "I cared little about her objections. I just went to say my piece and left."

Feeling compassion for his plight, she said, "I'm sorry. That must have been hard on you."

"Surprisingly, it was much easier than I expected," Samuel admitted. "It was a long time overdue."

"I know how much she meant to you."

Samuel reached for her hand and gently caressed it. "Not nearly as much as you mean to me."

Esther's heart took flight as he uttered those words. Did she dare believe him or was he just trying to be charming?

"You are beautiful, Esther, simply beautiful," he said as his eyes perused her face.

His words were spoken with such sincerity that she believed him. He had always made her feel beautiful, with his subtle glances and encouraging words. But that still did not mean there could be a future between them.

Her father let out a deep sigh from next to them, causing Samuel to release her hand and take a step back. "I was only gone for a moment," he said. "Perhaps I was unwise to leave you two alone."

Samuel turned towards her father. "I'm sorry, my lord, I was just trying to press my suit with your daughter."

"I think you managed to accomplish that quite nicely," her father muttered. "But do keep your hands to yourself from now on."

Gibson stepped into the room and said, "Lord Rushcliffe would like a—"

Lord Rushcliffe strode into the room, not waiting to be invited or announced. "I need to speak to everyone." He glanced around the room. "Where is Lady Mather?"

"She is resting," her father replied. "What is the meaning of barging into my home, Rushcliffe?"

"I will explain in the privacy of your study," Lord Rushcliffe said before departing from the dining room.

Her father looked baffled. "Do we follow him?"

"I think that would be wise," Samuel said as he offered Esther his arm. "May I escort you, my dear?"

My dear.

Esther didn't think she had ever heard anything so sweet, or so powerful, as those simple words. As she placed her hand on his sleeve, she wanted to believe that this was real. That he loved her, and all would be well. But he didn't love her.

And her heart broke all over again.

Chapter Nineteen

As Samuel escorted Esther into the study, he knew with a certainty that he had fallen in love with her. How could he not? She made him laugh, cry, and he wanted to be the man that was worthy of her.

But now he had to convince her that he was the one for her. Which was proving to be an impossible task since they kept getting interrupted. He just wanted to whisk her away and beg her to take a chance on him. Would she even listen to him after his last bungled attempt?

He led Esther into the study and saw Lord Rushcliffe was standing by the mantel with Lord Roswell, conversing in hushed tones.

"What is Roswell doing here?" Samuel asked.

Rushcliffe gestured towards the settees. "Have a seat and we will explain."

Samuel assisted Esther to the settee and waited until she sat down before he claimed the seat next to her.

Lord Mather sat down across from them and he had a disgruntled look on his face. "I do not like to be ordered around in my own home."

"I assure you that you will want to hear us out," Rushcliffe said. "It is a matter of life or death for your wife."

"Then out with it," Lord Mather growled.

Roswell spoke up. "Rushcliffe came to me with a vial, and we were able to confirm that it is a match for pennyroyal."

Lord Mather jumped up from his seat. "We have the proof now. Can we send for the constable?"

"Not yet," Rushcliffe replied.

"Whyever not?" Lord Mather asked in disbelief.

"Because we have discovered that Mr. Fairchild isn't content with pennyroyal anymore," Roswell said. "He intends to kill Lady Mather with arsenic."

Esther gasped. "How do you know this?"

"We were able to find the apothecary that created the pennyroyal oil for Mr. Fairchild, and we discovered that he recently purchased a high dose of arsenic," Rushcliffe revealed. "Mr. Fairchild claims that he was using it to kill the rats in his hunting lodge."

"What if he was telling the truth?" Samuel asked.

"We thought that, as well, so we did a little digging at his solicitor's office and we discovered he sold his hunting lodge to settle some debts," Roswell said.

Samuel lifted his brow. "The solicitor informed you of this?"

"Not exactly," Roswell replied. "He wasn't forthcoming with the information so we politely asked to see his files."

"Politely?" Samuel questioned.

"Threatened might be a better word," Roswell said with a smirk. "But I assure you that it was absolutely necessary."

Lord Mather crossed his arms over his chest. "If what you are saying is true, we need to protect Susanna."

"We have every intention of doing so," Rushcliffe said.

"No offense, Lord Rushcliffe, but why should I trust you? Or Lord Roswell for that matter?" Lord Mather asked.

Rushcliffe's gaze grew steadfast. "Because if you choose to

wait for the constable's arrival, your wife will already be dead."

"How do you know this?"

"Mr. Fairchild is determined to remain your heir and is willing to do anything necessary for that to happen," Rushcliffe explained.

"And how, pray tell, do you intend to stop Daniel from harming my wife?" Lord Mather demanded.

"That is simple." Rushcliffe hesitated before saying, "We are going to use Lady Esther as a decoy."

Lord Mather's brow shot up. "Absolutely not!"

Putting his hand up, Rushcliffe said, "Hear me out."

"No, this is madness," Lord Mather declared as he walked over to his desk. He slid open a drawer and pulled out his dueling pistols. "I will just ensure Susanna is protected. I am more than capable of doing that."

Roswell gave him a knowing look. "Do you truly think Mr. Fairchild is working alone?" he asked. "He won't strike until he is sure that Lady Mather is alone and unprotected."

"Who is he working with?" Lord Mather inquired.

"Our best guess is that he is working with one of your servants," Roswell said.

"Then I will dismiss the lot of them," Lord Mather stated.

Rushcliffe shook his head. "If you did do something so foolish, then you will let Mr. Fairchild know that you are onto him."

Lord Mather came around his desk and asked in exasperation, "So you just want me to do nothing?"

"Yes, that is right." Rushcliffe addressed Esther. "We need your help for this plan to work."

Esther squared her shoulders, exuding confidence and determination. How could he not love this woman, Samuel thought. "What do you want me to do?" she asked.

Rushcliffe nodded in approval. "You are going to act as a

decoy for your stepmother," he said. "In the dark, Mr. Fairchild won't be able to tell the difference."

Roswell stepped away from the mantel and revealed, "We suspect that Mr. Fairchild will enter Lady Mather's room and slip the arsenic into her tea."

"Then I will place guards outside of Lady Mather's bedchamber," Lord Mather interjected.

"We need to catch Mr. Fairchild in the act if we want a conviction," Rushcliffe explained. "Up until now, we don't have enough proof to have him transported."

Roswell walked over to the drink cart and picked up a decanter. "Furthermore, if you want Parliament to remove him as your heir, you will need to secure a conviction."

"I care more about my daughter than a conviction," Lord Mather declared.

Esther shifted in her seat to face her father. "I can do this, Father," she asserted. "It is not as if I am going to partake of the tea."

"Heavens, no!" Roswell exclaimed. "Besides, we will be hiding in the room to catch Mr. Fairchild in the act."

Lord Mather placed the pistol down onto the desk and demanded, "You still haven't explained why I should trust you two when there is so much at stake."

Rushcliffe put his hands out. "I know you are scared, but this is not the first time I have worked to catch a murderer."

With a huff, Lord Mather said, "I somehow doubt that."

Samuel bobbed his head. "It is true," he confirmed. "Lord Rushcliffe was the reason why Lady Eugenie was exonerated. He caught the real killers."

"And what about Lord Roswell?" Lord Mather asked.

As Samuel went to defend his friend, Roswell replied, "You have no reason to trust me, but you need me. You don't want to go about this alone."

Esther rose and spoke to her father. "I trust them, as should you," she said.

"You trust them with your life?" Lord Mather asked.

Without a moment's pause, Esther replied, "I do, whole-heartedly."

"Then I suppose I have no choice but to accept this plan of yours," Lord Mather sighed. "I do not like it."

"You do not have to like it, but it will work," Rushcliffe assured him.

"It better," Lord Mather said.

Samuel placed his hand on Esther's arm and turned her to face him. "You don't have to do this, you know. We can find another way." The thought of her being in harm's way unsettled him.

Rushcliffe leaned forward and said, "This is our best option."

"What if Mr. Fairchild decides arsenic isn't enough and plunges a dagger into her heart?" Samuel asked.

"We won't let that happen," Rushcliffe asserted.

Samuel trusted Rushcliffe and Roswell, but he still didn't want to take the chance that anything might go wrong. He refused to sit idly by when Esther was in danger. "I want to be in the room, as well," he said firmly.

"There are only so many places to hide," Roswell attempted.

Esther's eyes remained on him as she said, "I would prefer if Samuel was in the room."

Rushcliffe put his hands up in surrender. "We shall make room for him, but it might be uncomfortable."

Samuel tucked a piece of errant hair behind Esther's ear, his finger lingering on her delicate skin. "You must promise that you will not take any unnecessary risks."

"I promise," she replied.

"Good, because there are no trees to climb to escape if something goes awry," he teased.

Her eyes lit up. "That was just one time."

"Yes, but it made a lasting impression on me," he said.

"Although, I should say that *you* made a lasting impression on me."

Lord Mather cleared his throat. "You forget yourself, Mr. Moore."

Keeping his gaze firmly on Esther, he replied, "No, for the first time I see clearly."

"And what is that?" Esther asked in a soft voice.

Roswell came to stand next to him. "Not to intrude, but we are trying to stop someone from murdering Lady Mather."

Esther ducked her head and that was when Samuel realized that everyone was staring at them. Drats. When would they ever be able to finish their conversation?

Samuel took a step back. "My apologies," he said. "We shall continue this conversation once this is over."

"Very good," Rushcliffe responded. "Perhaps we should go over the plan?"

"Finally," Lord Mather muttered.

"Lady Esther will retire in Lady Mather's bedchamber, and her stepmother will stay in Lord Mather's bedchamber for the evening," Rushcliffe started. "Once she is situated, Lord Mather will inform her lady's maid that Lady Mather has retired for the evening and request for tea service to be brought in."

"How does Mr. Fairchild know that she will drink the tea?" Samuel asked.

"Susanna drinks the tea throughout the night to settle her stomach," Lord Mather said. "Any of the servants would know that."

Roswell took a sip of his drink before adding, "All Lady Esther has to do is remain in the bed and wait for Mr. Fairchild to arrive."

"What if he doesn't come tonight?" Esther asked.

"He will come," Rushcliffe said. "The apothecary said he appeared desperate for the arsenic to work."

"Why wouldn't he just give it to his accomplice to put into the tea?" Lord Mather asked.

"Because he needs to ensure she is dead," Rushcliffe replied. "Then Mr. Fairchild will move on to you."

Lord Mather furrowed his brows. "Why would he do such a thing?"

"That is simple," Roswell said. "Mr. Fairchild needs to inherit your title and estate or he will be thrown into debtor's prison soon. This is his last chance to save himself."

Rushcliffe grew solemn as he spoke to Lord Mather. "Mr. Fairchild bought enough arsenic to kill multiple people. It is not farfetched to believe one of those people will be you."

"Daniel won't get away with this!" Lord Mather exclaimed.

"No, he won't," Rushcliffe asserted. "That is why we are here."

With a glance out the darkened window, Roswell said, "It is time that we get into our positions."

Samuel reached for Esther's hand and whispered, "You can do this."

"I hope so," she replied.

"There is no one braver or stronger than you, my dear," he said.

She gazed into his eyes, searching for something. He was unsure of what she hoped to find, yet he prayed she would be satisfied. "It is only because of you that I am this way," she stated.

"You give me far too much credit," he said. "It has always been inside of you. I just helped you see how magnificent you truly are."

Her smile started off small but it grew into something that he could only describe as brilliant. "I'm glad that you didn't run off to be a pirate," she joked.

"So am I," he replied.

Rushcliffe's voice came from the doorway. "Lady Esther, we are waiting for you."

Samuel released her hand and said, "I won't be far behind you."

"You promise?" she asked.

"Always."

Esther lay in bed as she stared at the door in her step-mother's bedchamber. The trap had been set, and she was the decoy. All she had to do was lay in bed and partly cover her face, to conceal her identity.

Her father had informed the servants that Susanna had retired for the evening and for her tea service to be brought up. Alice had delivered the tea and placed it down onto the table next to her. She had poured a cup of tea and left it for her to drink. Fortunately, it was dark so Alice didn't get a good look at her.

Rushcliffe was sure that one of their servants had betrayed them, but who could it be? It couldn't be Alice. She had been Susanna's lady's maid since she had been out of the nursery and they shared a close relationship. Although, it had to be someone that her stepmother trusted and knew her routine. Who would do such a thing? And for what purpose?

Fortunately, she was entirely safe because Samuel wouldn't let anything happen to her. She was sure of that. He was hiding behind the curtains and she could see his boots peeking out from underneath.

Why couldn't he love her? She loved him, desperately. At times, she saw glimpses of what they could have, if only he would open his heart to her.

She let out a soft sigh. How much longer was she expected

to wait? It had been hours since Alice had delivered the tea. What if Daniel decided not to go through with his plan?

Esther saw movement coming from underneath the door before the handle slowly turned. The door opened and a tall, shadowed man stepped into the room. It must be her cousin.

Keeping her face partly concealed, the man approached the table and removed something from his jacket pocket. He held it up and she saw it was a vial of some sort. He took off the lid and poured the contents into the teacup.

Once he finished, he replaced the lid and slipped it back into his jacket pocket. He took a step back and looked towards the window, just as the moonlight hit his face.

Gibson.

It was their butler that had betrayed them.

Before she thought through the repercussions of her actions, Esther sat up in bed and removed the sheet from her face. "Gibson. What are you doing?" she demanded.

With a look of confusion etched on his features, Gibson asked, "Lady Esther?"

"It is me," she replied. "How could you betray us?"

He grew visibly tense. "Whatever do you mean?" he asked.

Gesturing towards the teacup, she replied, "You poured arsenic into my stepmother's teacup."

"I did no such thing," he attempted. "I came to ensure that she had received her tea and I added honey to it."

Esther was many things, but stupid was not one of them. "We know you are working for my cousin, Mr. Fairchild."

"I am not."

"How much did he offer you to kill my stepmother?"

Gibson's face paled. "I do not wish Lady Mather dead."

"I doubt that," she replied. "You poured enough arsenic into her teacup to ensure she would be killed, and quickly."

When his answer wasn't forthcoming, Esther shook her

head and continued. "How could you? You have worked for us since I was in the nursery."

"It is not what it seems, my lady."

"Then tell me what is truly going on."

Gibson glanced at the door before admitting, "Mr. Fairchild threatened me. If I didn't do as he instructed, he would kill my daughter."

"Why didn't you come to us?" she asked. "We could have helped you."

He gave her a blank look. "What would you have been able to do?"

"We could have gone to the constable and—"

Speaking over her, Gibson said, "By then, my daughter would already be dead." He slipped his hand into his jacket pocket and pulled out a pistol. "I won't lose her."

"Gibson..." she started, unsure of his intent.

He pointed the pistol at her. "You should have never interfered. This is your fault."

Rearing back, Esther asked, "Are you blaming this on me?"

"Why do you care anyways?" he spat out. "You don't even care for Lady Mather. You have been at odds since the moment your father married her."

Esther saw Samuel peek out from behind the curtain but she shook her head. Gibson wouldn't shoot her. He was just confused.

"My stepmother and I have come to an understanding," Esther said. "Put the pistol down."

Gibson thrust the pistol towards her. "I am tired of you ordering me around. I am in charge now."

"Do you truly intend to kill me?" she asked.

"I have no choice," Gibson replied. "If I don't, Mr. Fairchild will kill my daughter."

Esther shook her head. "No, he won't. If we go to the constable—"

"Absolutely not! I will not risk my daughter's life," Gibson said, shouting over her. "It is my word against Mr. Fairchild and I know who the constable will side with."

"You don't know that for certain."

"But I do," Gibson asserted. "Men like me don't get fair treatment."

Esther had to assume that the men were getting anxious to end this. But she didn't want Gibson to die. He was just doing what he thought was best, no matter how misguided it was.

"Gibson," she started, "if you shoot me, then the whole household will be woken up. How will you explain that?"

"I will say that I happened upon you first."

Esther put her legs over the side of the bed and rose. "You don't want to kill me."

"I do."

"If you do, my cousin has won," she said. "Is that what you want- for him to win?"

A deep frown creased his face, revealing a desperate expression. "No, but there is no other way."

"There is another way," she stated as she placed her hand out. "Give me the pistol and we both walk out of here alive."

He glanced down at her hand. "If I give you this pistol, my life is over. I will be thrown into Newgate, or worse, transported."

"I will ask the court to have mercy on you."

With a huff, he replied, "They won't listen to you. You are just a woman."

Samuel spoke up as he stepped out from behind the curtain. "No, but they will listen to me."

Gibson tightened his hold on the pistol. "Where did you come from?" he demanded, confusion on his features.

"You are surrounded," Samuel said as he pointed a pistol at the butler. "You won't make it out of here alive if you continue to threaten Lady Esther's life."

The butler's eyes darted around the bedchamber. "Who else is here?"

"It doesn't matter," Samuel said as he stepped closer. "I should warn you that I refuse to let any harm befall Lady Esther."

Gibson's eyes narrowed. "Put your pistol down or I will shoot Lady Esther."

Esther kept her voice calm as she tried to reason with Gibson. "It is over. Just do as Mr. Moore says."

"It is not over until I say it is over!" Gibson shouted.

She had known Gibson most of her life and she had to believe that he wouldn't shoot her. He was just frightened for his daughter's life and she didn't blame him. He was doing what he thought was best for his family.

Taking a step towards Gibson, she said, "I promise that I will see to your daughter. She will be provided for."

He looked at her in disbelief. "You would do that, despite everything that I have done?"

"I would because I know how much she means to you," Esther replied.

Gibson blinked and his face grew hard again. "Lord Mather would never allow that," he said.

Esther had to admit that Gibson wasn't entirely wrong, but this was a fight worth fighting. A daughter should not be held accountable for her father's decisions, no matter how terrible they are.

Samuel took a step closer to Gibson, keeping his pistol pointed at him. "We need your help to ensure that Mr. Fairchild is never in a position to hurt anyone else."

"How would I be able to do that?" Gibson asked.

"With your sworn testimony, Mr. Fairchild will be transported," Samuel replied. "He will be far, far away and he will suffer a fate far worse than death."

"What if they make me join him?"

Samuel lowered his pistol to his side. "I can't promise that you won't face some consequences for trying to kill Lady Mather, but the sentence won't be as severe if you agree to help us."

Gibson looked unsure. "I don't want to go to prison."

"Then you shouldn't have made a deal with the devil," Samuel said.

Esther watched Gibson with pleading eyes and hoped that he would do the right thing. "My cousin is a bad man, but you are not like him. You are good."

"How can you say that?" Gibson asked. "I tried to kill Lady Mather and I am holding a pistol at you."

"Yes, but if you wanted to kill me, you would already have," Esther said. "You are just scared and it is all right to admit that."

Gibson glanced down at the pistol in his hand. "Do I have your word that you will take care of my daughter?"

"You do," Esther said.

The butler closed his eyes for a long moment before saying, "I never meant for it to go this far."

"I believe you."

Gibson's face held regret as he lowered the pistol to his side. "I'm sorry, Lady Esther."

Before she could reply, Rushcliffe and Roswell emerged from under the bed. Roswell jumped to retrieve the pistol from Gibson.

Rushcliffe's eyes held approval. "You did well," he praised. "I don't think I could have done it better myself."

"And no one died," Roswell pointed out.

Rushcliffe nodded. "That is a relief. It will be much easier to explain this to the constable now."

Samuel approached Esther and stood in front of her. "You were brilliant, my dear."

"Thank you for your help," Esther said.

"Perhaps next time, you don't step closer to the person

who is threatening to shoot you," Samuel teased, but there was a seriousness to it.

"I hope there isn't a next time," Esther remarked.

Samuel placed his hand on her sleeve. "Not if I am around."

The door opened and her father stepped into the room. He looked at Gibson in surprise. "Why is Gibson here?" he asked. "Did Daniel not come yet?"

"It is a long story," Roswell said as he grabbed Gibson's arm. "We should get him to Newgate before we seek out the constable."

Rushcliffe stepped forward. "I will come with you."

Her father's brow creased. "Will someone please explain to me what the blazes is going on?" he asked as Roswell led Gibson out of the bedchamber.

Esther lowered to the bed as she explained, "Daniel threatened to kill Gibson's daughter if he didn't poison Susanna's tea with arsenic."

"Daniel didn't even have the decency to try to kill Susanna himself," her father said, his voice rising. "He had to ruin other people's lives in the process."

Samuel interjected, "Do not worry. Mr. Fairchild will not get away with this, especially with Gibson's testimony."

"What will happen to Gibson?" her father asked.

"It is tough to say but his sentence will be more lenient if he cooperates," Samuel replied.

Her father sighed. "I know he loves his daughter above all else but I am still disappointed that he didn't come to us right away when Daniel threatened him. We could have helped him."

"I know, Father," Esther responded with sadness in her voice.

"Since Daniel is still out there, I am just going to keep Susanna in my bedchamber for the evening," her father said.

A yawn escaped Esther's lips. "Excuse me. I must be more tired than I thought."

"It has been a long night, for everyone," Samuel said. "Why don't you go get some sleep?"

Esther bobbed her head in agreement. "I think that is wise." She glanced over at the teacup. "But, first, we should get rid of that tea that is laced with arsenic. I wouldn't want anyone to drink it accidently."

Samuel picked up the teacup and walked it over to the open window. He tossed the contents of the cup out the window. "That should do it," he said as he turned back around.

Her father gave Samuel an expectant look. "It is late and we need to go to bed. Allow me to walk you out."

"I will do it," Esther said.

With a shake of his head, her father responded, "No, I think it would be best if I do it. You two will dilly-dally and I need to get back to Susanna."

Samuel placed the teacup back on the tray before saying, "If you are not opposed, I shall call upon you tomorrow."

"I shall look forward to it," Esther responded.

"Good, because we have much to discuss."

"Do we?"

Samuel smiled. "We do." And she knew that everything would be all right. It had to be. She didn't think heartache could coexist in a world with one of Samuel's smiles.

Esther's heart took flight. "Tomorrow it is."

Chapter Twenty

The sun was still low in the sky as Samuel approached the main door of Mr. Fairchild's townhouse and knocked. He knew this was going to be a rather difficult conversation but it had to be done.

The door opened and a short, dark-haired butler answered. "How may I help you?"

"I need to speak to Mr. Fairchild."

"He is unavailable at the moment, sir, but if you leave your calling card—"

Samuel spoke over the butler. "You misunderstood me. I *will* be speaking to Mr. Fairchild."

"But, sir—"

Taking a commanding step forward, the butler staggered back, leaving the door open. "Where is he?" Samuel demanded.

The butler pointed towards the rear of the townhouse. "He is in his study."

As he started to walk away, the butler shouted, "I'm sending for the constable."

"Good," Samuel said over his shoulder.

He arrived at the study and he stepped inside. He saw Mr.

Fairchild was sitting at his desk, his head down. There were two open windows along the back wall and the curtains were blowing in the wind.

"We need to talk," Samuel said as he walked further into the room.

Mr. Fairchild looked up at him in surprise. "What are you doing here, Mr. Moore?"

"Did you truly think your plan would work?"

"What plan?" Mr. Fairchild asked, his brow furrowed. "What are you even talking about?"

Samuel sat down in front of the desk. The time to be direct was now. He didn't have the time or energy to beat around the bush. "You tried to have Lady Mather poisoned."

"I would never do anything so—"

"Spare me the lies," Samuel said, cutting him off. "Lord Mather's butler confessed to everything and he claimed you were threatening to kill his daughter if he didn't go along with your plan."

"He is clearly lying."

"Yes, just as you are," Samuel responded. "But at least Gibson had the decency to be ashamed of his role in all of this."

Mr. Fairchild put his hands out wide. "Why would I be ashamed? I did nothing wrong."

"It was just a coincidence that Lady Mather got sick after you offered her the mint ice and a mint biscuit?"

"I'm afraid so, and I felt awful for it," Mr. Fairchild declared.

"You won't get away with this."

Mr. Fairchild smirked. "I don't know what you are talking about, Mr. Moore, but my time is short. I need to see to a few things."

"You have gambled away all of your money and you are in desperate straits."

The smirk faded away as Mr. Fairchild asked, "What do you know about that?"

"I know you should be in debtor's prison, but being Lord Mather's heir presumptive has some advantages. Does it not?"

Mr. Fairchild's eyes sparked with annoyance. "What do you want?"

"The truth."

"Whose version of it?" Mr. Fairchild mocked.

"There is only one truth."

Mr. Fairchild shook his head. "You are wrong. There are many shades of gray and you are in the thick of it."

"Enlighten me."

"And why should I do that?" Mr. Fairchild asked. "You come in here and are making up ridiculous allegations."

"We both know they aren't 'ridiculous,'" Samuel said. "You poisoned Lady Mather with pennyroyal, and when you got tired of waiting, you sent Gibson to kill her with arsenic."

Mr. Fairchild huffed. "That is a good story."

"It isn't a story, and we found the apothecary that will testify that you purchased pennyroyal oil and arsenic from him."

"The arsenic is for the rat problem that we are having."

"And the pennyroyal?"

"I put it on my skin," Mr. Fairchild said. "It makes my hands soft."

Samuel lifted his brow. "You are going to have to come up with something more believable if you want the judge to believe that lie."

Mr. Fairchild glanced at the door before saying, "If you had any real proof, I would already be in Newgate."

"Don't worry, you will be," Samuel asserted. "I just came here to give you the courtesy of having you confess beforehand."

"Why would I do something so foolish?"

"Because it would be the right thing."

Mr. Fairchild's face grew hard. "The right thing?" he asked. "I have been waiting since I was born for that old man to die and give me his title."

"Lord Mather is hardly old. He could live many more years."

"Unfortunately, yes, but then he went and got a young wife to bear him an heir," Mr. Fairchild said. "He did so just so I wouldn't inherit."

Samuel shrugged. "Can you blame him?" he asked. "You are rather a terrible person."

Mr. Fairchild narrowed his eyes. "It is time for you to leave."

"I will, once you confess you poisoned Lady Mather."

"Then you shall leave disappointed."

Samuel stretched out his legs in front of him. "You think you are clever, but you are no different than the common criminal."

Mr. Fairchild opened his desk drawer and retrieved a pistol. He placed it on his desk. "I am no criminal."

"I want to discuss Miss Watson."

For the briefest of moments, Mr. Fairchild's demeanor slipped and he looked unsettled. "Why would you want to discuss her?" he asked. "She is in my past."

Samuel nodded. "Yes, but she died shortly after she told you that she was increasing."

"That was most unfortunate."

"Yes, but I suspect you killed her with pennyroyal."

Mr. Fairchild chuckled. "Now you are just grasping at straws, and it is embarrassing- for you. Not for me."

"So it is just a coincidence that you also purchased penny-royal around the time of her death?"

"I'm afraid so," Mr. Fairchild said. "Frankly, I am disappointed in you."

Samuel decided to humor the man and asked, "Why is that?"

"You are a renowned barrister and yet your attempt to get me to confess is pathetic."

Rising, Samuel said, "I am sorry that you feel that way." He paused. "Did you intend to kill Lord Mather once his wife was dead?"

Mr. Fairchild's eyes grew wide. "Why would I do such a terrible thing?"

Samuel gave him an amused look. "My apologies, you clearly have outwitted me." He paused. "But I should warn you that the constable is on his way to arrest you."

"Whatever for?"

"For some reason, when we went to the magistrate and we presented him with all of the evidence, he seemed to side with us," Samuel said.

Mr. Fairchild picked up the pistol. "Why did you come here?"

"I just thought I owed it to you since you are Lady Esther's cousin," Samuel said. "Fortunately for you, you did nothing wrong and this is just a misunderstanding."

Rising, Mr. Fairchild kept the pistol in his hand. "Leave, and do not come back," he ordered.

Samuel put his hands up in front of him. "I need to tell you one more thing and then I am done."

Mr. Fairchild gave him an expectant look.

"Miss Watson's body is getting exhumed, and the coroner will be looking for signs of pennyroyal poisoning. If there is any, you will be hanged for murder," Samuel revealed.

"There aren't any."

"Good, then you have no reason to worry."

As he turned to leave, Mr. Fairchild remarked in a hesitant voice, "I thought pennyroyal was undetectable in the body."

"You were misinformed," Samuel said. "There are telltale signs that point to pennyroyal poisoning."

A panicked look came to Mr. Fairchild's face and he pointed the pistol at Samuel. "You will help me."

"With what?" Samuel asked innocently. "I thought you didn't kill Miss Watson."

Mr. Fairchild looked at him like he was a simpleton. "Don't be daft. Of course, I killed her. I didn't want a baby."

Samuel kept his face expressionless. It would do no good to give away his advantage. "What would you have me do?"

"You will be my barrister."

"Or what?"

Mr. Fairchild's eyes became menacing. "Or I will kill you."

"That is a weak threat since we both know that you need me alive," Samuel said. "You can try again. I'll wait."

Coming around his desk, Mr. Fairchild kept the pistol pointed at him. "I would be blind to not notice the growing attraction between you and my cousin. If you don't do my bidding, I will kill her."

Samuel bobbed his head. "I believe you." He turned his head towards the windows. "Did you get all of that?"

Rushcliffe and Roswell's heads popped up in the open windows. "We did, and so did the constable."

Mr. Fairchild glared at him. "You set me up."

"Guilty as charged," Samuel said. "I told you that you weren't very clever."

"I'm going to kill you," Mr. Fairchild said, tightening his hold on the pistol.

Rushcliffe cleared his throat as he brought his pistol up. "You are outnumbered and outgunned. Put the pistol down and step away from Mr. Moore."

"Why would I do something so foolish?" Mr. Fairchild asked.

Roswell shook his head. "Did you not just hear Lord Rushcliffe say that you are outnumbered and outgunned? How embarrassing for you."

Mr. Fairchild pursed his lips. "I did nothing wrong. Mr. Moore coerced a confession out of me."

"Innocent people don't usually hold people at gunpoint,"

Samuel pointed out. "But you will have plenty of time to think on that when you are at Newgate."

As Rushcliffe climbed through the window, he said, "I am too old to be climbing through these small windows."

"You are hardly thirty," Roswell remarked.

"Yes, but do you know how hard it is for a man of my size to go through these openings?" Rushcliffe planted his feet on the ground of the study and pointed his pistol at Mr. Fairchild. "I am done playing games. Put the pistol down."

Mr. Fairchild's eyes spewed with hate. "This is all your fault," he shouted at Samuel. "You just couldn't mind your own business."

"It isn't really my fault since I didn't poison anyone," Samuel said.

"I should kill you and be done with it."

Samuel held Mr. Fairchild's gaze, showing no hint of fear. "If your finger even twitches on that trigger, Lord Rushcliffe will kill you."

Mr. Fairchild stewed for a long moment before lowering the pistol to his side. "Fine," he spat out. "It doesn't matter. I will have my day in court and the jury will side with me."

A tall, burly man stepped into the study with two men of equal size accompanying him. "Let's go, Mr. Fairchild."

"Who are you?" Mr. Fairchild asked.

"I am Constable Johnson and I heard every word that you said," he replied. "I hope you have a good barrister because you are going to need it."

"It won't be me," Samuel rushed to say.

While Mr. Fairchild was being led away, Rushcliffe came to stand next to him. "I had my doubts but you managed to get justice for Miss Watson."

"I hope now she can rest beyond the grave."

"I thought pennyroyal was undetectable in the body," Rushcliffe said.

Samuel grinned. "It is."

Roswell climbed through the window and dusted off his trousers. "Shall we celebrate with a drink at White's?"

"I can't," Samuel said. "I need to speak to Lady Esther."

With a knowing look, Roswell asked, "Are you going to offer for her… again?"

"Yes, but this time I have worked out what I am going to say beforehand," Samuel replied.

Rushcliffe placed a hand on his shoulder. "Good luck, and just know that there is no shame in groveling when you are trying to convince the woman that you love to marry you."

"Duly noted," Samuel said. "Good day, gentlemen."

As Samuel departed from the study, he knew that the time had come. He loved Esther with all that he had and he needed her in his life, desperately. Now he just had to convince her of it.

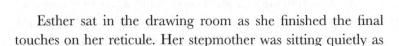

Esther sat in the drawing room as she finished the final touches on her reticule. Her stepmother was sitting quietly as she read a book.

She was just biding her time until Samuel came to call. He told her that he would and she believed him. He said they had much to discuss and she wasn't entirely sure how she felt about that. She knew he cared for her since he had told her as much, but she wouldn't marry him unless he loved her. She deserved to be loved the way she loved him.

Her stepmother glanced up from her book. "He will come," she encouraged.

"I know that, but when?" Esther asked, glancing out the window. "I am growing tired of waiting."

"Patience is a virtue," Susanna teased.

Esther brought the reticule to her lap. "It is a virtue that I am not in possession of."

Susanna offered her a sad smile before saying, "I was wrong, you know."

"About what?"

"I should never have tried to force you into a marriage with Lord Warley," Susanna said. "You deserve so much more."

"So do you."

"Your father is good to me, but I hope with time, his heart will soften towards me and he will look at me the way Mr. Moore looks at you," Susanna said.

"I believe he will."

Susanna's eyes became moist. "My apologies, I seem to have turned into a watering pot since I started increasing."

"There is no shame in crying."

"I just want what is best for you. That is all I have ever wanted," Susanna said.

Esther fidgeted with the reticule in her hand. "Do you think Mr. Moore is what is best for me?"

"Don't you?"

"I don't know if he loves me or not," she admitted.

Susanna's face softened. "Trust yourself to do what your heart is guiding you to do."

"But what if it is wrong?"

"Only you can be the judge of that," Susanna responded.

The heavy-set underbutler stepped into the room. "Mr. Moore has come to call upon Lady Esther," Brown announced. "Shall I—"

"Yes, send him in," Esther said eagerly. Perhaps too eagerly.

Brown tipped his head. "Yes, my lady."

A moment later, Samuel stepped into the room with a smile on his face. He was dressed in a blue jacket and buff trousers. His dark hair was swept to the side and his long side-burns had been neatly trimmed.

As she admired his handsome face, he bowed. "Ladies," he greeted. "I have come bearing news about Mr. Fairchild."

"Must we speak of that horrid man?" Susanna asked.

Samuel looked amused. "It would please you to know that he is in Newgate and he no doubt will be hung for the murder of Miss Watson."

"Who is that?" Esther asked.

"It was his mistress and she made the mistake of getting pregnant with his child," Samuel said. "He poisoned her with pennyroyal and she died."

Susanna gasped, bringing a hand to her mouth. "How terrible."

"Even if he confesses to poisoning you, the worst punishment they could have inflicted on him would be transportation," Samuel explained. "But since he murdered someone, he will ultimately pay with his life."

"I wish I could say that I feel sorry for him, but I don't," Susanna said.

"Neither do I, but onto much more pleasurable things." Samuel's gaze fixated on Esther, as if trying to communicate something without words. "Would you care to take a stroll in the gardens with me?"

Esther glanced at her stepmother for permission, who promptly nodded. "I would like that very much," she said, rising.

Samuel approached her and offered his arm. "Shall we?"

After placing her hand on his sleeve, he led her towards the rear of the townhouse and out the back door. They started walking down a path and Esther could feel how tense he was.

"Is everything all right?" she asked.

Samuel nodded. "Yes. Why do you ask?"

"You seem tense," she replied.

"Do I?" He stopped on the path and turned to face her, his boots grinding on the gravel. "I must speak to you."

Esther couldn't resist the urge to tease him. "But you are speaking."

Ignoring her attempt at humor, his voice was uncharacteristically firm. "Yes, but it is of the utmost importance that you listen."

"I am listening."

Samuel's jaw clenched. "I spoke to your father and he granted his permission for me to marry you."

Esther removed her hand off his sleeve and asked, "Is that what you want?"

"It is," Samuel replied. "Why do you ask?"

"Perhaps because you don't seem pleased by that prospect."

Samuel brought a smile to his lips, but it appeared forced. "Nothing would make me happier than you being my wife."

That was hardly convincing, she thought. "Is my father forcing you to marry me?"

"What? No!" Samuel shouted. "I want to marry you but I'm afraid you will say no again."

Esther felt her heart drop. Nothing had changed for either of them. She was still in love with him and he was only doing the honorable thing by offering for her.

Samuel ran a hand through his hair, making it terribly disheveled. "I am making a blunder of this proposal," he said. "Allow me to start over, please."

It was on the tip of her tongue to refuse his request, but his eyes pleaded with her to listen to him. "Very well."

Samuel brought a hand to his heart and said, "I stand here, humbled before you, begging you to marry me. I know I am not a perfect man, and I won't ever be, but I can't lose you. I won't lose you, not with everything that we have been through."

It would be so easy to say yes and marry him. But she couldn't do that, not if he didn't love her. "Samuel, I..."

"Before you say no, you must know that I love you. You

must be able to feel it in your heart," he said. "Because I feel it. Every time I am with you, I feel it."

"You love me?" Esther asked.

"With all my heart," Samuel said. "I have never loved another as much as I have loved you."

In a timid voice, she asked, "Even Lady Bedlington?"

Samuel reached for her hand and tenderly brought it up to his lips. "There was a time that I thought Phoebe was my match, but I was wrong. It is you that holds my heart."

Esther felt tears well up in her eyes, but she didn't swipe them away. These were happy tears. "I don't know what to say…"

"You don't have to say anything."

"… the only thing I can say is that I love you, too."

Samuel took a step closer to her. "I started falling in love with you the moment I saw you trying to climb that ridiculously tall tree."

She laughed. "It was a perfectly logical escape plan."

"No, it wasn't," Samuel joked before he sobered. "I'm sorry that it took me this long to realize how much I love you."

"It is all right."

"It isn't, and I will spend the rest of my life making it up to you," Samuel said. "If you will allow me to."

Esther watched as Samuel dropped down to one knee, all while keeping hold of her hand.

"Marry me, Lady Esther, and we will start a new life together," Samuel said. "A better life because we will do so together."

The bright smile that came to her face gathered up everything inside her and directed it towards him. "I will," she replied.

Samuel returned her smile as he slowly rose. "I wonder how on earth I was lucky enough to find you, my love. You plague my thoughts, unceasingly."

"I feel the same," she said.

He wrapped his arms around her waist, pulling her close. "You have no idea what you do to me."

"What do I do to you?" she asked in a breathless voice.

His eyes dropped to her lips. "May I show you?"

"Yes, please."

He leaned closer and brushed his lips against hers. "You and me, forever and ever," he breathed.

"Sounds perfect."

Her words had barely left her mouth before he kissed her again. Only this kiss was long and slow and full of promise. How she loved this man, more than she could ever find words for. And he loved her. Never had she thought her reality would be better than her dreams.

Samuel broke the kiss but remained close. "I should not have kissed you in such a fashion."

"It was perfect." Her lips still tingled from his kiss and she wished that he would do it again.

"I will go post the banns at once, assuming you have no objections," Samuel said.

"I have none, but must you leave now?"

Samuel's lips twitched. "I suppose I can tarry for a little longer," he said before he pressed his lips against hers.

Epilogue

One month later...

Samuel sat in an uncomfortable pew as he watched Mr. Whitmore and Miss Keene get married. He hoped they had gotten married for the right reasons, but by all accounts, they appeared to be genuinely happy. Both had broad smiles on their faces as they snuck glances at one another throughout the ceremony.

He shifted his gaze to Esther and smiled. They had been married for a week now. One glorious week. They had decided to postpone their wedding tour to watch his friend get married, but he couldn't wait to finally get Esther alone.

He had never been so happy. If his heart could burst from happiness, it would already have. He loved everything about Esther, and even the things that she wished he didn't. He couldn't wait to spend the rest of his life with her.

Esther leaned closer to him and whispered, "You should be paying attention."

"I would rather be alone with you," he said flirtatiously.

A blush came to her cheeks, just as he hoped it would. "You shouldn't say such things."

"Why not?" he asked. "There is nothing wrong with flirting with my wife."

"True, but other people might overhear you."

Samuel kissed her cheek. "Then let them talk," he said.

A cheer went up around the room and Samuel sat back in his seat. Mr. Whitmore and his wife were walking down the center aisle and they only appeared to have eyes for one another.

After they had left the chapel, Esther turned in her seat to face him. "I do believe we can leave for our wedding tour now."

"Didn't you promise your stepmother that you would stop by and see the new baby?"

Esther blew out a puff of air. "I did."

"You don't seem excited to see your brother."

"I am," she replied, "but I am more excited to be in Scotland for a fortnight."

Samuel rose and held his hand out to assist his wife. "We will strive to hurry, but I fear Susanna won't let us leave so quickly."

"Most likely not," Esther responded as she accepted his assistance in rising. "She probably will insist that we join them for dinner."

"I am glad that you have set your differences aside with Susanna."

Esther nodded. "We were at odds for far too long."

As they walked out of the chapel, Lord Roswell came to stand next to them. "Another good man has been lost to the parson's mousetrap."

"Perhaps you will be next," Samuel remarked.

Lord Roswell shook his head. "I have far more important things to do than take a wife."

"Such as?" Samuel asked.

"The list is far too long for me to mention," Lord Roswell said, dismissively.

Samuel lifted his brow. "Appease me," he said. "Just name one thing that a younger son of a marquess must do."

"Aren't you being rather inquisitive today?" Lord Roswell remarked.

He noticed that his friend still hadn't answered his question, but he decided to let it go. Roswell was entitled to his secrets, just as he was.

Esther put up her hand in greeting when she saw Miss Bolingbroke and her brother, Caleb, approaching them.

Miss Bolingbroke kissed Esther on the cheek. "What a surprise!" she exclaimed. "I just assumed you would be on your wedding tour."

"We decided to delay it so we could attend the wedding today," Esther shared.

"It was a beautiful ceremony." Miss Bolingbroke turned her attention towards Samuel and tipped her head. "Mr. Moore."

"I would prefer if you would call me Samuel, especially since I suspect we will be seeing a lot of one another."

Miss Bolingbroke grinned. "It was your choice to marry my dear friend."

"That it was and it was the best decision of my life," Samuel said.

Lord Roswell cleared his throat, making his presence known. "Good morning, Miss Bolingbroke."

Her smile dimmed. "Good morning, Lord Roswell," she said, her voice tight. "I hadn't expected to see you today."

"Mr. Whitmore and I have been friends for many years," Lord Roswell explained.

"Oh, that is nice," Miss Bolingbroke murmured.

Lord Roswell leaned closer to Miss Bolingbroke and said, "You look especially lovely today."

"There is nothing special about the way I look," Miss Bolingbroke responded as she smoothed down her gown.

Samuel could feel tension between Miss Bolingbroke and Lord Roswell, and he wasn't sure why that was. He would need to ask his friend the next time they were alone.

Caleb did not seem to share his sister's standoffish behavior with Lord Roswell because he greeted him warmly. "It has been far too long since we have had a drink at White's," he declared.

"That it has been," Lord Roswell agreed. "Will you join me tonight?"

"I would be honored," Caleb said.

Miss Bolingbroke lifted her brow at her brother. "Do you truly intend to let me contend with Mother and Father alone this evening?"

"You will be fine," Caleb encouraged.

"They will find fault with something I did or might do and will spend the whole evening lecturing me," Miss Bolingbroke complained. "I would rather go to White's with you."

Caleb's eyes grew wide. "No, absolutely not!"

"I didn't say I would go, but just that I would 'rather' go with you," Miss Bolingbroke said.

"Knowing you, you would wear a pair of trousers and try to sneak in," Caleb remarked.

Miss Bolingbroke seemed to consider Caleb's words. "You are right—"

Caleb placed a hand on her sleeve, stilling her words. "Father would disown you if you did something so outlandish. A gentlemen's club is no place for a lady."

"I should start a women's club," Miss Bolingbroke declared. "We could sit around, drink tea and debate with one another."

"You mean gossip," Caleb teased.

Miss Bolingbroke placed a hand on her hip. "Women are capable of having opinions on a myriad of things."

"I am well aware of *your* opinions since you share them all the time, whether or not I ask for them," Caleb stated with a smile.

Lord Roswell spoke up. "I would be glad to hear some of Miss Bolingbroke's opinions."

"No, you wouldn't," Caleb said. "Trust me. Run away while you still have the chance."

Miss Bolingbroke dropped her hand from her hip as she offered Lord Roswell the briefest of smiles. "Thank you, my lord, but I'm afraid our time is short. I have a painting lesson that I am late for."

"I thought you were terrible at painting," Esther said.

"I am, but my mother thinks I will have a better chance of finding a suitor if I suddenly become good at painting," Miss Bolingbroke shared.

Caleb shrugged. "I think Mother is grasping at straws since nothing else has seemed to help."

"That is because I am not looking to get married," Miss Bolingbroke said.

"On that note, I should depart." Lord Roswell bowed. "Good day."

As Lord Roswell walked off, Samuel noticed Miss Bolingbroke's eyes watching his retreating figure with a look of longing, and dare he believe, regret?

Samuel placed his hand on Esther's back. "We should go, as well. Your stepmother is expecting us."

Esther placed a hand on her friend's sleeve. "Just promise me that you won't rule out the possibility of falling in love," she counseled.

Miss Bolingbroke grew solemn. "Not everyone is so lucky to have a happily ever after like you."

"But you can be one of those people," Esther pressed as she dropped her arm to her side.

"You are wrong but thank you."

While Samuel led Esther towards their coach, he asked,

"Is there something going on between Lord Roswell and Miss Bolingbroke?"

"I don't believe so. Why do you ask?"

"Forget I said anything," he replied. "Besides, I would much rather focus on more pleasurable topics."

Esther stepped into the coach and he sat next to her on the bench. He slipped his arm around her shoulders and asked, "Have I thanked you yet for marrying me?"

"I don't believe so and I was just about to chide you on your impertinence."

He leaned in and pressed his lips to hers. "Thank you," he murmured, against her lips. "A hundred million times, thank you."

"I daresay that you could stand to thank me more," she joked.

Samuel pulled back slightly so he could gaze into her eyes and ensure she felt the love conveyed in his words. "You and me, forever," he said.

Her lips curled into a smile as she repeated his words, "You and me, forever."

The End

Coming Soon...

SECRETS OF A BLUESTOCKING

A secret has kept them apart, but can that secret bring them together?

Miss Anette Bolingbroke was not like most girls of the *ton*. She dreamed of writing a book and had no grand illusions that she would ever wed. Which was fine by her. Her heart had been irretrievably broken by a man that wanted nothing to do with her. Rather than wallowing in her own self-pity, she focuses on her own hopes and dreams, determined to make it on her own.

Lord Roswell Westlake had a secret; one that could ruin him and his family if revealed. He played the role of a carefree younger son of a marquess well, but it was just an act to maintain his cover as an agent of the Crown. When he is assigned to root out a traitor amongst the peerage, it causes him to come face-to-face with the one person he had promised to avoid- Miss Bolingbroke.

Roswell's usual tactic of indifference towards Anette soon backfires as he finds himself enjoying her company once more. And much to her dismay, Anette starts letting Roswell back into her life. When Anette's life is threatened, Roswell must keep secrets from her to ensure her safety. But as time goes on, he begins to question whether or not he is truly doing the right thing by keeping her at arm's length from his heart.

As the fifth novel in the series by author Laura Beers, *Secrets of a Bluestocking* continues the Lords & Ladies of Mayfair series. This is a light-hearted, clean and wholesome romance set in the Regency era. All books in this series have their own Happily-Ever-After and are best enjoyed in proper order.

About the Author

Laura Beers is an award-winning author. She attended Brigham Young University, earning a Bachelor of Science degree in Construction Management. She can't sing, doesn't dance and loves naps.

Laura lives in Utah with her husband, three kids, and her dysfunctional dog. When not writing regency romance, she loves waterskiing, hiking, and drinking Dr Pepper.

You can connect with Laura on Facebook, Instagram, or on her site at www.authorlaurabeers.com.

Made in United States
Orlando, FL
26 December 2024

56551951R00173